What reviewers are saying about the stories in

Agency of Extraordinary Mates Vol. 1

Kate Douglas -- Finding Magic

"Finding Magic is a fast, sexy read that has a wildly romantic thread woven into its steamy 'lust at first sight' premise... It's a wonderful fantasy that will keep you hot and bothered but leave you with a satisfied smile!"
    -- Patrice Storie, Just Erotic Romance Reviews

4 Play by Eve Vaughn

"The sex is hot, hot, hot, but how could it be anything else considering this is a ménage or should I say 4 Play romance! Eve Vaughn's Agency of Extraordinary Mates: 4 Play is one book you don't want to miss."
    -- Lady Amethyst, Fallen Angel Reviews

Sea God's Pleasure by Alice Gaines

"If you're looking for a hotter than Hades fantasy with love scenes that will scare the fish in the sea, then look no further. This reviewer highly recommends it. Get your copy of A.O.E.M.: Sea God's Pleasure by Alice Gaines pronto!"
    -- Janalee, The Romance Studio

Changeling Press, LLC

www.ChangelingPress.com

Agency of Extraordinary Mates Vol. 1

Kate Douglas -- Finding Magic
Eve Vaughn -- 4 Play
Alice Gaines -- Sea God's Pleasure

ISBN 1-59596-362-6
ISBN 978-1-59596-362-8

Publisher:
Changeling Press LLC
PO Box 1561
Shepherdstown, WV 25443-1561
www.ChangelingPress.com

Printed in the U.S.A.
Lightning Source, Inc.
1246 Heil Quaker Blvd
La Vergne TN 37086
www.lightningsource.com

Anthology Editors: Margaret Riley & Sheri Ross Fogarty
Cover Artist: Sahara Kelly
Cover design: Bryan Keller

The individual stories in this anthology have been previously released in E-Book format.

A.O.E.M.: Finding Magic
Kate Douglas

Prologue

"Cut, people. That's a wrap. You've done a great job on this film. *Tomorrow* is finito!"

Amanda Carlisle didn't acknowledge the cheers, nor did she join in. Head down, she rushed from the soundstage and headed for her trailer.

Her personal assistant and bodyguard, all six foot six of big, black male, blocked her entrance. "What's the rush, missy? That's not the face I'm used to seeing at the end of a shoot."

Amanda curled her lip and wished she felt like smiling. "Who the hell do you think you are? Mr. Clean? What's with the shaved head, Lester?"

Les grinned and tugged at the big gold ring hanging from his left ear. "I thought it complemented the bling. You mean you don't like the look?"

"You look so damned sexy you make my teeth itch." Amanda ran her hand down his bare chest. Everything about Lester Ondáge was perfect.

Well, almost everything.

"Ms. Carlisle? Over here!"

A flash bulb momentarily blinded her.

"Oh shit." Amanda ducked her head and slipped around Les. He moved his big frame aside and she raced into the trailer.

Les closed the door behind her, but she still heard his deep voice and the mumbles of disgruntled paparazzi.

"No pictures of Ms. Carlisle, fellas. Now, how'd you get back here? This area is off limits to press."

"Is it true? Has Franklin dumped Amanda from *No Love Again*?"

"What's the deal, Lester? Rumors are flying fast and furious. What about the reports of all the dissent on the set of *Tomorrow*?

Word's out Ms. Carlisle is getting real hard to work with, that she put the film way over budget."

"Ms. Carlisle is always a professional. Word of her being replaced on the *No Love Again* cast is pure rumor. You know how it is in this business. Now, the lady is tired and she needs her rest. We'll see you at the cast party, I imagine."

Amanda groaned and buried her head in her hands. She'd forgotten about the damned party. She heard the door close, felt the warm strength of Lester's hands working the strained muscles in her neck.

"Good Lord, Les. Now that's magic."

"You're tight as a spring, missy. Can I get you some Ibuprofen?"

"I'd rather have a glass of brandy. A big one."

"You can have a small one and that's it. As tired as you are, you'd be on your cute little ass by dinnertime. I'm sure those jokers would love a picture of that."

Les poured a small shot of amber liquid into a plastic cup, then squatted down in front of Amanda and handed it to her. He wrapped her small hands in his big ones, cradling hers as she held the cup. "It'll be fine, sweetie. Relax."

Amanda leaned close and brushed her lips over Les's extraordinary mouth. He kissed her back, his full lips caressing hers with just the right pressure to hint of more.

"Damn you, Lester. You're perfect. Why the hell are you gay?"

He leaned back and grinned at Amanda. "That's the way the good Lord made me, sweetie. Just like he made you the most gorgeous woman on earth with a heart so full of love you sometimes make me think of putting the moves on you, just to feel your glow."

Amanda snorted. "Yeah. Right." She cupped the side of his face with the palm of her hand. "Thank you, Les. You always make it better."

Les sighed. "I can't fix this, though, can I?"

Amanda shook her head. "The magic's gone. I felt it from the first line of the script. It was a damned good story and I blew what could have been an Oscar quality performance. Les, I don't know what to do. Those guys were right. Franklin's trying to force me off his movie. William said…"

"William's an ass."

"He's also my agent, and a damned good one. He said Franklin's people are planting the word all over town that I'm through, that I'll kill the project." She sniffed and took a sip of brandy.

Les brushed her hair, bleached silver blonde for the film, back from her face. "You're a professional, but you're human. You're tired. You've done three films, back to back, and you haven't taken even a weekend break."

There wouldn't be a break for her now, either. *No Love Again* was due to start shooting on Monday. In Chicago. Damn, she hated Chicago.

"I've got an idea, but you might not like it." Les stood up and reached into the overhead compartment where he kept her papers. He pulled a long envelope out of the stack then sat down in the small chair next to Amanda's.

Les didn't open it. He sat there, tapping the envelope on his knee, staring at Amanda as if he were contemplating the end of the world.

Amanda opened her mouth to ask him what the hell was going on, when he took a deep breath and held up the envelope. "You're not going to like what I think you should do, but hear me out, okay?"

Amanda frowned and nodded. This was so unlike Les. He actually seemed nervous.

"I want you to have William contact Franklin, tell him you think Ashley Jenson would make a better Lisa than you. Pull yourself off the film. Don't give him the chance to do it… it would hurt your career too much. You know Franklin would love to get out of the contract and…"

Amanda sat back and blinked. No way in hell would... "I don't break contracts, Les. You know that."

"I said, hear me out." He stood up, paced a few steps away, then whirled around. "This is an invitation to a very special resort. I've heard of it but never knew for sure it really existed. I checked. This invitation is for real and it's addressed to you. It's an island called Chimera -- a Caribbean island smack-dab in the middle of the Bermuda Triangle. No paparazzi, no one who knows who you are, no make-up people knocking on your door at four in the morning, just a beautiful island where you can relax, regroup..."

Amanda sighed, caught up in the mesmerizing cadence of Les's soft words. He described heaven. Warm sands, endless miles of beach, an elite clientele completely disinterested in her Hollywood status.

"Think about it, sweetie. It's your chance to..."

"Get the magic back."

Amanda's whisper hung between them. She looked up at Lester and smiled. Suddenly it all felt right. "Maybe you're right, Les. Tell you what, I'll do exactly what you say, but there's one condition."

Les blinked. Obviously he hadn't expected her to give in so quickly.

"I'll drop out of *No Love Again* and I'll take this vacation you're so convinced I need, but only if you go with me."

The expression on Lester's face was worth any contract for any movie ever made. "Close your mouth, Lester. You'll catch a fly." Amanda reached across the small space between them and snatched the envelope out of his suddenly lifeless fingers. "I'm not trying to seduce you, Lester. Think about it. You work just as hard as I do. You're just as lonely as I am. Separate rooms, we go our own way, but I'll feel safer knowing you're nearby. Will you come with me?"

Les cleared his throat. "Uh, I'm not on the invitation."

Amanda stood up, feeling more energized, more alive, than she'd felt in ages. "You are now. Here." She handed the envelope back to Les. "Make the arrangements and see how soon we can arrive. I think it's time for both of us to find the magic."

* * *

Prince Lorcan, heir to the Northern Realm of the Lands of Eldar, ruler of the Northern Eldar, direct descendent of the First Kindred, Dragon Clan and a man in his physical and mental prime leaned over the stone basin and puked.

His manservant, Tady, stood beside him, holding a clean damp towel and a glass of minted water.

Lorcan raised his head, took the towel from Tady and carefully wiped his face. "I swear, I am going to kill my mother. Where does she find these hideous females? I can't do it anymore. By the gods, that last woman tasted of six-day-old fish! I will not kiss another, nor will I pick one of these damned fortune hunters to be my bride. My mother *will not* select my Chosen One."

He grabbed the glass of minted water, rinsed his mouth and spit.

Tady nodded, his eyes downcast, his hands now folded over his chest. "As my Lord wishes."

Lorcan tossed the towel in the basin. "Cut the crap, Tady. I'm serious."

"I understand, milord. No crap. Your dinner awaits you."

"Ya know, Tady, you'd make a damned fine wife." Lorcan wiped his mouth with the back of his hand and sauntered over to the table, lifted a silver lid and sniffed the savory fowl simmering within a blend of mixed vegetables and sauce.

"I'm perfectly willing, milord."

Lorcan's laughter burst out of him. "I know you are, you twit. I'm the one who prefers the opposite gender. It's merely that, other than the physical, you have all the qualities I want in a wife. You're loyal, entertaining and a wonderful cook." Lorcan patted his loyal manservant on the shoulder. "You're not bad looking, either, but as much as I wish it, you just don't turn me on."

"I'm sorry, milord."

Lorcan laughed again, shaking his head as Tady carefully pulled the royal chair away from the table and seated his master. "Join me? There's more than enough."

"T'wouldn't be proper, milord."

"Proper, hell... I'm in charge and I command you to join me for dinner. It looks delicious."

Tady sighed.

Lorcan knew exactly what went through the smaller Elf's mind. No matter how hard he tried, he couldn't get his master to act the part of the prince of the realm.

So be it. Lorcan had made his decision. There would be no nuptials. No new Elven queen for the Dragon Clan. Not unless he found his Chosen One, a long shot by anyone's standards. He'd been perfectly happy for all these many years cheerfully screwing whichever sweet young thing crossed his path. He'd not had any complaints, merely the occasional whimper from a wench who expected more than the princely cock thrust between her thighs.

So, he'd make the decree himself, that he, Lorcan of the Northern Realm, should hereafter be known as the Bachelor Prince, a playboy among men... or Elves. If Tady read it, standing on the uppermost balcony of the castle while dressed in his finest livery, it should go over quite well.

Or not. Lorcan stared at his plate, his appetite gone. Even the chilled mug of dark ale didn't tempt him. What he needed was a break, a short vacation from his mother's insistence that he wed, from the constant parade of horribly ineligible, eligible women.

"Why is it," Lorcan asked, raising his head to glare across the table at Tady, "that the word *eligible* equates with tedious?"

Tady's snort was surprisingly unprofessional. "Possibly, milord, because your mother determines who is eligible?" Tady lifted his mug of ale and took a long, slow swallow. He smacked his lips with obvious relish. "Have you thought of searching on your own?"

Lorcan shook his head. "It's not a bad idea. Unfortunately, can you see me running that one by dear old mom? Besides, I really don't intend to wed."

"There's always Chimera."

Lorcan raised his head and blinked. Now why the hell hadn't he thought of Chimera? It was the perfect solution. A beautiful tropical island hidden in the midst of the Bermuda Triangle, accessible by humans -- appropriate humans -- only by invitation. Accessible by creatures such as Lorcan whenever the need for escape -- or a suitable mate -- grew strong.

"I swear, Tady. I just might choose you for my bride. That's a brilliant idea! We'll leave in the morning."

"We, milord?"

"We. Pack your bags. We're going on vacation."

Chapter 1

Tady set Lorcan's bags down just inside the door to the prince's private bungalow. One entire wall of clear windows opened to the gleaming ocean where the sun hovered just above the western horizon. Shades of gold and silver spilled across the calm waters. Lorcan stared out the window a moment, then quickly shed his lightweight jacket.

"It's a beautiful night, Tady. Get yourself settled and enjoy the evening. It's yours. I'm going to take a walk on the beach... check out the women."

"Alone, milord?" Lorcan rarely did anything on his own. Tady knew he made an unusually small, but effective, entourage.

"Yes, Tady. Alone. I told you, this is your vacation as well. You're more than welcome to ignore me entirely." Lorcan turned and stared out the window as a matched pair of gorgeous young women passed by on the beach just outside. Their long blonde hair swung in rhythm with their steps, brushing nicely rounded hips. Make that *bare* hips... Lorcan grinned. He did love a thong bikini...

"In fact, Tady. I think I'd prefer you ignore me. Talk to you later."

Lorcan ran his fingers through his dark hair to cover his Elven ears, the only obvious feature that set him apart from ordinary human males -- other than his propensity to shift to Dragon form on occasion. Then he loosened the upper two buttons on his brightly patterned cotton shirt and nonchalantly headed for the beach at a perfect angle to intercept the two young women.

Tady sighed. The concept of leaving Lorcan to his own devices for a full week on an island filled with nubile young women was enough to give any self-respecting Elf nightmares.

Grumbling under his breath, Tady grabbed his bags and headed across the warm sands to his own bungalow. Only a few yards from the prince's, it was just as secluded by thick palms and ferns, giving it a sense of total isolation.

Tady laughed when he saw the size of the bed, designed to accommodate the largest of guests. At barely five foot two, Tady figured he could hold a party in the damned thing and have room to spare.

As if he'd have the chance to share it with anyone.

He sat heavily on the edge of the bed. Lorcan needed a wife, if for no other reason than to keep him out of trouble. Between the queen mother and his loyal manservant, the prince would eventually find the perfect mate, whether he wanted her or not.

But what of me? Tady looked around the beautifully appointed room. Luxurious yet tasteful, it was the perfect setting for seduction. Chimera, however, didn't seem like the best of places for a rather small, gay Elf to find that perfect-ever-after kind of love.

Hell, he'd be happy for any kind of love.

"It's thinkin' like that'll get ya nowhere." Tady shoved himself to his feet, grabbed his bags and began putting his clothing into the closets and drawers. The lower drawer on the dresser stuck. He tugged and the drawer flew open.

It was filled to the brim with neatly packaged sex toys, floggers and shackles. Everything he needed for a night of hot sex, except the man. Tady poked through the collection, chuckling quietly at the impressive array, then carefully shut the drawer.

He left his empty bags stacked on two of the chairs and thought of going back to Lorcan's bungalow to unpack for the prince.

The sound of music drifted across the still night air. Tady's stomach growled. It'd been a long journey and Lorcan was a grown man.

Let him put his own clothes away. Tady straightened his shirt, ran his fingers through his short blond hair, taking care to cover his ears, and headed for the nearest restaurant.

* * *

Lester watched Amanda as she strolled slowly away from him, her long skirts whipping about her slim legs, her thick, honey blonde hair, so much prettier in its natural shade, falling heavily across her shoulders, spilling down her back.

Damn but she was one fine woman. It amazed him, especially when he saw her like this, free of the cares of work and the pressures from an intrusive press, that he didn't feel the slightest sexual attraction to her at all. She loved him. He loved her. There was nothing one wouldn't do for the other... except *that.*

Laughing, Les raised his hand to wave when Amanda turned around. He caught the gleam of her bright smile in the last rays of the sun as she returned his wave, then he turned away and left her on the beach. Amanda Carlisle might eat like the proverbial bird, but the flight had been long and there was a lot of Lester Ondáge that needed filling.

* * *

The restaurant closest to their bungalows was bursting with beautiful people. There was no other way to describe the mix of obviously powerful, wealthy men and woman who lounged against the long, polished teak bar or sat at small tables beneath a canopy of palm fronds. Candles cast a romantic glow on the faces of lovers bent over exotic looking meals.

Les might have felt totally out of place, but his stomach growled again and he searched over the heads of the shorter patrons, looking for an empty table.

He noticed a booth toward the back of the patio that appeared empty. There wouldn't be much of a view, but it was close to the kitchen and food sounded more appealing than the ocean right now.

Les worked his way through the crowd, hoping to reach the booth before someone else beat him to it.

"Oh. Sorry. I thought this one was empty."

The diminutive blond man sitting back in the dark corner of the booth glanced up at Les and smiled. "Just me. I was doing my best to disappear. Didn't realize I was that effective."

Lester couldn't help it. He burst out laughing. "You don't have a date, either?"

"Definitely the odd man out. Care to join me?"

Still laughing, Lester slipped into the booth across from the smaller man. "As the odd man out, or at your table?"

"Take your pick." The blond held out his hand. "Tady O'Shea, personal valet and manservant to Prince Lorcan of the Northern Realm."

Lester engulfed the man's hand in his much larger one. "Lester Ondáge, personal assistant and bodyguard to Amanda Carlisle. Where the hell's the Northern Realm?"

Tady blinked, then frowned, almost as if he'd been caught at something illicit. "Of Ireland. The Northern Realm of Ireland. It's a small county that keeps its old traditions."

"Ah. I see." Les didn't, actually, but it wasn't important. There was something absolutely fascinating about the little blond dude. *Tady O'Shea*? Definitely an Irish name, and obviously he was not a fan of American movies. He hadn't even blinked at Amanda's name. This trip was looking better all the time. Amanda needed a break.

So did Les.

He wondered about the man sitting across from him. There was nothing feminine about Tady O'Shea, nothing obvious to explain the strong attraction Les felt, the almost magnetic pull toward the Irishman. Small he might be, but he was well muscled and moved with the sense of a man comfortable in his own skin.

The waitress left a couple of menus and quickly departed with orders for a cold draft beer and a tankard of ale. Tady glanced up from his menu and caught Les looking back at him. Lester wondered if the need roiling in his gut was visible in his own eyes... as visible as the need in Tady's?

His hands were shaking when he took the cold mug of beer from the waitress. Tady mumbled his thanks, ordered quickly and grabbed his ale, then proceeded to down it so fast he choked. Les leaned across the table and slapped Tady's back.

Tady raised his head, eyes streaming, and once more Lester felt a connection, a sense of mutual need, of desire so intense it turned the pressure of his hand, preparing for another slap against Tady's back, to a warm caress.

Caught there, his massive arm stretched across the table, palm planted solidly against Tady's lean back, Lester tried to take a deep breath and couldn't.

The waitress brought their meal. The glue holding Les's hand to Tady's spine released. Les sat back in his seat and turned his attention to his lobster dinner, but all his senses keyed on Tady. What was the other man thinking? Did he feel it? Was Les imagining the sudden, gut-wrenching attraction?

The cock pressing against his zipper wasn't a figment of his imagination. Damn, if he was wrong, if Tady wasn't interested in him *that* way, Les was going to feel like a fool.

He finished his dinner without speaking. Tady ate steadily as well, then sat back from his plate. This time when he looked at Lester, there was a speculative gleam in his blue eyes. Damn, Les couldn't recall seeing eyes so blue on a man before. They sparkled, clear and bright, surrounded by lashes as dark and thick as any starlet's.

In fact, Tady was absolutely the most beautiful man Les could remember seeing. High cheekbones, eyes tilted slightly up at the corners, a broad, full-lipped mouth, blond hair cut short but covering just the tops of his ears. He was slightly built, but still well muscled, his biceps flexing with each move of his arms.

Les's thoughts kept returning to that perfect mouth.

He pictured those lips sliding around the erection that was beginning to cry out for attention. Damn, his cock was usually better behaved than this, but something about the look Tady was giving him had Les squirming in his seat. Not an easy feat for a man his size.

"I'm full. Are ya up for a walk?" Tady tilted his head and smiled. If Les weren't so unsure of himself right now, he'd guess the little guy was flirting.

"Uh, sure. I don't have to be anywhere else. C'mon."

Amanda had assured him there were no charges of any kind for their stay, but Les tossed a few dollars tip on the table as they left. Tady left something that appeared to be gold coins.

Les wondered once more about that strange Northern Realm Tady'd mentioned.

The moon was high, the waves crashing like quicksilver against the shore. Other couples passed them in the darkness. Lester noticed they were the only same sex couple, but Tady didn't seem the least bit concerned. In fact, he walked close to Les.

Invading his space.

Hips almost touching, arms occasionally brushing.

Tady barely came to the middle of his chest, but he moved with a fluid rhythm that was pure poetry to watch.

Les realized he'd been watching Tady walk without really hearing him talk. He'd been breathing in the scent of him, the clean, fresh smell of crisp cotton, after-shave and sun-heated male skin.

They stopped at one of the small cabana bars along the beach and each man grabbed a drink, one of those fussy looking things with lots of ice and too much alcohol and a parasol stuck in the top.

"It's like drinking fruit punch." Les finished his in a couple of swallows and grabbed another. Tady laughed.

"Take it slow. They pack a wallop. Of course, you're a big man and I imagine you hold your liquor better'n most."

Les laughed, downed the second drink and grabbed a third as they continued their walk. He wondered where Amanda was, and said as much.

"She'll be out enjoying the moonlight. Maybe she'll meet Prince Lorcan. He's a fine man."

Lester finished his third drink and nodded. It seemed to take his eyes a long time to catch up to the movement of his head and he was aware of a pronounced buzzing over the sound of crashing waves.

"I told you that drink would sneak up on you." Tady stopped, put his hands on his hips and stared up at Les. He shook his head and nodded to his left. Les watched both blond heads move slowly back and forth. "Here's my bungalow. Come with me, I'll make you some coffee."

Grinning like a fool, Les followed Tady into the neat little hut, an exact copy of his own luxurious bungalow. Once inside, he looked for a place to sit, but there were suitcases stacked on the two chairs. Les sat on the edge of the bed.

Tady closed the door behind him, then stepped close to Les as if sizing him up. Les spread his knees wide.

Tady stepped between them, almost eye to eye with Les sitting down. He stared for a long telling moment, then slowly smiled. "Who'd have thought?"

Les shook his head. The buzzing subsided just a bit. "My thoughts exactly." He reached out and swept his hand over Tady's smooth hair, ebony fingers sliding through blond silk.

Tady leaned close and pressed his lips against Les's mouth, pressed his tongue along the seam between his lips, found the sharp edge of Les's teeth, found his tongue.

Almost afraid to move, Les let the smaller man kiss him, make love to his mouth with a most amazing tongue, delving deep, then retreating to place tiny kisses along his jaw, down his throat. Les's cock burned and throbbed against his zipper, begging for release.

Tady stepped back, hands on his hips, and stared at the bulge between Les's legs. "I'm almost afraid to release that beast. A man your size could kill me."

Tady grinned when he said it, but looking at the small man in front of him and knowing well the size of the beast in question, Les didn't argue.

Tady reached down and stroked the length of Les's cock through the soft denim. Les groaned and arched, thrusting his hips forward. Tady left his hand, large for a man of his small stature, cupped around the full mass of Les's testicles. "Of course, if you were willin' to offer up a little control in the situation, sort of let me take charge, I imagine we could figure out something to make both of us happy."

The buzz slowly building behind Les's eyes sounded like a swarm of bees. Hungry, horny bees.

Which is why, within a few minutes, Les found himself stark naked, shackled hand and foot to Tady's bed with soft, leather restraints. Tady sat on the edge, still fully dressed and wearing a huge grin on his face. He stared at Les's cock, standing at full mast and at least ten inches long.

"My oh, my…" Tady leaned over and licked a single drop of white fluid from the tip.

Les's hips jerked. "I've never done this before."

"What? Had sex?"

"No. Never let anyone tie me up." He took a deep breath and tugged futilely at the shackles. A bit of sweat broke out on his brow. What if the little guy was nuts? He'd heard about people in situations like this… not all the stories good.

He suddenly felt a lot more sober than he'd been a few minutes ago.

Tady ran a hand along Les's ribs, fondling each muscle as he passed. "All you need to do is say 'enough,' and I will release you. I'm not one to hurt a man. To be honest, I've never done this either, but it's a fantasy that's lived with me for much too long. When I found that drawer full of all this stuff… when I met you…"

He dipped his chin and looked a bit ashamed. "I'm a small man, Lester Ondáge, and you're very large. You're used to being in control. I've always had to follow orders. I'm attracted to you. You're attracted to me. I guess I should have asked…"

Les shook his head. For some odd reason he was no longer worried. He realized he felt comfortable with Tady, as if they'd known each other for ages, not hours. "Have your way with me, boss. I'll tell you up front, though, I am most definitely not into pain."

Tady laughed, his relief obvious. "Me neither. Though I have to admit, I have a few ideas that should drive you nuts. Are you game?"

Lester sighed. "Yeah. Do your worst... or best."

Tady stood up and grabbed a black silk scarf out of the dresser. The last thing Lester saw before the blindfold slipped over his eyes was the mischievous twinkle in Tady's bright blue eyes.

"Now, don't move unless I give you permission and don't talk, unless it's to say the safe word."

Okay. I can do this. Lester nodded but kept his mouth shut. He'd read enough to know the rules, and to tell the truth, he'd always been just a little bit curious.

Of course, he'd imagined himself in the more dominant role. Not that he didn't find it terribly erotic, lying here naked with his eyes blindfolded, not knowing what was to come.

Not knowing. A shiver raced along his spine, and his cock, if such a thing were possible, grew harder... longer. His balls drew up close against his body. Les couldn't remember ever feeling as aware of all his parts as he did right at this moment.

Where was Tady? Something brushed against his foot. Les decided it was the fabric from Tady's chinos. A hand swept slowly along his thigh, tangled in the thick mat of hair at his groin. Tugged.

His cock grew harder.

Les heard a familiar sound, as if Tady were shaking liquid in a can. Felt the cold, wet weight of something sprayed around and above his cock. Shivered when slick fingers spread it about his groin.

Whipping cream?

Les bit down on his lip to keep from groaning when a warm mouth drew his cock deep inside, dragged teeth along the crown, licked the tip and released him. The air blew coolly over his damp skin. His cock jerked in response.

He held perfectly still, muscles locked in place. Tady's lips moved along Lester's jawbone. Warm breath tickled his ear when Tady whispered, "Now don't move. This razor is very sharp."

Razor? Holy shit.

Lester didn't even breathe.

Chapter 2

The sky was a deep purple globe sprinkled with diamonds by the time Amanda paused on a sharp stone pinnacle high above the waterline. She stared far below at the silver tips of waves crashing against the rocks and felt at peace for the first time in forever. Thank goodness for Lester. Only he would have known how very badly she needed this break.

Most women at thirty-eight were just reaching their prime. Not in Hollywood. Amanda knew she'd already begun her personal roller-coaster slide from the top. William had been handing her projects geared to the more mature woman for the past year.

She should have taken a closer look. Sighing, Amanda consigned her lousy performance on *Tomorrow* to the rolling sea. Along with it, she tossed her decision to pull out of Franklin's new project, a move that would turn that bitchy little Ashley Jensen into the next Amanda Carlisle.

Maybe it's time.

Amanda flung her hands in the air and held them wide, stretched over her head. She imagined Hollywood and contracts, agents and deals -- all tossed away, swept out to sea on the tides of her life like so much detritus and debris.

All thanks to Lester and his wonderful habit of keeping her world in order.

What was he doing tonight? She'd wanted him in her bed since the first time she saw him, working as a bouncer at one of the clubs she'd visited in Las Vegas. Unfortunately for that little fantasy, Lester had been upfront about his sexuality, but she'd liked him from the very beginning and not once regretted hiring him, first as her bodyguard, then adding the role of personal assistant.

PA, friend and bodyguard -- big enough and fierce enough to make her feel safe in any situation, yet gentle and loving and perfectly capable of organizing even a scatterbrained actress.

Damn. He was the perfect husband. Almost. Amanda hoped he wasn't bored, stuck away on this tropical paradise for lovers.

She spread her arms wider and let the wind catch her. Hair whipped around her face, stung her eyes, and she closed them, bathing in the spray from the crashing surf, the clean scent of saltwater and fresh air.

It caressed her in a sense of lightness, of life and excitement.

No photographers, no autograph hounds, no phone calls or beepers. Lester close by in case she needed him. Beautiful sea and sand and absolute privacy. Chimera, living up to its name, certainly gave the illusion of heaven.

"The footing there is a mite precarious, miss... I do hope you can fly."

"What?" A strong arm caught Amanda's wrist as she spun around and stumbled. Prepared to scream, she looked up into the greenest eyes she'd ever seen, emeralds set in the face of an angel. Coal black hair swept casually back from his face, his smile was wide and open, his teeth perfectly straight and white.

There was no threat in the man, merely smiling good humor, the sense of laughter and a thick Irish brogue that sent instant shivers racing along her spine.

"You startled me." She placed a hand over her racing heart, gasped for a quick breath and wondered if it was the fright that took her breath or the exotic, sensual look of the man still holding onto her arm.

"I apologize." He turned her loose and stepped back, leaving Amanda feeling oddly bereft. "You were so close to the edge, so caught in the moment, I feared for your safety. I didn't mean to frighten you."

"I'm fine. Thank you." She glanced behind her and realized she *had* been precariously close to the edge. It was a long, long way down. "It probably wasn't all that smart, standing on the edge of a cliff with my eyes closed."

He laughed.

She shivered.

He held out his hand. "I'm Lorcan. Just arrived today. It's lovely here, isn't it?"

"I'm... Mandy." Her tongue tripped over the nickname she hadn't answered to in years. No way did she want anyone to connect her with the famous Amanda Carlisle. "We just got here a couple of hours ago."

Lorcan tipped his head. "We?"

She smiled. "I came with my personal assistant. I'm not really comfortable traveling alone."

"Nor am I. My valet is here, though I've told him it's his vacation as well as mine."

"I said the same to Lester."

"Lester? Your assistant is a man?"

They'd somehow started walking back along the trail. Lorcan held his arm out, his gesture so smooth and practiced that she grasped his muscular forearm almost without thinking. "He's also my bodyguard and my friend." She smiled up at him. Odd, how quickly she'd fallen into step with this lean, tall male, their bodies moving together as if they'd walked this way before.

"So, why have you come to Chimera?"

Lorcan's question caught her by surprise. Why did anyone take a vacation? "I needed a break. It was Les's idea, really. He thinks I've been working too hard." Amanda cast a glance at Lorcan. "Why are you here?"

He laughed. She decided she could grow used to the sound of his laughter.

"I needed a break as well. My mother insists on finding me a bride. I've tried to explain it's a choice I'll make -- or not make -- entirely on my own. She didn't take the hint. Tady suggested Chimera. I jumped at the chance to get away."

"Tady? He's...?"

"My manservant... valet. My PA, to be politically correct."

"So, marriage isn't in your future, either?" Amanda thought of the years past, of the times when she'd wondered if she'd ever marry. Now, nearing forty, she realized marriage was no longer her holy grail. She'd chosen career over love, a choice she'd come to terms with long ago.

A serious relationship was something else. It would certainly be nice to have someone to share things with in the dark of night when the day was over and hours stretched on forever until she could go *back* to work. Someone with a lean, sexy body like Lorcan's. Someone with the lilting brogue of Ireland tripping off his tongue, someone...

"Never, at least if I can help it." Lorcan's soft laughter brought Amanda thudding back to earth. "I'm not cut out for marriage, nor for long-term relationships of any kind. I like women too much." He glanced at her, his grin light and definitely flirtatious, then gave her a long, slow perusal that left her feeling naked... and somewhat disappointed.

"There are too many beautiful women in this world to tie myself to one." Lorcan tilted his head and ogled Amanda as if she had an invitation taped to her boobs.

"Too many lovely breasts to suckle, too many warm, dark places to explore. Just think... if I'd listened to dear old Mom, I'd never have chanced upon a lovely sea nymph prepared to dash herself upon the rocks."

"Dashing wasn't in my plan." She slipped her hand free of his arm and walked on, a step ahead. His slimy attitude was a wet, stinky blanket thrown over her desire. "I was merely enjoying the moment, the freedom of the sea wind."

"As was I. Enjoying the moment. I stood and watched you for a moment or two before rushing to your rescue. The wind molding your dress to each lovely curve was more beautiful than the sunset. My imagination filled in the blanks."

Amanda turned and cocked her head, flashing a brittle smile at Lorcan. "You were spying on me?"

"Not spying. Appreciating the view. There's nothing more lovely in all Chimera than you, my lovely Mandy."

Talk about smarmy.

"Well, I thank you for my non-rescue and bid you good evening. Enjoy your walk."

"Aren't we going the same direction?" Lorcan rushed to catch up with her quick steps.

"I'm going back to my bungalow. Alone. I imagine you've another direction to head, more island beauties to rescue."

"I'll see you to your door. Maybe we could share a glass of wine?"

"It's not necessary and no." Amanda turned to face him. The last thing she needed was a handsome lothario looking for a quick lay.

Not that she was thinking of marriage. Not anymore. No, all she really wanted was a break from reality. Unfortunately, Lorcan's cynical line was all too familiar and not the least bit appealing... not nearly as appealing as his appearance. Too bad he was such a jerk when he opened his mouth.

Turning her back on him, she quickly unlocked her door and stepped inside. She closed it without saying a word.

His laughing, "Good night, m'dear," left her shivering, with her back pressed tightly against the door.

* * *

The soft towel was warm and slightly damp. Lester's skin tingled where the razor had obviously removed every last pubic hair within reach. He lay quietly, his body rigid with anticipation, while Tady cleaned the shaving cream off his groin.

This was so unlike him, this quiet acquiescence, but something about the island, the calm, easy-going sense of quiet and peace, lulled him. Allowed him to be someone entirely unlike his usual focused, controlling self.

The blindfold had warmed to his skin. The air chilled his damp flesh. Les felt strangely relaxed, as if the restraints and blindfold had removed all desire for control. He never would have imagined himself in such a position, giving another man complete charge of his body.

"I'm going to turn you now. Just relax."

Yeah, like that little guy was going to move his big bod? Les grinned, wondering just how Tady intended to flip 280 pounds of rock-solid muscle, when he suddenly found himself unshackled, lifted, flipped, and the shackles re-fastened before he could hardly draw a breath.

"Unh."

"Sorry, big guy. Didn't mean to startle you. No talking, now... remember?"

Les's cock pressed against the satin bedspread and the cool fabric rippled sensuously against his newly shorn skin. His hands were stretched tightly over his head, but his ankles were free.

Suddenly Tady was slipping a hand beneath his belly, lifting his massive weight as if he were a child, pressing a stack of pillows beneath Les to raise his ass in the air.

His ass? Shit! No one took Les Ondáge in the ass. He didn't do bottom. Hell, he didn't suck cock, either. What the hell did Tady think...

"Relax. I'm only finishing what I started."

Once again, Les felt the cool shaving cream spread over his ass, between his legs, right up the crack between his cheeks. He squirmed when some of the astringent foam found its way inside his ass, but he managed to keep his mouth shut.

As stupid as he felt, having his tail end shaved smooth as a baby's butt, this was the most erotic thing he'd ever experienced. The razor was sharp but Tady wielded it with great care. It swept over Lester's muscled buttocks, across the underside of his balls, then fingers spread his cheeks and Les felt the blade go right over his asshole. He tensed, but he didn't move.

Once more, Tady wiped the shaving foam away, then tucked the towel under Les's hips.

"Hold still. This might sting. Don't talk."

The sound of a cork pulled from a bottle. The splash of icy cold liquid spilling over his ass, between his legs, soaking his balls.

Fire! Burning, stinging, screaming fire!

"Uhmph!" Les buried his face in the bedspread. Tried to pull his knees together but realized the pillows held them firmly apart. Fumes assaulted his nostrils. Whisky! The bastard had poured whisky all over his ass!

The stinging slowly subsided, gave way to a warm, deep-seated tingle. He was still trying to figure out what the hell Tady was up to, when once again Les found himself on his back, his hands and feet shackled to the bedposts.

How the hell does he do that?

Then Lester really didn't care. A warm mouth encircled his cock. Lips tightened, stroked him up and down, licked the smooth skin around his balls, skin that only minutes earlier had been neatly covered in coarse black hair.

Now, with nothing to impede the sensation of tongue and lips and nipping teeth, Les suddenly understood what Tady had been up to.

Never, in all his thirty-five years, had he ever been so aware. Damn, if he'd known this kind of sensitivity even existed... still tingling from the whisky, skin ultra-sensitive from the close shave, Les felt his entire being center in the smooth skin of his groin and butt.

The mouth was gone. Les felt Tady sliding up his outstretched, shackled body, waited for his kiss. Instead, the round tip of a fully erect cock brushed his lips. A drop of hot semen spread across the closed seam of his mouth.

Now wait a minute... He'd never sucked a man before. Always thought of himself as the *suckee*, not the *sucker*. It was one thing to shove his cock down someone's throat, another altogether to be on the receiving end.

"C'mon, big boy. Open wide. Unless you want to use the safe word?"

Damn. Tady made it sound like a challenge, like Les was afraid. Les opened his mouth. Tady's cock teased at his lips, the head hard and smooth, and a lot wider than a guy Tady's size should carry around between his legs.

Les wondered just what kind of package the little guy had. He felt the bed shift, realized Tady had switched around so that he knelt at Les's shoulders. This time, when Tady lowered his cock into Les's mouth, Les swallowed him down as far as he could, until the smooth sack of Tady's balls rested lightly at his upper lip and pressed against his nose.

At the same time, Tady's mouth came down on Les. Tady moaned around the hard shaft stretching his jaws wide, licked the veined underside, nibbled at the round tip. Whatever Les did to Tady, the other man copied, until it almost felt as if Les was sucking himself.

Caught up in the mind-blowing sensations of a mouth full of cock and his own cock filling a mouth, Les knew he wouldn't last. Hell, he'd been celibate for months, almost as if he'd been saving it up for this one, mind-blowing fuck with a little guy barely half his size.

Tady's cock jerked in Les's mouth, reminding him that not all of Tady was proportionally small. Les felt the burning in his balls, the tight pleasure that was almost pain as a load of sperm made its convoluted journey from testicles to take-off.

He was so caught up in his own climax, he almost choked on Tady's load. Sucking and swallowing for all he was worth, Les knew he'd give anything to free his hands and rub on Tady's balls the way Tady was doing his.

Body spent and cock fading fast, he licked the last drops off of Tady, turned his head to plant a kiss on the quivering thighs on either side of his head and nipped at the tight ball sac.

With a groan, Tady rolled to one side. "Oh, my. That was exquisite. Absolutely exquisite." He leaned over and removed Les's blindfold, then unshackled his hands, planting a kiss on Les's mouth as he reached across his body to undo the left one. Les opened his mouth to Tady's kiss, sharing the taste of one man to another.

When Tady crawled across Les's thighs to unshackle his left foot, Les got his first good look at Tady's package.

"Can I talk now?"

Tady turned and grinned at him. "Oh, yes. Of course." He laughed. "You had something in particular you wanted to say?"

"Yeah. How'd a little turd like you end up with a cock as big as mine?"

Tady grinned and looked down at himself. "Haven't a clue. It's nice to know, however, we're equally matched in some areas."

He released the leather restraint around Les's ankle, then caressed the dark skin, moving up past Les's knee, over the bulge of his muscular thigh. Tady's long fingers left reactive shivers wherever they stroked. Les felt his cock rising once more.

Tady looked at him and grinned. "Okay. I guess this means you had as good a time as I did. Do you want to do it again?"

"Oh, yeah. You wanna rub a little higher?"

Tady rocked back on his knees and sat on his heels. "Not tonight. I have other plans. Lester... here's the way this works. You will go back to your bungalow, but first you will stop at one of the shops and choose a sarong. There's no charge for anything on the island... you just pick one you like. You will wear a sarong and nothing more while you are on Chimera. You will feel the air against your smooth balls and hairless butt and you're going to think of me and what I'm planning for you tomorrow... and the day after that, and the day after that one."

While he talked, Tady continued stroking Les's thigh, his fingers growing ever closer to Les's re-awakening cock. "You will not touch yourself. No jacking off. I want you ready when you arrive here tomorrow night at seven o'clock. We will have dinner here, in my bungalow. You will serve me. Then I will service you."

He leaned over and kissed Les on the mouth. Les sucked the other man's tongue deep, sighed and let him go. He had no idea what Tady had planned, but he already wanted to jack off.

Of course, he wouldn't do it. This was too much fun. Fantasy. Pure, unadulterated fantasy. Sex with a little guy with attitude like Les's drill sergeant back in basic.

Lester dressed quietly and slipped out the door. He started to head back to the bungalow, then remembered the sarong. Hell, there were plenty of other dudes on the island wearing the brightly colored skirts. He might as well follow orders.

The selection was endless, but Les finally found a bold tie-dye in blacks, blues and deep orange. He wrapped it up with instructions on how to wear it, and headed back to his bungalow without meeting a soul. The lights were on in Amanda's little hut. Normally, Les would've gone to check on her, but not tonight.

Tonight he had a lot to think about.

I sucked cock. Shit.

He'd really done it. More amazing, he'd really liked it. Of course, it was the blindfold. The blindfold and the shave job.

He'd never felt so naked in his life, lying there on the bed with his butt in the air, pillows under his belly, his eyes covered and his hands tied to the bed. Naked and vulnerable, so turned on his cock ached with the need to come, his balls wanted to crawl up inside his gut and he'd actually, for a moment there, wondered what it would feel like to take a cock up his ass.

Take it deep inside, thrusting hard and fast the way he liked to take a man.

He was still thinking about it when he crawled naked into bed. Still thinking about it hours later, unable to sleep because of the erection that wouldn't subside. The erection he'd promised the little guy he wouldn't touch.

* * *

Tady crawled into bed, sliding between cool sheets, beneath a satin spread still warm from Lester's body. He still couldn't believe it.

Shivering with reaction, the adrenaline nowhere close to subsiding, Tady relived the past couple of hours with the sexiest man he'd ever seen.

Six and a half feet tall if he was an inch, Lester Ondáge radiated pure, unadulterated power and sex, a combination sure to drive a sane man nuts. The effect on a horny gay Elf was practically lethal.

Soft spoken, his voice rumbling up out of that broad, smooth chest, Lester'd laughed as if the world were there for his pleasure. Lester was obviously a man used to being obeyed, even feared. An amazing man.

A man who'd allowed himself to be shackled and shaved, who'd taken Tady's huge cock all the way down his throat and swallowed every drop of the huge load of sperm he'd shot. A man confident enough to take orders, strong enough to let himself experience every fantasy Tady'd ever had in his lonely bed.

Not that Tady hadn't had sex, before. He'd had plenty of sex, but he'd always been the one taking orders, taking a cock down his throat or up his ass, making do with hand jobs and occasional blow jobs.

Nothing like tonight. Nothing so wonderful, so fulfilling as tonight.

Tady lay awake for hours, grinning into the darkness. Imagining tomorrow. Planning his evening with Lester.

Chapter 3

Lorcan awoke with a Dragon-sized headache. He squinted against the bright slash of sunlight beaming through the open windows, then groaned when he rolled over to bury his face in his pillow.

Carefully, he opened one eye again, just to make sure he was alone in the bed. One never knew, when one had gone drinking. Relieved the coast was clear, Lorcan rolled over on his back and covered his eyes with his forearm.

Right now, he'd give that arm -- or a leg -- to have Tady standing beside him with a cup of hot coffee...

Damn. Where was Tady, anyway? He'd never taken Lorcan's offer of time off so seriously before.

Worried, concerned something might have happened to his assistant, Lorcan hauled his butt out of bed and staggered to the shower. He kept trying to recall what had happened last night, but all he could remember was a sea of nameless faces, loud music and many tankards of ale.

A face drifted into his consciousness and brought him up short. *Mandy.* Honey blonde hair, flashing gray eyes and enough attitude to put any Elf in his place.

Now why would he think of her? She'd dismissed him as if he'd been less than nothing. Turned down his kind offer to escort her as if he'd been scum beneath her perfectly shaped little feet.

Of course, the minute she'd said the *M* word, he'd panicked and gone into his *Lorcan the louse* routine, as Tady had once dubbed it.

Damn. Where the hell was Tady?

Growling, aware he'd suddenly developed a morning hard-on to equal all others, Lorcan turned on the shower as hot as he could stand it and stepped beneath the spray.

He leaned his cheek against the cool tile, both hands splayed wide, and let the water pound his back and neck. His head cleared slowly. There'd been two other blondes. He remembered them now... sort of. Twins... Lola and Lila? Lilly? Lora... hell, he couldn't recall much, other than they'd wanted to come back here with him. He'd turned them down for some reason...

Mandy.

Lorcan shook his head. Damn. It was coming back to him, but it didn't make sense. The two blondes, the same women he'd followed from his bungalow. *Lola and Lila... yeah.* They'd been more than willing to return with him and he'd turned them down!

All because of Mandy!

That made absolutely no sense at all... why in the Dragon's name would he turn down a sure romp with two gorgeous sirens for a woman who had essentially told him to get lost?

Even more curious, why, when he thought of Mandy, did his cock decide to stand up and join the mental conversation? She was beautiful. There was no doubt in his mind about that, but not nearly as sexy as the two blondes.

Yet it was Mandy who filled his mind.

She couldn't be... no. No, he was not going there. Mandy was not his Chosen One. Not a woman with an attitude like hers.

So why didn't his cock get the message?

Lorcan looked down at the broad plum-colored crown staring straight up at him, almost as if the little eye was winking at him. Steam rose all around; his balls didn't know whether to hang low and cool off or crawl up inside and ache. Sighing, Lorcan soaped his hand and slowly, methodically, took care of the problem himself.

* * *

Amanda relaxed in a comfortable wicker chair out on the deck, nibbled at a croissant and sipped her coffee. The morning sun filtered through palms and ferns, and the ocean glimmered a brilliant sapphire blue, lapping against pristine sands as white as freshly fallen snow. She'd slept like the dead last night, but memories of dreams lingered this morning.

Dreams of Dragons and Elves and strange, towering trees. Dreams with strange, sensual images that flitted in and out of her mind this morning, leaving her confused and unsettled... and most decidedly aroused.

She leaned back in her chair and grinned. Lester's idea of a vacation must be working if her libido was coming alive. Sex had been the last thing on her mind for months.

Immediately, the image of Lorcan popped into Amanda's mind.

No. Don't go there.

The man had been sex appeal incarnate -- and was way too aware of his power over women. He was a jerk and a heartache waiting to happen.

"Mornin', sweetie."

"Lester!" She turned at the familiar greeting and almost dropped her croissant. "Lester? What are you wearing?"

Any other man might have looked ridiculous in a brightly colored sarong. Les Ondáge was a massive native god, his bare chest gleaming, his trim hips neatly encased in yards of silk. With his shaved head and one gold earring he might have stepped out of a dugout canoe after crossing miles of ocean.

"It's a sarong. Do you like it?" He turned his huge body in a graceful arc.

Amanda practically drooled. "I never would have imagined you going native, Les, but you look absolutely gorgeous. Is it silk?"

"Sure is. Really slippery."

He canted a hip close and she ran her hand along his flank. He could have been naked, the silk was so sheer, though she couldn't see through it. She could, however, feel every muscle and tendon.

Amanda laughed. "I need to get me one of those. Actually, let me rephrase that. I need to get me a *man* in one of those." She winked at Lester. "A man who's interested in me. In the meantime, do you want some coffee?"

Lester nodded. "I'll get it." He grabbed her cup for a refill, leaned over and gave Amanda a quick peck on the cheek.

She watched him walk into the bungalow, his muscular buttocks perfectly outlined in dark silk, his calves rippling below the hem. Even knowing he wasn't for her, she couldn't help but sigh.

Almost perfect.

A minute later, Les walked back outside and handed Amanda's cup back to her. She took a sip of the strong brew and practically purred. "So, what did you do last night, Les?"

He turned a sly smile on her. "You'll never guess." Then he laughed. "You tell me what you did first."

Amanda grinned. Les was hiding something -- or someone. This was a side of him she'd not seen before. "Well... I went for a walk, enjoyed the world's most gorgeous sunset and managed to get free of a sleazy pick-up artist."

That caught Les's attention. "Was some dude hassling you?"

She shook her head. "No. Just the typical guy who thinks he's God's gift to the feminine race. I get enough of that in LA. I'm certainly not interested in it here. Now, tell me about your night?"

Les stared down at his bare toes for a moment, then looked up at Amanda and flashed her a dazzling smile. "I met someone. He's... special. Don't know how to explain it. We're meeting again tonight."

"Oh, Les." Amanda grabbed his hand. "I'm glad. You haven't seen anyone as long as I've known you. It's not right to be alone for so long. Just be careful, okay?"

Les nodded his head. "I will. What are you up to today?"

Amanda thought about the hours stretching ahead of her and realized she had absolutely nothing planned. "I'm going to slap sunscreen all over my body and go lie on the beach. I'm going to wade in the ocean and think of nothing important. I might even take a walk. What about you?"

"I think I'll explore a bit. The island is beautiful and it's supposed to be very mysterious. We are in the midst of the Bermuda Triangle, you know."

"Well, be careful. Don't get sucked up by any aliens, okay?"

Les leaned over and kissed her full on the mouth. "Well, you watch out for Dragons."

Dragons. Now why would Les mention Dragons?

Last night's dream spun its way through Amanda's mind, then the thread disappeared. She sipped her coffee and watched the sea birds fly along the coast.

* * *

Les stuck a water bottle in a fold of his sarong and headed out along the beach. He'd expected to wake up to scratchy, itchy balls as his hair started growing back, but he was still as slick and cleanly shaved as he'd been last night.

Smooth balls, smooth ass, slick as a newborn and twice as sensitive. *Damn.*

Smooth skin sliding under a silk sarong was going to keep him hard all day long. He'd had to tie the silk extra tight across his groin to keep from showing off his damned cock, but the way the fabric slipped and slithered over his slick butt and balls was making him crazy.

What did Tady have planned for tonight? Last night had certainly been a surprise. Les hardly noticed the thick foliage along the narrow path he followed away from the beach. His mind was full of Tady, of the emotional as well as physical reaction he'd had to the little man.

There was no denying the fact Tady was his physical opposite. Blond hair, fair skin, twinkling blue eyes, a tiny elf of a man… except where it counted.

Swish, swish, swish… Les groaned. All he'd done was picture that perfect package between Tady's legs and all his blood rushed to his damned cock. The silk rode over his sensitive skin like… *shit.* Just like silk.

Les paused, unwilling to take another step until he got his wayward libido under control. How the hell was he going to last until tonight?

The leaves around him rustled, as if a strong wind blew past. Shadow darkened the trail, then all was once again quiet.

Had a plane flown over? No, he would have heard the engine. Les glanced overhead at the thick, green canopy of luxuriant jungle. Maybe folks were hang gliding off the mountaintop. That must be what caused the wind. He'd always wanted to try that.

Les stood a moment on the quiet trail and imagined himself flying, held aloft by nothing more than a flimsy kite... with the wind whistling up inside his silk sarong.

Gentle wind. Caressing his smooth balls and baby-smooth butt, caressing him with the same tenderness as Tady's fingers, as his talented lips, his warm, moist tongue.

Ah, shit.

The sarong tented out in front. Lester glanced up the trail and saw light where the jungle thinned on high ground. He'd heard this was an ancient volcano. From the jagged rock outcroppings he saw above, it looked as if there was at least some sort of old lava bed. Maybe a little island exploration would take his mind off the long hours between now and his date with Tady O'Shea.

* * *

Tady, resplendent in clan form, preened in the morning sunlight, straightening each iridescent scale in order to catch as much of the morning warmth upon his long Dragon's back as he possibly could. From this high point on the island, he had a full view of the pristine beach, the tiny bungalows scattered about the water's edge, and the thick wall of green jungle between the shoreline and the western shoulder of the volcano.

The ground here was warm, heated from within by the slumbering molten core, from above by the full rays of the sun. Tady stretched one huge wing, flexed his claws and scratched his belly. It had been much too long since he'd last shifted.

Damn, it felt good to be a Dragon the morning after a good fuck.

He glanced up as a dark shadow obscured his sunlight.

Lorcan?

Now what on earth would bring the Prince of the Northern Realm out this early in the day?

Lorcan pulled off a perfect landing on the small patch of bare ground next to Tady. His huge wings swept back, throwing up swirling dust devils. His thick legs came forward and clawed feet caught the rough ground and held.

Lorcan's green eyes swirled in the morning light, his nostrils flared, and he settled himself on the warm ground next to Tady. "G'mornin', Tady. You're up early."

"I was about to say the same of you, milord." Tady dipped his head in a habitual sign of respect for his prince. "Did you sleep well?"

"No." Lorcan's throaty growl hinted at a bit of a hangover along with a sleepless night. "No, I did not sleep well. You?"

"Like the proverbial dead, milord."

"Umph." Lorcan shifted, found a position that appeared to please him more and laid his scaly chin down on his forelegs.

"Is there something I can do, milord?" Tady sighed quietly... it had been so nice up here, reliving the touch and taste of Lester's magic. He'd rarely thought of Lorcan as an intrusion... at least not until today.

Lorcan's deep sigh stirred the dust. "You can tell me if I've lost my touch."

"Your touch, milord?"

"With women."

"Ah... the island appears to be filled with beautiful women, milord."

"Hrumph."

"What of the two you went in pursuit of last night, if I might ask?"

"They were willing. I wasn't."

Tady's head came up. Lorcan not interested? In two gorgeous blondes? "Milord?"

"Cut the milord crap, Tady. I could have had both of them if I'd wanted. I didn't want." Lorcan raised his head, the princely hauteur even more evident in his Dragon form.

Finally accepting the fact his peaceful morning had come completely to an end, Tady turned and sat up. "You, milord, did not want two gorgeous blondes? Are you ill?"

"It's all her fault."

"Her?"

"Mandy."

"Mandy? Who is Mandy?"

"A woman I met on the beach last night. She caught my interest. I didn't catch hers."

"I find that hard to believe, milord. I've never seen a woman who wasn't interested in you." *Or a man, for that matter…*

"Well, this one wasn't. I need to figure out why."

Tady hadn't seen this side of the prince before. Generally Lorcan was so cocky, so terribly self-assured. Generally, of course, he had women falling all over him… women well aware of his princely status.

"How did you approach her, this… Mandy?" Tady tapped one clawed nail against his cheek as he watched his prince.

Lorcan had the good grace to look sheepish. "In my usual fashion. It always works at home."

"Ah." Tady nodded and almost bit his lip to keep from chuckling. "At home, milord, if I may be so bold, the women know you are a prince. Maybe your approach, as a simple man, needs help." Tady took a deep breath and put his future employment at risk. "Do you really want my opinion, man to man?"

Lorcan stared long and hard at Tady, then he nodded. "You are my manservant, Tady O'Shea, but before that I have always considered you my friend. In many ways, my only friend. I would welcome the truth from you."

Tady nodded. Lorcan's words touched him deeply. At the same time, he wondered if it was the woman who intrigued his prince, or the mere fact she'd turned him down.

"I imagine, milord, you approached her as if you were her better, as if she should be thrilled to have you pay her the least bit of attention. Knowing your aversion to commitment, you probably managed to inject something in the first words of conversation to let her know you do not involve yourself romantically for more than a night. Essentially, you probably met the young woman, flirted outrageously, then in your less than subtle manner, let her know you were looking for a good fuck."

Lorcan's glittering eyes told Tady he was very close to the truth, if not literally tripping all over it.

"In other words, Prince Lorcan, you behaved in your usual boorish manner, a man much too full of himself to ever romance a woman in the proper manner."

"I could have you shot for that." Lorcan canted a sideways glance in Tady's direction.

Tady laughed. Coming from the mouth of a Dragon, it was more of a snort. Still, he knew he'd gotten his point across. "But you won't, milord, because I have just given you a truth you need to hear if you're ever to find a woman interested in you, not your crown. Go to her. Apologize. Ask for a second chance to get to know her, and try, for once in your life, to put someone else's pleasure before your own."

Lorcan nodded slowly, then turned his huge, scaled head and took a close look at Tady. His lip curled, showing just a hint of ivory. "You're certainly ballsy this morning, I'll give you that. What did you end up doing last night?"

Tady glanced down at his feet and studied the huge claws at the end of each elongated toe. He wasn't ready to share anything specific about Lester. Not yet. His feelings were too new. Too fresh.

Too special and definitely too confused.

"I had a nice dinner. Met a chap of the same persuasion. We're planning to get together tonight."

Lorcan blinked, as if surprised. Then he grinned, fully exposing his six-inch fangs. "Good. I'm glad you've met someone. At least one of us might get laid…" He looked away and sighed dramatically.

Tady wondered if, for once in his privileged life, Lorcan felt as lonely as Tady often did.

"I'm going back to the bungalow, Tady. Thought I'd try snorkeling, maybe spend some time on the beach. Maybe I'll even follow your advice."

Before Tady could reply, Lorcan launched himself off the narrow shelf and disappeared in a swirl of wings and reflected light, skimming low over the jungle to avoid detection.

It wasn't that the various and sundry beings who visited Chimera couldn't be who and what they were while on the island, but it was never a good idea -- or good manners -- to startle the human guests.

Tady prepared to settle back in the sunlight when a rustling in the jungle just below his rocky perch caught his attention. Holding perfectly still, tilting his scales to avoid as much shine and reflection as possible, Tady went into chameleon mode, hoping against hope he'd blend into the background.

Lester burst out of the forest. Wrapped in a shimmering, darkly patterned sarong wrapped low on his narrow hips, he strode up the rocky trail, picking his way quickly yet carefully over the ground in bare feet. His chest was bare. Sweat glistened off his broad shoulders and sunlight caught the single gold ring in his left ear.

Lord almighty, he was wearing a sarong, just as Tady had ordered. A gorgeous silk sarong over that perfect, dark-as-night, freshly shorn body.

Picking his way along the trail, dressed in native garb, Les might have been an island god, a powerful, perfect entity born of the heat and fire of the volcano. Tady swallowed back a greeting. The last thing he wanted was for Lester to see him like this, nothing more than a big shiny lizard lying on a rock in the sun. That would take more explanation than any Elf wanted to tackle, especially one hoping to get laid in a few hours.

No, not merely get laid. Last night was so much more than sex. Tady's heart rate sped up as images of Lester's big, strong body tied to the bed in Tady's bungalow suddenly popped into his mind's eye. He shivered. His scales rattled.

Control, idiot. Get control! Tady thought of shifting, but then he'd have to explain what he was doing up here, naked. Damnation and Dragons, why in the hell hadn't he thought to bring a pair of pants?

Les passed on the trail below him without noticing the huge Dragon tucked back against the cliff face just a few feet away. Tady watched Les move on down the trail, his strong, ebony back glinting in the sun, his perfect butt tightly wrapped in silk.

He ran his forked tongue across his lips, imagining the taste of all that skin -- sun-heated, slightly sweaty. Imagined Lester beneath him, knowing it was the Dragon that licked his ass and balls, knowing Tady's true self when they made love.

Tady imagined what Les must be feeling now -- the shimmer of warm silk against a smoothly shaved ass and the hot sun beating down on his back. His balls smooth and ultra-sensitive, brushing between his slick thighs with each step. Tady wondered if Les's beautiful cock was hard, if he was aware of it as well with each step he took.

Tady felt his own cock grow in response.

Les disappeared around a large lava outcropping. Tady didn't hesitate. He launched himself into the air, iridescent wings outspread and tail streaming behind like a long, scaled rudder, and coasted low on warm air currents, heading for the beach.

He heard a shout behind him. Reacting quickly, Tady dove beneath the canopy of the trees and made the rest of the journey on foot. So much for a relaxing morning as his Dragon self. Smiling grimly, Tady raced through the jungle, a rather small, naked Elf with huge plans for tonight.

Chapter 4

Amanda adjusted her floppy straw hat against the noonday sun, spread her lightly woven caftan to protect her legs from the tropical heat and took a sip of her iced tea. The mystery she'd been reading had almost succeeded in putting her to sleep, so she set the book down beside her on her lounge chair and laid her head back on the soft pillow.

Her dreams of Dragons and Elves and strange, sensual acts had made her restless all morning long, but now Amanda's body felt loose and languid, the tension draining away with each beat of her heart, each soft breath she took. Lester was right. She definitely needed this vacation. She couldn't recall ever being this relaxed, ever feeling so carefree.

She'd never been so bored in her life.

Less than twenty-four hours on this perfect island and she was already wondering about her next script, thinking of excuses to contact her agent and praying for something, anything, to bring a little excitement into her life.

"Good morning, my lovely Mandy. How are you this fine day?"

Anything but him.

Lorcan squatted down on the sand beside her. He was shirtless, hatless, wearing only faded shorts and a gorgeous light tan over his perfectly sculpted torso.

Amanda tipped the brim of her hat up and glared at him over the tops of her dark glasses. "What are you doing here?"

She couldn't make her annoyance much clearer than that.

"Looking for you." Lorcan did just the opposite -- he looked away, shielding his eyes against the glare of sun on the turquoise bay in front of them. "I owe you an apology for my boorish behavior last night." He turned back to her and grinned. His green eyes twinkled merrily. "According to my personal assistant, I occasionally act a bit too full of myself."

"Your assistant is right. Thank you. I accept your apology. Now, go away."

Lorcan slapped his hand over his heart. A heart on the left side of the most beautiful chest Amanda had ever seen, now covered with a smattering of dark, curly hair and the hand of an artist... long fingers, nicely trimmed nails... A man could do amazing things with a hand like that -- if he knew how to use it.

"Mandy, you wound me. I have apologized, something that comes neither easily or naturally to me. I beg of you, a second chance to redeem myself in your lovely gray eyes."

"I'm not interested." Amanda turned away and lay back down on her lounger. Her heart raced, her blood pounded in her veins. He might be a bore, but he was a gorgeous bore.

Strangely enough, she no longer felt bored.

Lorcan didn't go. He merely grinned at her, spread his long legs out in the sand and kicked his sandals off. How could such a jerk look so damned good? Lorcan rivaled any of Hollywood's leading men. His face on the cover of *People* would break every sales record ever set for any magazine.

Amanda studied him surreptitiously, checking out the long, lean length of him, peering at his perfect profile from beneath the rim of her hat, behind her dark glasses.

She hadn't really appreciated his appearance last night, at least not after the first serious glance. Not after he'd come on to her like a sleazy lounge lizard with his shirt partially unbuttoned and his "God's gift to women" attitude.

Today he seemed almost boyishly contrite. Her gaze swept along his muscled thighs and paused below his waist. Amanda's heart rate picked up a notch. No, correct that -- there was nothing at all boyish about Lorcan, if the bulge in his denim cutoffs was anything to go by.

He cleared his throat, sounding somewhat hesitant. "I actually planned to go snorkeling today. Would you care to join me?"

Damn, even his voice was sexy -- velvet soft and thick with Irish.

Snorkeling?

Amanda stared out at the colorful coral reef shimmering just beneath the clear waters of the bay. She'd thought of snorkeling, something she'd never done before. She'd feared going alone.

The beach here was deserted, except for the two of them. Did she really have the nerve? She glanced once more at Lorcan. She hadn't planned on this, not really.

He smiled at her.

Well, maybe, way in the back of her mind...

Did it really matter?

Amanda lifted her glasses and smiled back at him, willing to accept his apology after all. Even willing to take a chance. He *was* acting the perfect gentleman this morning... and damn, but Lorcan was one gorgeous male.

This was a vacation, after all. Amanda took a breath, made her decision and threw caution to the winds. "I don't have the equipment."

"I do." Lorcan lifted a mesh bag filled with two sets of flippers, diving masks and snorkels. "Join me?"

Amanda nodded, then set her straw hat and glasses aside. Her heart pounded so hard she wondered if Lorcan could hear it, thudding away inside her chest. She'd never done this before, not even on a closed set. So what if it was typical island garb? She sucked her stomach in and said a quick little prayer for support, if nothing else.

Lorcan stood up and helped Amanda to her feet. His big hand was warm and strong, surrounding hers with just enough pressure to tug her lightly out of her comfortable lounger. When he touched her, she saw him blink, almost wide-eyed, as if he might be feeling the same, electric connection she had zinging through her veins.

The paperback toppled to the sand. Amanda ignored it. Lorcan almost reluctantly freed her hand and grabbed the bag of gear. Amanda hesitated only a moment longer, then swept her colorful caftan over her head.

All her nervousness was worth the look on his face when she stepped out of the folds of woven cotton wearing nothing but a bright red thong bikini bottom... and barely enough blonde hair to cover the tips of her bare breasts.

Lorcan really tried to play it cool. He didn't stare, controlled the desire to drool... didn't even reach out to touch one of those perfectly formed globes attached to an absolutely gorgeous chest.

No, he handed fins and snorkel to Mandy and controlled the whimper caught in his throat until they'd both submerged in the warm, crystalline waters of the bay.

He was swimming with the woman of his dreams and she was practically naked!

More important, his hand still tingled where he'd touched her. Was she truly the one? Lorcan had heard of the magical connection, the link that existed between an heir to the throne of the Dragon clan and his Chosen One. Of all the women Lorcan had touched over the years, not once had he felt anything remotely close to the shock that raced from Mandy's warm fingers, through Lorcan's hand to spread like white fire throughout his body before lodging deeply in his groin.

Now, paddling slowly through the clear, warm waters, Lorcan watched Mandy with a new fascination, a knowledge he'd not had before. He had to touch her again, had to find out if his senses were telling him the truth.

He wasn't quite sure how he felt about any of this. Did he really want a mate? Did he have a choice?

Mandy might have been a sea nymph, her body so perfect, her thick hair flowing around her beautiful breasts, the tiny red thong merely an accent to her glorious backside and perfectly rounded tummy.

Lorcan wasn't wearing much more, just a tiny strip of fabric to cup his privates and a thin strap bisecting his buttocks, but Mandy didn't pay him a bit of attention.

No, she appeared totally focused on the glorious sea life beneath the surface, the flashes of brightly colored fish, the deceptively beautiful coral with its knife-like edges, even the occasional sea turtle lumbering slowly yet gracefully through the clear waters.

They danced with the fishes, played tag with a huge, ferocious looking eel, even posed beside a rather calm giant stingray. Lorcan pushed his concern over Mandy's status as his Chosen One to the back of his mind and let his worries go with the tides.

It was a day of magic. A day when a prince felt like a child again, when the magic of Chimera claimed two more sentient converts.

He'd lost track of time, but the sun had lowered on the horizon by the time Lorcan decided there had to be a missed meal somewhere. He dragged Mandy away from the coral beds and the two of them crawled up on the white sands like a pair of stranded dolphins.

Gasping, laughing, Mandy rolled to one side, her sand-sprinkled breasts mere inches from Lorcan's hungry lips. "Thank you. That was amazing. I never would have gone on my own."

He couldn't help himself. His fingers reached for her, found the swell of her breast, the sharp peak of her turgid nipple. "No, Mandy. Thank you. This has been the most amazing day. Watching you, watching the life beneath the sea... wonderful. All of it."

She smiled, leaned closer and kissed him. He knew she meant a quick peck to his lips. He caught her, his mouth waiting for her touch, his tongue primed to invade.

Lorcan reached out, held her by the back of the head, pulled her close and tasted her for the first time. Her mouth was closed, but his tongue gained entrance. She moaned, opening to him, flowering for him, her tongue sparring with his, her lips exploring, her teeth nipping at his lower lip.

He pulled her close and she came, willingly. Her breasts met his chest, her well-muscled thigh covered his hip. Lorcan surged forward, found her center, barely hidden behind the tiny scrap of red.

Groaning, he pulled his mouth free, tilted his head and found her right breast. The nipple was raised, hard and blushing a deep rose, inviting his mouth. He brushed the sand from her warm skin with a brush of his cheek, licked the peak, nipped it with his teeth then settled his lips around it for some serious suckling.

Mandy arched her back, forcing her breast against his mouth, her pubic mound hard against Lorcan's groin. A wave washed over their ankles as the tide slowly but surely rose.

Lorcan fumbled with the bare scrap of fabric that covered him, ripped away the smaller piece that covered Mandy. Her hands grasped his shoulders and she whimpered, a small, needy sound deep in her throat that caught him, held him in thrall.

She was hot, wet and ready, her folds of flesh swollen and wet from seawater and feminine dew. Lorcan teased her first, rubbing the broad head of his cock against her clit, dipping it briefly inside her wet vagina, then returning once more to the swollen bud awaiting him.

He'd fully expected sand. Somehow, not a single grain clung to his cock or Mandy's sweet pussy.

Only on Chimera...

Lorcan dragged the solid crown of his cock over her clit. Mandy cried out, a strangled sound of need, of desperate desire. Shifting to lie beside her, Lorcan found her opening with his fingers, explored deeply, swept his fingers over her clit, then rolled back between her long legs and aimed his cock for the hottest, wettest spot. Mandy was ready, her hands fluttering over his ribs and across his back, her body straining, tissues swollen and hot, primed for his invasion.

Lorcan thrust once, hard and fast, driving deep, then again. Mandy shattered around him. The tight, grasping muscles inside her hot pussy clung to his cock, clenching and releasing him as Lorcan slowed his assault to long, slow strokes in and out. Mandy whimpered when he changed his speed and direction, and cried out when he occasionally pulled all the way out to brush her hot juices across her swollen clit.

Mandy shuddered beneath him and whimpered. He thrust harder. She screamed, tightened her legs around his waist and climaxed again in his arms. Lorcan buried himself all the way, his balls pressed against her ass, his cock seated so deeply he bruised his pubic bone against hers.

Gloved within her wet heat, Lorcan paused, caught on the edge of orgasm. Then, hips driving, mouth open in a silent scream of pain and pleasure, he rammed deep and hard, filling Mandy for all he was worth. His cock swelled more within her tight channel, clasped in Mandy's tight muscles.

Like a driving piston, Lorcan thrust faster, harder... balls aching, lungs bursting, heart more engaged than it had any right to be...

Lorcan threw his head back and shouted. His climax exploded, powerful, overwhelming, frightening and intense. His semen shot up out of his balls and down the length of his hard cock, flooding Mandy's wet heat. His hips continued rocking against her, as if of their own accord.

Mandy grasped Lorcan's shoulders and screamed. Her heels dug into the small of his back. Her pussy closed tightly around his cock and she shuddered, giving up one more climax as Lorcan's heart pounded in his chest and his breath whooshed out of straining lungs.

His head spun. Blood pounded in his ears and when he opened his eyes, Lorcan saw black spots instead of Mandy's lovely face. A buzzing filled his head, the sound of a thousand bees, and the Dragon within fought for release, fought to claim the woman in his arms.

Lorcan had heard about such as this, but never expected to experience the full majesty of finding his mate. He'd not expected any of this. Definitely didn't want it, the mystical attachment between two souls. A mating such as theirs was a covenant, unbreakable, unending.

He felt it. Defied it. Denied it... and pumped his fertile Elven seed deep in the waiting nest of a seriously feministic, modern human woman.

Amanda had never felt so replete, so completely drained and satisfied. Even covered in sand, she couldn't recall an orgasm as emotionally and physically complete as the one still thrumming through her body. Lorcan lay, half on, half off her, his lungs expanding like a bellows, the pounding of his heart against her chest outpacing even the cadence of her own speeding rate.

Amazing. There was no other way to explain what she'd just experienced with what was, in essence, a total stranger. The most complex, fulfilling, overwhelming sexual climax of her life and it had to be with a guy who had insincerity nailed.

She brushed her fingertips through his thick, black hair. Lord but he was a gorgeous man. Perfect body, perfect smile, perfect technique... perfectly pointed ears?

Amanda frowned, swept the hair back from his ears and stroked the smooth tips. His ears were definitely pointed. Not just little points, either. No, they were unlike anything she'd ever seen.

Just then, Lorcan's lips found the pulse point in her throat. He nuzzled closely, his tongue finding the line of her jaw, the corner of her mouth.

Amanda forgot about his ears.

Lorcan licked and kissed his way down her body, spending a great deal of time on first her left breast, then her right. When she was arching her back and moaning, he moved on, licking tight swirls in her navel, then nipping at the tiny, neatly trimmed thatch of pubic hair just above the juncture of her thighs.

Warm seawater reached Amanda's knees, lapped softly, bathing her between her legs, then receded. Lorcan's mouth followed, his tongue finding her swollen clit, his teeth nipping the lips of her vulva.

Filled with his seed, her pussy wet and swollen, she shifted, unwilling to have him taste her. Lorcan's hands found her buttocks and he knelt between her legs. He grabbed her hips, tilted her pelvis and drove his tongue into her hot center.

The sun beat down on them. The beach was open to anyone who wanted to walk this way. Birds flew overhead. They could be discovered at any time.

Throwing caution to the winds, Amanda moaned once more, raised her knees to offer Lorcan better access and gave herself up to his licking, biting, searching mouth.

This was, after all, Chimera. The island of illusion, of love.

He nibbled gently at her clit, then licked. Long, slow, hot strokes of his tongue, each time delving deeper inside, until she felt his upper lip pressing on her clit and his tongue twisting and turning against tissues already sensitive to his touch. Amanda whimpered, her fingers diggin deep furrows in the wet sand, then reached up to grab Lorcan's shoulders.

Lorcan's fingers massaged her buttocks, traced the seam between her cheeks, swirled around her tightly puckered ass. He found a rhythm, his tongue going deep, his fingertip pressing against her sphincter. The waves rose a bit more, cresting over her mound, covering Lorcan briefly with each pass.

His finger pressed harder, his tongue went deeper, and Amanda's head spun with the multitude of sensations. He breached her anus at the same time his teeth found her clit. A wave covered him completely, but Lorcan's tempo never altered. Amanda screamed. Her body convulsed, her thighs coming together, holding Lorcan as yet another climax took control.

He soothed her with his tongue, his lips, even his teeth, then planted gentle kisses all about her neatly trimmed mons. His fingertip softly circled the sensitive ring of her ass and he brought Amanda slowly, but surely down from her orgasm.

Amanda's body went limp and boneless as Lorcan dragged her gently up the sandy wave-swept beach, just beyond reach of the froth. It came to her then, as she lay there in the warm tropical sands, gasping for breath, her eyes closed against the brilliant afternoon sun, her hands caught in the thick, black hair of a man with unusual ears and extraordinary skill, that now, after so many long, empty years, she'd finally found the magic.

Chapter 5

Gone was the smarmy, lounge-lizard pick-up artist who'd approached Amanda the day before. Lorcan was amazing, funny, sensitive, self-deprecating. They talked for hours, showered beneath a stream of fresh water falling from the cliffs, made love more than once, then went back into the warm waters of the bay to clean the sweat from their bodies. There, in the soft blue waters of Chimera Bay, Lorcan made love to her again.

He held her with an unusual reverence and this time, when he looked at Amanda, there was a deep question lurking in his brilliant green eyes. "Am I the only one who feels something magical about this day?"

Amanda shook her head. "No. I felt it the very first time you entered me. As if all the questions I've ever asked finally had answers. As if the empty parts of my soul were filled. Is it us, or is it the magic of the island?" She swept her hands along his finely shaped jaw, then lifted the dark hair covering beautifully pointed ears.

"Who are you, Lorcan? What are you?"

He dipped his head. "Can you love me, my Mandy? Can you feel the magic for more than today?"

She nodded, mesmerized by the depth of passion in his voice. Had it only been a day since he'd first touched her?

He stepped away from her then, gloriously naked, his body as perfect as any carved in marble by the artists of old. His gaze was intent, his eyes glowing. Lorcan's chest expanded as he took a deep breath, and then he began to speak.

"I am not human. I am Elven, of royal blood. I am Prince Lorcan of the Northern Realm of the Lands of Eldar, ruler of the Northern Eldar, direct descendent of the First Kindred, Dragon Clan. I believe, with all my heart and soul, that you are my Chosen One. I find you, my lovely Mandy, to be a woman befitting the title of Princess of the Northern Realm. I pray you heed my call, that I might court you in the manner befitting one who would wed the prince."

Amanda blinked. *What the hell?* She was still assimilating the northern realm-prince-wedding jargon when Lorcan suddenly wavered in front of her. His form shimmered, glowed, then slowly shifted and stretched until she faced, not the man she'd made love to all afternoon, but a full-blown, gossamer-winged, sharp-taloned, large-toothed, green-eyed Dragon.

Amanda did the only thing any modern woman under the circumstances could do.

She fainted dead away.

Lorcan frowned, stared down at her perfect, prostrate form. "Well, that approach needs some work," he said. Then he curled up beside her to wait for Mandy to awaken.

Lorcan watched over her, soaking up her scent, her womanly tastes still lingering on his tongue and lips. He'd never experienced anything like the lovemaking he and Mandy had shared over the course of the past day. There was no longer any doubt in his mind she was his chosen mate, ergo, there was no way he could -- or would -- give her up.

He sighed and nuzzled her prostrate form. Somehow he'd have to help her get over this odd reaction to his shift. Of course, he knew very little of human women. Lorcan wondered if they were all so easily frightened.

Waiting grew tedious when Mandy didn't stir. The day had been long and they both needed time to rest. Unfortunately, Lorcan hadn't been able to keep his hands off of Mandy at all during the day. Even now he wanted her, if only to have her sleeping beside him where she belonged.

After a bit, Lorcan regained his princely form, gathered the unconscious -- or was she merely sleeping? -- Mandy in his arms, and carried her back to her bungalow. He left her sleeping soundly on her bed, her blonde hair spread out like a golden halo, with a note on the pillow beside her. Kissing her lightly on her parted lips, he tip-toed from the room.

* * *

Les stepped out of the shower and grabbed a large towel. His dick was so hard it almost hurt to dry himself and he'd practically come when the shower spray hit the damned thing, so he toweled carefully between his legs and over his belly.

Tady said to save it. Damn it all, Les intended to save it, but the little guy better be prepared for a whole lot of Lester Ondáge tonight!

Les rubbed the soft cotton towel across his chest, glanced at himself again and sighed. His balls were still as slick and smooth as when Tady'd shaved him the night before. Not a single whisker marred his groin or butt. Les rubbed his hand across his bewhiskered chin and wondered what magic Tady had that kept hair from growing back.

He grabbed the silk sarong he'd tossed over a towel rack and carefully wound it about his waist and hips, folding the top under the way he'd learned, to keep it from falling off.

Les's sensitivity to the air currents alone was enough to keep him turned on, much less the relentless slip and slide of that blasted silk sarong. He hitched it as tight as he could, but there was still an obvious protrusion in the front. Sighing, he reached for his razor and the shaving cream.

What a day. The image of that Dragon, or whatever he'd seen coasting over the treetops, slipped into his mind. Les had never seen anything remotely like it, more beautiful than any bird, unimaginably graceful, almost sensual, in flight.

Chimera was supposed to be special. Maybe it was one of the indigenous life forms, something that lived here and nowhere else? As the razor swept over his jaw, Les let his mind fly free. What would it be like, to be a Dragon? To fly free and far, to have the power of those huge muscles, those scythe-like teeth?

Rubbing his hands across his smooth jaw and shaved skull, Les caught himself grinning. He'd have to ask Tady what he thought of Dragons. For some reason, they'd always fascinated Les.

Until today, he'd considered them figments of imagination. Maybe the Dragon was a sign...

Light sparkled through the ferns and palms separating his bungalow from Amanda's. Les put his razor away and headed in her direction. It was a bit too early to meet Tady... the least he could do was check in and see how Ms. Carlisle's day had gone.

"Sweetie, you in there?" Les rapped softly on the door.

"That you, Les? C'mon in."

She sat in a wicker chair, her hair all undone and falling free, a light robe covering her sun-kissed skin. As usual, Les caught his breath at Amanda's natural beauty. She might be almost forty, but the experience in her eyes and the glow that was a part of her nature merely added to the image of perfection.

He leaned over and kissed her cheek. Her hand slid over his shoulder and stayed, a fiery brand against his left biceps.

Obviously something was not right.

"What's up, sweetie? Something bothering you?"

She shook her head. "Dreams, maybe? I saw something today I still can't quite reconcile..."

"So did I!" Les sat on the edge of the rumpled bed. "I hiked up the hills toward the volcano and by damn, I think I saw a Dragon!"

Amanda's head came up. She stared at him with a tiny frown marring the smooth skin between her eyebrows. "A Dragon?"

"Yep. It must have been sunning itself on a ledge above me... I saw it gliding down over the jungle, then it disappeared into the trees and I lost it, but the damned thing was huge. Way bigger than a lizard... wings about twenty feet from tip to tip, a long tail with a spike at the end, shiny scales that reflected the sun, it..."

Caught up in his description, Les hadn't noticed how pale Amanda had suddenly grown. "Sweetie, are you okay?"

She nodded, then licked her lips. "I'm fine, Les. Really. I..." She glanced around, grabbed a sheet of notepaper off the table beside her. "I need to get going, love. I'm meeting someone for dinner."

"Anyone I should know about?"

This time the color returned to her face full force. "Uhm, not yet, okay? He's definitely someone interesting, though. I'll tell you about him later." She glanced up and seemed to truly see Les for the first time. "I do love that sarong, Les. You look absolutely marvelous. Going somewhere?"

He laughed. "You could say that. I've got a date tonight, too. What say we get together tomorrow and compare notes?"

Amanda's smile lit up her face. "Works for me." She leaned over and kissed him full on the mouth. "Have a wonderful night. Be careful."

Les kissed her back, then headed out the door. The silk swished back and forth across his swollen cock, swept over his smooth butt. The cool evening air found his naked balls and he walked a little faster, heading toward Tady's secluded bungalow.

* * *

Amanda squinted into the mirror and applied a touch-up coat of lipstick. The entire day had an almost dreamlike quality about it, but as sore as she was between her legs she knew at least part of it was real.

It was that last, final moment, that shimmery, foggy, almost believable image of Lorcan standing tall in front of her, announcing he was an Elf of royal blood, then turning himself into a Dragon that went way beyond credibility.

Except, Les saw a Dragon today... She didn't doubt for a moment what he'd seen. Somehow, the impossible seemed merely improbable on Chimera.

Which meant, if Les had seen a Dragon, maybe she'd seen one too.

The slip of paper with directions to the restaurant caught Amanda's eye. She glanced at her watch. Lorcan should be there by now. Would he have an explanation for what she had or had not witnessed?

He did have the most delightfully sexy pointed ears...

Amanda grabbed her small clutch bag and wrapped a pale blue silk shawl around her shoulders. Knowing she would see Lorcan in less than five minutes gave her a wonderfully warm ache between her thighs, a hollow, hungry sense of expectation in her womb.

She mentally replayed the last few minutes she'd spent with Lorcan on the beach. He'd said he was a prince, an Elven prince.

Well, he certainly has the ears.

He'd called her his *Chosen One*, as if it were some sort of ritual, binding them together.

The way her heart felt tied to his made that all too believable.

Then he'd shimmered, wavered and sort of... *shifted*... from human to Dragon.

Amanda shook her head. That was pushing it just a bit too far.

I did not see Lorcan turn into a Dragon.

Lester saw a Dragon today.

She laughed out loud. *Magic.* It was all about the magic.

Light spilled across the wooden veranda at the edge of the seaside bar and grill. A few couples chatted at small tables, their faces lit by flickering candles. One man sat alone at the bar.

Lorcan!

His back was to her, but Amanda knew she'd recognize those broad shoulders and narrow waist anywhere. She paused a moment, drinking in the sight of him, the sense her destiny waited mere steps across the teak floor. What had she seen today?

An Elven prince who shifted from sexy male into fierce Dragon before her eyes?

Amanda took a deep breath. There was only one way to find out.

Two blondes swept by her, headed directly for the bar.

Directly for Lorcan. He looked up, smiling, as first one then the other planted a wet kiss directly on his mouth.

"Lola! Lila... how nice to see you!" Lorcan gave each woman a very familiar hug.

Lola, or was it Lila, slipped her hand in the back of his loose-fitting chinos. The other blonde thrust her full breasts forward and stepped between Lorcan's widespread thighs.

They were obviously already very well acquainted.

Amanda felt her skin go hot, then icy cold. Her blood pressure rose way beyond the explosion point. She stalked across the small space and planted herself directly in front of Lorcan.

"Looks like you're already busy tonight, dear."

Lorcan's chin snapped up. His eyes went wide. "Mandy!"

"You rotten, lying, two-timing, pointy-eared lizard. How dare you!"

"You don't un..." He rose to his feet, dumping one clinging blonde to the deck, shoving the other aside.

"You're damned right I don't. After what we... how we... oh hell!"

Her vision blurred and Amanda frantically blinked back the unwelcome tears, but her voice was low and ragged when she finally cleared her throat. "Why did I believe anything you said? You bastard." Spinning on her heel, Amanda charged out of the bar.

She thought she heard Lorcan behind her and walked faster. When she finally looked back, there was no one there.

A large man loomed up, out of the darkness. At first she thought it was Les. Amanda gave a sigh of relief.

A complete stranger stepped into the light. "Do you need any help?"

Amanda shook her head. "No, I..." Then she took a closer look. Damn, he was beautiful. Weren't there any homely guys on this island? As tall as Lester, with short, spiky blond hair and broad shoulders of the sort that sent a woman's heart into overdrive, he carried himself with the kind of presence that turned any woman's heart.

"Actually, I'd love a drink. Would you care to join me?"

He hesitated a moment and glanced toward the bar, then held his arm out to her. Amanda took it. She hoped Lorcan noticed. Damn, she was not going to cry. How could he do this to her? They'd made love all day long. He'd acted as if it meant something to him. He said he wanted to *court* her, damn him, like some otherworldly prince! Then he'd pulled that damned trick and scared her half to death… and now he was in there crawling all over a couple of sexy blondes.

Amanda smiled up at the blond giant beside her.

"My name's Amanda. And you are…"

"Roar. My name is Roar." He handed a glass of sparkling wine to Amanda. "Is everything okay? You looked distressed."

Only because the jerk inside ripped my heart out… well, okay. That's a little melodramatic… "I'm okay. I was a little upset over, well, nothing." She looked up at the huge man and smiled brightly. "I'm fine. Thank you."

He found a table for the two of them, well within view of Lorcan and his twin bombshells. Amanda tried not to look in their direction, but her eyes seemed to have a mind of their own… When she stole another glance, Lorcan was alone at the bar, his back to her, a row of empty glasses in front of him.

Good. It served him right. She smiled at Roar. He smiled back. His teeth were very white, perfect, in fact. Everything about him was perfect.

Everything except the fact he wasn't Lorcan. Amanda sipped her wine and tried to answer his friendly questions appropriately. Inside, she felt as if her heart were breaking.

It was almost a relief when, an hour later, two equally gorgeous hunks appeared at their table. Obviously, they were close to Roar. Very close. One of them leaned over and whispered in Roar's ear. The other smiled sympathetically at Amanda.

Roar nodded, shrugged his shoulders and gave Amanda an apologetic smile. "I have to leave. May we walk you home?"

She shook her head. As brush-offs went, this one had been pretty painless. "I'm fine. Thank you, though, for the company. For helping me out."

Roar dipped his head. "My pleasure." He reached across the table and covered Amanda's hand. "Thank you. May all your dreams come true."

Amanda watched the three men walk away. There was something about them, something not quite what she would have expected... she thought of Roar's wish... *May all your dreams come true.*

Of their own volition, her eyes focused on the bar where Lorcan had been sitting.

The stool was empty. All that remained was an empty row of glasses.

Chapter 6

Les paused just outside Tady's bungalow. Soft lights glowed through the open windows, along with some absolutely mouth-watering scents. The air about him was alive, the soft chirp of crickets awakening, the twittering, clicking sounds of birds settling in to sleep.

Caught on the bridge between day and night, Les experienced a sense of enchantment, an awareness of both his body and his surroundings unlike anything he'd known before.

He tried to picture himself as he must appear to Tady. Large and muscular, his skin was an overall deep, coffee brown that added size to an already over-sized man. With his shaved head, amber eyes and one big, gold earring, Les knew he easily intimidated most people he met for the first time.

Not Tady. No, that little guy had balls. He'd sized Lester up and not found him fearful or wanting.

Les sighed. Not found him wanting at all… to the contrary. Tady found him desirable.

Just as Les found Tady. He grinned and stepped forward to knock on the door. It swung open as he raised his fist.

Tady stood in the open doorway, his blond hair slightly ruffled, his perfectly formed body hidden beneath a soft blue silk shirt and white cotton drawstring pants. He smiled at Les without speaking a word, then stepped back and waved him through the door.

"You're just in time. Dinner's ready." Tady pointed to a chair and handed Les a glass of sparkling wine. Bubbles danced in the golden depths. The table was set with fine china, linen napkins, sterling silver. A bouquet of exotic flowers decorated one end, placed so as not to interfere with conversation.

Les took the fragile crystal glass and stood awkwardly by his chair. He felt like a bull in a china shop, horribly big and awkward next to such a petite and obviously stylish man. Damn, he hoped he remembered which fork to use!

"Sit, Lester. Relax." Tady raised up on his toes and kissed Les's cheek. "I have a full night planned for us. I want you well fed and comfortable, not looking as if you're afraid to touch anything."

Lester glanced at Tady out of the corner of his eye, then tipped his wine glass and finished the whole thing in a couple of swallows.

Tady laughed and refilled Les's glass. He set a huge plate laden with all kinds of succulent morsels on the table. "Well, it doesn't have the kick of those little numbers you scarfed down last night, but whatever works..."

Les sat down the moment Tady did. He took a serving of the baked fish and some of the vegetables, then followed Tady's lead on the proper utensils to grab.

Within minutes their conversation flowed, along with the wine.

"... and I told the prince he'd better quit acting so full of himself if he wanted to attract a woman. I'm amazed I had the nerve to say that, but the poor boy's needed to hear it for years."

"Any idea who he's trying to impress?" Lester took another serving of fish. Tady really had outdone himself.

"Some woman he met here on the island. Her name's Mandy. Do you know her?"

Les shook his head. "No one I know, but then I've hardly met anyone. I went hiking today... saw the most amazing thing."

Tady looked up from his meal. "What was that?"

"I could swear I saw a Dragon." Les laughed out loud. Tady'd think he was nuts. "I hiked up the western flank of the volcano and it took off from one of the ledges up there. Coasted down over the jungle and disappeared."

"A Dragon?" Tady nodded his head. "Could be. The island is known for the unusual. What did you think of it? Did it scare you?"

Les shook his head. "Scare me? Are you kidding? It was gorgeous... absolutely gorgeous. Wish I could have gotten closer. There is something magical about a creature that big, that unbelievable, flying. The sun glinted off the scales like fire over ice... I'll tell you, Tady, it was the most thrilling thing I've ever seen."

Tady nodded. "I'm glad."

He stood up abruptly and began clearing away the dishes. Les helped stack them in the dishwasher, sensing the building awareness between the two of them each time their arms brushed or their hips touched. By the time the small kitchen area was clean, Les felt as if he were ready to explode.

Tady went around the room, dousing the lights until only a couple of candles burned. He reached into the dresser drawer and withdrew a black scarf, the same he'd tied over Les's eyes the night before.

Without waiting for instructions, Les leaned over so Tady could blindfold him. The small man still had to stretch to place it securely over Les's eyes. Les straightened up once more, held in thrall by the darkness, caught in an erotic world of Tady's design.

He'd spent the last twenty-four hours in a state of arousal. His groin cleanly shaved and sensitive to every draft of cool air, every wisp of fabric that made contact. He'd not touched himself, not found relief no matter how strong the urge.

No, Lester had stuck to Tady's directions as if they'd been carved in stone.

He sensed Tady's nearness as he stepped close to Lester and brushed his wide palm down the front of Les's sarong. Les sucked in his breath, his body went rigid, and he closed his eyes behind the silk, silently begging for control.

"Have ye found release since last we met?" Tady's brogue was suddenly more pronounced, his voice deeper.

"No, I've not. I wanted to, though." Les grinned nervously and shifted beneath Tady's slowly moving fingers.

"Answer the question only. No speaking, unless you feel the need to tell me *Enough*. You're mine tonight, Lester Ondáge. Mine to do with as I wish. This is my cock..."

He lightly squeezed Lester's full erection. Lester bit back the whimper in his throat.

"These are my balls..."

Tady's fingers stroked Les's testicles through the shimmering silk. A tiny drop of fluid escaped the end of his cock and soaked into the material. The damp spot felt cold against flesh that had to be nearing combustion.

Tady's hand slipped around Les's thigh. Thick fingers traced the crease in his buttocks through the silk. "This is my ass... I might screw it. I might spank it... I will do whatever I want with it. It's mine, is it not, Lester?"

"Yes, Tady." Les's voice cracked.

"I am pleased with the sarong. Has it been comfortable? Do you like the way the fabric slips over your smooth ass, the way it sucks up so close to your perfectly shaved balls?"

"Yes, Tady."

Tady stripped the sarong from Les's hips in one smooth maneuver. The silk whispered as it slipped over his bare skin.

Les shivered from the nape of his neck to his toes, a jolt of pure energy that left him covered in goose bumps.

"I want you to lean over and place your palms on the edge of the bed." Tady guided Les as he spoke, bending him over the bed so that his butt stuck out behind him.

Another shiver raced along Les's spine. He felt totally vulnerable like this, shaved and naked... blindfolded. Though he wasn't at all restrained, Les knew he was helpless to stop whatever Tady chose to do to him.

It was, after all, a matter of choice.

Something cool and wet dribbled over his buttocks. Tady's hand smoothed the cream, rubbing slow circles over the hard muscles of Les's rear, occasionally sliding up and down the crease in his ass.

Les wasn't used to being touched there, but he found himself subtly shifting his hips to bring himself closer to Tady's fingers. On about every third pass, Tady pressed harder against Les's anus.

Then every other pass.

Then he stopped.

Les's lungs expanded like a bellows, his cock felt ready to explode, and he waited, engulfed in his personal darkness, to see what Tady would do next.

Warm, damp fingers found his cock, then something tightened around the base, tightened almost to the point of pain.

"That's to keep you from coming. Please tell me if it hurts. I don'na want to hurt you."

Les nodded. He wasn't sure he could speak at this point.

Something warm and smooth brushed over his ass. Was Tady going to fuck him? Did the little man with the big cock know he was a virgin, at least in that particular part of his anatomy?

Les blew out a couple of quick breaths. Tady's hand pressed low on his back. "It's not my cock you're feeling, Les. It's a simple plug. Something to make you more aware of yourself."

Les relaxed a bit just as Tady's slick fingers found entrance. One finger, then two filled him, thrusting slowly in and out. His cock strained, his balls ached, but the band around his cock kept him from coming.

Then something hard and smooth and very large slipped inside him. Les grunted. He wanted to ask Tady if he'd just shoved a doorknob up his ass, but he wasn't ready to break the rules.

Whatever was in there felt huge, though Les knew his sphincter had tightened around a smaller, narrower end. He was still trying to adjust to the sensation when Tady helped him straighten up.

"Feel okay?"

Les nodded. If feeling as if every nerve in his body were exposed, as if his cock must be swollen to ten times normal size, as if his balls might explode was okay then, yeah... he was okay.

"Good. Now this might pinch."

A soft tongue swept over his left nipple. Teeth nibbled and lips sucked until shivers ran over Les's entire chest. If this was Tady's idea of a pinch, Les figured he could stand it for at least a week or two.

"Ouch! Shit... sorry. It's okay... I..." Les's breath huffed in and out like a freight train climbing a steep hill.

"Nipple clamp." There was laughter in Tady's voice. "Sorry, thought I warned you."

Les was ready for the second one. At first it hurt like hell, then settled down to a dull ache that took his attention off the plug in his butt and the band around his cock.

At least, for a moment.

Tady was obviously having a wonderful time with all this. Les wondered where it was leading. He felt trussed, probed and pinched and so damned horny he fully expected something to blow any minute.

"On your knees, Lester."

Okay, this wasn't quite what he meant when he thought about blowing. Les knelt down on the floor, surprised to find a pillow waiting to cushion his knees. Tady was nothing if not thoughtful.

"Use your hands and your mouth. Show me what you would like someone to do to you."

Well, if he's gonna put it that way...

Les reached out blindly, found Tady's surprisingly solid thigh with his left hand. Grasped his other thigh, then walked his fingers around to grab Tady's buttocks. He might not be a large man, but Tady's muscles were hard as rocks. They flexed beneath Les's searching fingers.

He nuzzled Tady's smooth groin, licked the root of his swollen cock. Just like Tady's butt, this muscle felt like solid steel.

Hot steel, encased in smooth silk.

Les dipped his head, licked the hard length of the other man, then ran his tongue over Tady's balls. It was gratifying to hear a choked whimper. Les bit back a smile as he set about showing Tady exactly what he liked.

Oh, Tady thought, he'd had this planned so well, how he was going to take control, how he'd love to have the big man on his knees with Elven cock down his throat. Tady hadn't given a thought to how hard it would be to have any kind of control once he actually implemented this long-held fantasy.

Tady threw back his head and ground his teeth together as Lester slowly ran his tongue the length of Tady's cock. His lips were moist velvet, his tongue hot and searching, teeth nipping and teasing.

Damn. Tady's knees quivered, his thighs barely held him upright, and Les hadn't worked on him but a few seconds.

This was going to be horribly embarrassing. Hell, he'd almost come just putting that plug in Les's ass, watching the dark pink muscle slowly stretch to accommodate the smooth, metal plug, then tighten back down around the base. Tady'd imagined that same muscle doing the identical maneuver around his cock and had to resort to his multiplication tables.

Now, glancing down at Les, at the golden nipple clamps firmly attached to his slightly swollen, dark nipples, to the red ring encircling his equally swollen cock, Tady realized he'd bitten off more than he could chew… literally. How was he ever going to satisfy this gorgeous giant of a man? How could a little Elf with a big imagination possibly pull off an evening powerful enough to make Lester want to stay?

Les obviously took this project seriously. Tady rested his hands on the big man's shoulders to steady himself, though Les's hands had his butt in such a firm grip, Tady knew he wouldn't fall.

Damn, Les's skin was dark chocolate satin, smooth and slick, totally without blemish or scar. Muscles rippled as he sucked and licked Tady's balls, dipping his head low to swipe his tongue completely around the sac, then sucking first one, then the other gland between his lips.

Les paused a moment, as if considering his next move, then he opened his mouth and took Tady's cock deep, swallowing the thick head, taking him down his throat.

No, Tady didn't want to come, didn't want to lose it so quickly, he…

Lester found a rhythm, in and out, his tongue licking, his teeth scraping, hands squeezing.

Tady moaned. It felt too good, too perfect to stop. He centered himself, finding his own marginal control, then let himself go with the rhythm, let his body open to whatever Lester did, found the freedom in giving himself over to Les's mouth, his hands, his lips and teeth.

Les's thick forefinger found the ring of muscle between his buttocks. Tady tensed at first, then relaxed with the subtle press and release, press and release. Suddenly, Les thrust his finger hard and deep inside his ass, clamped down on Tady's cock and sucked like a Hoover. At the same time, his free hand slipped between Tady's legs and squeezed his testicles, hanging there so firm and solid, almost but not quite to the point of pain.

Les could, at that point, have ripped them off. Tady wouldn't have noticed. The combination of thrusting finger and compressed lips, nipping teeth, licking tongue and enough suction to take paint off walls, tipped the scales.

Tady's knees buckled, the air whooshed from his lungs, and a load of sperm exploded way before either he or Lester was prepared to deal with it.

Gasping, whimpering, practically sobbing for breath, Tady leaned into Les's embrace. Damn, he felt so foolish to have lost it so quickly. Foolish and so damned good he wanted to cry.

Lester continued sucking, then licked his cock clean, running his tongue over it until Tady was totally flaccid and reduced to tiny whimpers deep in his throat. Then Les picked him up like a child and carried Tady the two short steps where he laid him on the bed without saying a word.

Les stood beside the bed and waited. His eyes remained hidden behind the blindfold. His cock was so swollen it looked as if it might burst. His nipples, almost black beneath the tight clamps, looked like huge berries.

He still wore the plug in his butt, still waited for Tady's instructions. Still carried himself like a proud, if subjugated, island god. Watching Lester Ondáge standing tall and proud, yet still under control was the most heartwarming, emotional experience in Tady's life.

Somewhere between one breath and the next, Tady O'Shea fell completely, irrevocably, head over heels in love.

Lester waited, his body pulsing with an overload of sensations ranging from exquisite pain to overwhelming pleasure. His heart thudded in his chest, the salty taste of Tady's sperm filled his mouth, and he tried to imagine a time beyond Chimera, a time away from this island and the little man who had snared him as completely as if he'd been a fish on a line.

Not one of his lovers had ever suggested putting Lester in a submissive role. No, they'd taken one look at his size, his presence, and assumed he would always be in charge.

Even Les had made the same assumption. Then along came this little elf of a man with the big ideas and bigger cock and *wham*! Les might not be physically restrained, but his heart felt shackled all the same.

After a few long moments waiting, something warm and moist brushed his arm.

Tady's lips. They traveled across his chest to the clamped nipple over his heart. Les had heard of nipple clamps. Never before had he experienced them. The pain was subversive, dragging his thoughts into a sensual spiral from nipples to balls and back to his nipples, an unending circuit of sensation.

Tady released the left clamp and blood rushed back in. Warm lips suckled the swollen flesh, a tongue stroking the tip, soothing it. Les sighed, even more aware of the tactile connection between nipple and balls, balls and cock.

The right clamp came off next. Swollen nipple licked, suckled and soothed, just as the left had been. Next, Tady helped

Lester lean over a small bench. Les had noticed it earlier, sitting unobtrusively near the end of the bed with a rolled towel lying on the floor in front of it. Carved wood, padded seat, about two and a half feet high. He hadn't given it much thought at the time.

Still blindfolded, Les followed Tady's silent instructions that left him lying with his chest across the padded surface, his knees cushioned by the towel, his ass in the air and his ringed cock bouncing vainly against the edge of the bench.

Les grabbed the legs of the bench and held on tightly.

Knowing what would most likely come next raised his heart rate. His breathing went from long, slow pulls to short, sharp gasps. Tady had to know he'd never done this before.

That didn't mean Les wasn't willing to try.

Gentle fingers brushed the end of the plug, gave it a slight twist.

Damn... the sensation was like a shock through his entire body. Les realized he'd raised his hips without thinking, making himself more accessible.

His cock ached. He wanted to reach down and pull that damned strap off, but he kept his grip tight on the bench legs. Forced himself to relax.

Warm fingers traced the shape of his butt, trailed lightly between his legs and gently rubbed his aching balls. Anticipation warred with fear and desire... Les groaned and spread his knees wider. His legs -- hell, his entire body -- trembled.

Damn, he didn't know how much more of this he could take.

In the same thought, Les knew he didn't want it to end, not this amazing sense of closeness to Tady, not the wonder of each new sensation, each fresh touch.

Once more Les felt warm lotion rubbed between his legs, over his ass, even on his balls and cock. Tady tugged at the plug, rotated it again very slowly, tipped it back and forth, pushed it deeper, pulled it back against the tight muscle... back and forth, back and forth until Les felt his sphincter relax, winced slightly as Tady pulled the plug free, then sighed as the broad head of Tady's smooth cock slipped easily inside, passing through the now relaxed muscle without any pain at all.

Rock solid thighs spread Les's legs wider. Smooth, hot balls rubbed lightly against his own cleanly shaved set as Tady slowly but surely buried himself completely inside Les.

Les didn't breath, didn't move. He waited for expected pain. There was none. Tady held completely still as well, as if giving Les time to adjust to the huge cock filling his ass.

Les let out a long, slow breath, then pulled a deep draught of air into his lungs. He settled his knees more comfortably on the rolled towel and let sensation set him free.

Tady leaned forward and draped his body over Les's back. Les felt each breath where Tady's lips rested against his skin. He bit back a whimper when Tady's fingers found his cock, slick from all that lotion, aching from the ring still pressing into the base.

"Does this feel good to ye, man? Do you like the whole of my big cock shoved balls deep in your gorgeous ass? You can talk, now. I give you permission to speak at will."

Les opened his mouth just as Tady reached down and stroked his balls. All that came out was a groan. It took him a moment to catch his breath, to find his voice. "Oh, God, man... my God that feels good."

"I thought you might like it." Tady pulled his cock out slowly, then just as slowly thrust deep. This time, his fingers found the catch on the cock ring. He released it on the next drive, replacing the tight band with a circle of his thumb and forefinger.

In, out, Tady's huge cock filling and then retreating, his fingers repeating the action along the length of Les's cock. Lester's legs trembled. His knuckles gripping the legs of the bench lost feeling. Tady replaced his fingers with both his hands, fingers tightly laced around Les. He continued his steady penetration, his slow, smooth slide up and down Les's erection.

Lester's entire world centered on the huge cock sliding in and out of his ass and the hands slipping back and forth on his cock. He felt Tady's hot breath against his back, felt his own climax building, the sperm finding its way to the surface as Tady suddenly stiffened behind him and howled.

Les felt every thrust and spurt as Tady climaxed deep inside. Felt every gasping breath, every muscle lock in his own overwhelming climax. Black spots, bright stars and shafts of light burst behind the blindfold. Moaning, practically weeping with relief, Les collapsed on the sturdy bench.

Draped across Les's back, his cock deeply embedded inside Les's ass, Tady continued to stroke Lester's dwindling erection, rubbing the thick ejaculate along the length of his cock.

Les's full weight rested on the small bench, but his heart and soul soared free. Tears dampened the blindfold still covering his eyes, but he felt suffused in light. He'd never known this connection, this sense of oneness with another person.

Had not thought it possible.

How, Les wondered, would he ever be able to leave this man?

How could he manage to stay?

Chapter 7

Tady awoke in the middle of the night, his back pressed firmly against Lester's broad chest, his body engulfed in the huge man's powerful arms. A long, thick cock wedged between his butt cheeks and the soft even puffs of breath against his neck told him Lester was sound asleep.

Tady smiled but his heart ached. Was it possible to fall in love in just a couple of days?

Yes. Of course it is. You've gone and done it, haven't you, ya dumb shit.

He'd never felt so safe, so secure, so loved in his entire life. Nor had he felt as frightened. What was Lester going to say when Tady told him of his true self?

It's never gonna work... never.

Tady shifted his hips to press more firmly against Les's cock. He felt a hitch in his lover's breathing and realized his subtle motion had just brought the sleeping giant awake.

Tady shifted, rolled over so he could face Lester in the darkness. Moonlight glinting off amber eyes confirmed Les had truly awakened. Les hugged him close and stroked his back.

"Tady, I..."

"Lester, there's..." Tady chuckled. "You go first." Tady pressed his cheek against Les's chest and listened to the rhythmic pounding of his heart.

"Tady, I may sound like a fool, but is it possible to fall in love in so short a time? I... I feel things for you I've never felt for anyone else, man or woman. I don't want to lose this, whatever it is."

Tady felt the tears rise in his throat, so hot and burning they almost choked him. He pressed a damp kiss to the muscle just above Lester's nipple. "Aye, I must be as big a fool as you, Lester

Ondáge, because I feel the same way. A bigger fool, actually, because I've not been truthful with you."

Tady felt Les stiffen beneath him and knew he had to tell the truth.

"I'm not like you, Les. I'm..."

"Of course you're not. You're little and white. I'm big and black. We can get past that."

Tady knew his laughter sounded more like a sob. "Ah, if only it were so simple. Les, I'm not human. I'm an Elf... and more than that, I'm an Elf of Clan Dragon."

"Huh?" Lester leaned back to get a better look, but his arms remained firmly locked around Tady's waist. The movement brought their cocks into close contact.

Neither of them had an erection.

Tady reached up and flipped his blond hair back to display his perfectly pointed ears.

"Well, I'll be damned."

Les stroked the upper edge of Tady's ear with the broad tip of his finger. "I can live with this." He chuckled. "They're really kinda cute. What's a Dragon clan?"

"Come with me." Tady slipped out of bed, waited for Les to follow him, then walked out on to the lanai. Moonlight cast a silver gleam across the teak deck. Candles burned in two torches near the door. "Sit here, okay?" Tady held out a chair for Les.

The big man sat.

"Watch very carefully. Don't be afraid." Tady stared into Les's eyes, waiting for the look of fear he fully expected.

He shifted. Almost, but not quite an instantaneous process, he knew there would be a moment of disorientation as his brain adjusted to seeing the world through his many-faceted Dragon eyes.

The moment passed. Tady gazed down on Les from his much taller self -- and looked into eyes of wonder and a smile of amazement.

"Holy shit." Les stood up, then grabbed the back of the chair for support. He hadn't realized how hard his knees were shaking. "Holy fuckin' shit. You're a goddamned Dragon, Tady. A big fucking Dragon. How? I mean..."

Les stood there and stared. He had to believe his eyes. He'd seen the man change, just sort of melt, reform and get bigger. A lot bigger. The Dragon had a body bigger than a horse. It was hard to tell how large his wings were, all folded up the way he held them, but if this was the Dragon Les had seen yesterday, those wings had been at least twenty feet from tip to tip.

The Dragon -- no, *Tady*, this was definitely Tady -- curled one lip in what had to be a grin. His ivory-colored teeth were at least six inches long. His voice, when he spoke, rumbled up out of his chest like the sound of a drum. "I might be a little man, Lester Ondáge, but I become a very large Dragon."

"No shit, Sherlock." Lester reached out slowly and ran his fingers over the scaled neck. He'd expected something almost metallic because of their iridescent sheen, but instead the silver-dollar-sized scales were warm and pliable to the touch.

He shook his head, well aware he couldn't shake the stupid grin off his face. "You're beautiful, Tady. An absolute fantasy creature. I had no idea..."

Tady slowly lowered his heavy head and rested it lightly on Les's shoulder. "I was afraid you wouldn't understand, that you'd think me a freak."

Les ran his palm across Tady's broad, scaled cheek. "Never, Tady. You're not a freak when you're a little Elf with big blue eyes, pointy ears and a package that belongs on a bull. How could I think you're a freak when you're more beautiful than any creature I've ever seen in my life, more magical than anything I could ever imagine?"

Tady nuzzled Les's shoulder. "Fly with me, Lester. Let me show you Chimera."

Feeling as if he'd entered a dream, Les grabbed his sarong out of the bedroom, tied it around himself like a silk diaper and crawled up on Tady's strong neck. With a powerful beat of his wings, Tady lifted the two of them into the nighttime sky.

The sun was peeking over the flank of the volcano when Tady coasted down onto the lanai with Les clinging tightly to his scaled neck. He and Les were both exhausted as well as exhilarated, but they'd come to a definite agreement -- if they were going to give their newfound love time to grow, they had one, and only one, option -- get their respective employers together.

Somehow, Prince Lorcan of the Northern Realm and Ms. Amanda Carlisle, Hollywood star, had damned well better fall in love.

* * *

Amanda glanced up from her morning coffee and croissant just as Lester rounded the path from his bungalow, headed directly toward hers. He walked like a man with a mission, his bare feet slapping the packed sand hard enough to send dust flying.

Amanda pulled her dark glasses down her nose and peered over the top of the frames. "So, who put the bee up your butt, Lester?"

His head snapped up. "Oh, I ah... wasn't sure you'd be awake yet, not after a date. Good morning, sweetie. How was your night?"

"It sucked... and not in a friendly way." Amanda sighed and took another sip of her coffee. "I got to the restaurant just in time to see him fondling a matched set of blondes."

"Ah, sweetie. I'm sorry." Les leaned over, hugged her shoulders and kissed her cheek. "The guy's a complete jerk. Want me to break some bones?"

Amanda smiled thinly. "It's tempting, but not this morning. What about you, Les? How was your date?"

Lester poured himself a cup of coffee and sat across from Amanda. He took a sip and grinned. His entire face lit up. "Can I say fantastic? Amazing?" He sighed. "I've never felt this way, not ever, about anyone. I know it seems sudden but... Ms. Carlisle, would you be so kind as to join me for dinner this evening. I want you to meet my friend."

Amanda grabbed his huge paws in her hands and squeezed. Damn, at least one of them was happy. Les deserved love. "I'd like nothing more. You're sure he won't mind?"

Les shook his head. "I was trying to figure out how to get you away from your new love so you'd come with me. Guess now I don't have to worry about that. I'll pick you up at seven, okay?"

Pain sliced Amanda's chest and settled deep in her heart. She'd expected the feelings for Lorcan to be gone by now... she'd only known him a day, not nearly long enough to really care one way or another what he did.

So why in the hell did she still hurt so much?

"I'll be ready. What are you going to do today?"

Les rubbed the back of his closely shaved head. "Sleep. I'm gonna sleep all day long." He blushed again when he looked back at Amanda. "We didn't do much sleeping last night."

"I guess I do need to meet this special someone... if he kept Lester Ondáge awake all night, he must be special." It was the best she could do. Amanda felt horribly petty at having to force any joy over Les's happiness.

Les leaned over and kissed Amanda's cheek, then wandered back to his bungalow. Amanda lay back and covered her eyes with her forearm. She would not cry. No more tears. She'd only known Lorcan for a day, long enough to fall in and out of love with the biggest jerk she'd ever met.

Had she really seen him change from human to Dragon? No way. Damn, she must be losing her mind. Maybe she needed stress to function properly! She certainly didn't need a pointy-eared shape shifter with roaming hands.

Crap. The tears Amanda'd been fighting leaked from beneath her closed eyelids. She'd never had a lousier vacation in her entire life. All she wanted was to go home, back to the smog and stink and cutthroat business typical of life in Los Angeles.

Now how the hell was she going to talk Les into cutting the trip short? He was obviously having the time of his life.

Amanda sniffed. Les could stay on Chimera if he wanted. She'd just go without him. It was time to go home. Time to face reality again, to find a new project, a new reason for living.

Chimera's illusions, so far as Amanda could tell, had been exactly that -- illusions and lies.

Lester picked her up at seven. He wore a different sarong tonight, one of deep reds and shades of orange and turquoise. Amanda thought he looked even more like an ancient island god... but then he'd looked like a god in the last sarong he'd worn, too.

She hated to tell him it was time for her to leave the island. Maybe tomorrow. There was no point in ruining his evening tonight. She knew he wouldn't want her to go alone. Les took his position so seriously, cared about her so deeply.

Why couldn't Lorcan be more like Lester?

Amanda looped her arm in Lester's and walked beside him to the restaurant. There was something terribly erotic about walking along a jungle path with a half naked man, even if the man was unequivocally gay. Amanda squeezed his arm and leaned against his strong body.

"Les, has anyone ever told you how gorgeous you are?"

Lester laughed, a deep, booming sound that started low in his chest and worked its way out. "Why, Ms. Carlisle... I do believe you're flirting with me."

"Of course I am, Lester." She sighed. "The problem is, Les, you're the standard I find myself judging all other men by, and they always come up short."

He stopped and drew her into a warm, comforting hug. His smooth chest felt warm against her cheek and his laughter tickled the top of her head. "That's only 'cause I'm so tall, sweetie. Don't worry. You'll find your man. He's out there, just waiting for you." He ran one finger along her cheekbone. "You never know... maybe you'll meet him tonight."

Les gave Amanda a quick kiss on top of her head and they walked on toward the restaurant. The night was warm and humid. The scents of jungle and humus, flowers and ripe earth enfolded them as they followed the trail. It was still bright enough the torches hadn't been lit, but Amanda knew they'd each spring to life the moment light was needed.

All part of the magic that was Chimera... a magic she wished she were more willing to accept. Had she really seen Lorcan shift from man to Dragon?

Nothing seemed clear anymore.

Had she really seen him encouraging those women, or was he just being friendly?

"I wish I could believe you, truly believe there was someone waiting for me. I honestly thought I'd found him..." Amanda *had* felt it with Lorcan. Felt the magic. *If only...* "Tell me about your man, Les. I've never seen you serious about anyone before. What's he like?"

Les chuckled. "Tady? He's little, not even as tall as you. He's smart and funny with a wicked sense of humor... He's got blond hair and the brightest blue eyes you ever saw, but he could be seven feet tall and covered with shiny scales and I'd love him just as much."

Covered with... Amanda planted her feet and stopped. "Lester, if there was something really unusual about Tady, you'd tell me, wouldn't you?"

"Uh..." His amber eyes shifted away from hers.

This was not like Les at all. "Lester? Have you *seen* Tady standing seven feet tall with scales? Shiny, iridescent scales and huge wings?"

Les looked away, sighed then nodded, but he didn't look happy about giving away Tady's secret. "Have you seen him, too?"

Amanda grinned. "No, but I think I've seen a close double. I thought I was losing my mind. C'mon. I want to meet this new love of yours."

Les grabbed her hand and they reached the restaurant in record time. A diminutive but very attractive blond man waved to them from a corner booth. Amanda smiled and said hello, all the while trying to picture this very tiny man with Lester.

It was easier to imagine him turning into a seven-foot-tall Dragon. Now *that* was something she'd already seen.

"Tady, I'd like you to meet Amanda Carlisle, my employer and very good friend."

"My pleasure, Ms. Carlisle." Tady stood and bowed. "My employer should be here any... ah, there he is, now. Milord?" Tady waved his arm.

Amanda turned around.

Lorcan stopped dead in his tracks.

"Mandy?"

"He's the jerk who..."

"Ms. Carlisle is Mandy?"

Lorcan stepped forward before Amanda could catch her breath. "Yes, Tady. It appears Ms. Carlisle and Mandy are one and the same." He took her hand in his, and for all his smooth talk she could feel his fingers tremble. "I'm so glad you've decided to join us for dinner, Mandy. You will dine with us, won't you?"

Unable to speak, Amanda merely nodded. Lester was still scowling at the prince, but he made way for Lorcan to seat Mandy and slide into the booth beside her. His body felt lean, long and very warm pressed close beside hers. Both Tady and Lester glared at them from across the table.

Les stared at Lorcan as if he'd only be happy when he got a chance to tear the man in two. Tady appeared just as furious with Amanda. She wondered what Lorcan had told his manservant.

Lorcan's hand found hers, a strong, warm anchor in the swirling sea of emotions filling the small booth. He squeezed her fingers and smiled at her. Amanda smiled back. She blinked away sudden, unexpected tears.

The tension around them eased.

They ordered, ate and talked, their conversation flowing comfortably within a few minutes. Lorcan described the Northern

Realm, Amanda told silly stories of Hollywood. Lester and Tady nodded in all the right places, even added a word or two, but their attention was paid mostly one to the other. Amanda felt a warm glow in her heart watching Lester.

Obviously Les was just as besotted with Tady as the small man was with his giant. Amanda couldn't bring herself to look at Lorcan, so afraid of what she'd see.

"Dinner was excellent." Lorcan wiped his mouth with his napkin and set it beside his plate. He smiled at Tady. "I imagine you two have plans for the evening." He held his hand out to Lester. "I've enjoyed meeting you, Lester. Now, if you gentlemen will excuse us, I think Man... uh, Amanda and I are going for a walk."

Amanda turned her head slowly and found herself staring directly into Lorcan's green eyes. "We are?"

"Yes, my love. We are. I'm not willing to waste another day with any anger between us. Please... there have been too many misunderstandings. Will you walk with me?"

She nodded her head, smiled weakly at Lester, and allowed Lorcan to lead her from the restaurant.

Chapter 8

Amanda slipped her hand around Lorcan's arm as they strolled along the quiet beach. The area where they walked was near the spot they'd made love. Had that only been yesterday?

Neither of them spoke, yet Amanda didn't feel the least bit uncomfortable. It was as if something about this night were fated, no longer in her control.

She thought of the looks of expectation on both Lester and Tady's faces. Of course they would want their employers to get along. It was obvious the two of them were already deeply in love.

Could one fall in love so fast?

How should I know? The only man I've ever loved is Lester.

No, that's not true... She took a quick glance at Lorcan and caught him watching her, his eyes dark emerald chips in the waning moonlight. She loved him. That's why she'd been devastated last night, to see him kiss those two women. He'd obviously already gotten to know them quite well.

"They meant nothing to me, you know."

Amanda smiled. "Are you reading my mind?"

"I wish I could." Lorcan stopped and turned Amanda to face him. He cupped her shoulders in his elegant hands. "I met them briefly on the beach shortly after I arrived, and then I saw you, standing alone on that high pinnacle over the sea, and I no longer saw the two blondes beside me. Of course, that particular meeting between us did not go so well."

Amanda laughed out loud. "You were smarmy and insincere and obnoxious as hell. What could go right?"

Lorcan had the good grace to blush. He looked away and chuckled. "I figured that out, later." He looped his arm around Amanda's waist and they continued their slow stroll along the sand.

"In my country, I am a prince, a much sought after member of the royal family. I can act the jerk and still get the girl. That doesn't make me any less a jerk, as Tady helped me realize." He laughed, obviously embarrassed with his admission.

Amanda's heart began to melt.

"After you told me to get lost, I went to the bar to drown my sorrows. I already knew then I wanted you... not merely for one night. I wanted you for all time, beside me. I just wasn't sure how to repair the damage I'd already done."

"Ah, so that's when you ran into Lola and Lila."

"Oh yes. After too many tankards of ale and much self-recrimination, I once more met Lola and Lila. They were more than willing to take me back to their bungalow and help ease my pain."

Amanda felt a cold fist surround her heart. Was he that shallow?

"Of course, I did not go. That alone told me I was in terrible trouble." He squeezed Amanda's waist and pulled her close against his side. "I have never before turned down an invitation like the one those girls offered. Believe me, leaving the two of them alone in that bar was not in my nature. Amanda? Look at me."

She turned in his arms and looked into hooded eyes, almost hidden behind silky dark lashes. He gazed at her with such longing she felt her own desire leap to the surface. "It *is* my nature, now. Now that I have met you, there's no need for another woman. Ever. You are the only one I want. The only one I will ever want. I've never asked a woman for her hand in marriage and I won't ask you yet, not until I have properly courted you. But, know this. Marriage is my ultimate goal. I never fail. It is not an option."

Almost of its own volition, Amanda's hand rose and she gently caressed his cheek. "Is that a dare, my Elven prince?"

"Not a dare, lovely Amanda. A promise." His lips found hers, warm and sweet, inviting her total surrender. When he finally broke their kiss and led her toward his bungalow, Amanda followed him without question.

Lorcan's small hut was much like hers and Lester's. Private and secluded, they might have been the only inhabitants of Chimera. Lorcan closed the door behind them and lit a couple of candles. Flickering shadows and light reflected off a large gilded mirror that covered most of one wall. The satin bedspread glowed a deep ruby red.

Lorcan tangled his fingers in Amanda's thick hair and he drew her close to his mouth for another heated kiss. She felt languid, boneless in his embrace, her mouth opening to his, her tongue sparring gently with Lorcan's.

Their bodies met, sealed together by heat and desire. His hands were in her hair, caressing her breasts, trailing along her ribs to the rounded curve of her hip.

Amanda tore her mouth free, catching air with each heaving gasp. She looked into his eyes, focused on the deep green filled with need and want, then slid her hands inside his shirt, ripped the buttons free and bared his chest.

She put her mouth on the firm muscle just above his breast, trailed kisses along his throat until he lifted her, his arms strong and sure as he stretched her out on the bed.

The mirror to her left reflected both Lorcan and Amanda… She watched their reflections in the glass as Lorcan slowly peeled her dress down over her thighs, slipped her panties off along with the silk. When Lorcan stood beside the bed and stripped himself bare, Amanda watched him in the mirror, her head turned away from his perfect form.

"Look at me, not at the reflection of the man who needs you."

Amanda slowly turned to face him. "Need is not love, Lorcan. Do you love me? Can you love me, a simple human when you, yourself, are someone of another world?"

"Ah, my love." Lorcan knelt on the edge of the bed, one hand in her hair, the other brushing the flesh covering her ribs. "You are my love, my one true love, my Chosen One. I knew it the moment I saw you, but I denied the truth. When we swam together, I accepted my fate. When we made love I welcomed it. When you left me, when you smiled at that other man, I felt my life had ended. I love you. I can say it no plainer than that. I love you and want you for my wife."

"Will you shift for me? I promise not to faint." Amanda's body pulsed with need but she had to see this, had to accept all of Lorcan before she could make love to him again.

He nodded. Stepped back from the bed. Glanced about him as if checking the amount of space he had. As Amanda watched, Lorcan rippled, faded, shifted, all within a few beats of her heart.

Knowing now what to expect, Amanda fully appreciated the mystery, the beauty of the Dragon kneeling in the room. Naked, curious, more aroused than she could recall, Amanda rose from the bed and reached out to touch the iridescent scales covering Lorcan's throat. He leaned his huge head close and nuzzled her shoulder.

He ran his long, rough tongue across her chest, leaving a trail of heat from one breast to the other. Followed that with an equally slow, unbelievably arousing lick between her legs. Amanda stepped closer. Her nipples were on fire, their tender tips abraded by the Dragon's tongue, the sensitive tissues between her legs already weeping with need.

She wanted more. He was beautiful. More beautiful than any creature she'd ever seen. Magical. He was magic incarnate. Amanda wrapped her arms around his neck and pressed her face close.

Lorcan's voice rumbled out of the Dragon's chest, deeper, rougher, yet still the same. "I cannot hold this form when the man in me wants you so badly, my sweet Amanda. Now you've seen, do you believe?"

Tears streaming down her cheeks, Amanda hugged Lorcan's neck even tighter than before. She nodded against the warm scales and felt him shift once more, becoming Lorcan in her arms.

He lifted her, carried her to the bed and knelt beside her.

Then, very slowly, very thoroughly, Lorcan made love to her.

His elegant hands with their long fingers played music upon her body. Amanda arched beneath his touch and cried out when his mouth followed where his fingers had blazed a path. Lorcan moved between her legs and nipped at the tender skin of her inner thighs, suckled her blood-rich labia between his lips, then laved her swollen clitoris with the flat of his tongue. He brought her to the very edge of orgasm, then backed away.

Her body tingled and trembled with need, every inch of her on fire. She whimpered, raised her hips in blatant invitation and sighed when his tongue found her once again. Teasing, licking, suckling, from long, slow sweeps of his tongue to sharp little nips of his teeth, Lorcan brought her once more to the peak.

Then he left her, shivering and gasping, her body burning, needy and wanting.

His hands grasped her buttocks, kneading and massaging until her muscles felt malleable as warm clay. His fingertips teased the sensitive ring of muscle between her cheeks, pressed and released without entering, held her closer to his searching mouth, but still he wouldn't let her come.

Moaning, whimpering deep in her throat, Amanda fisted the satin bedcover in her grasping fingers. Her head thrashed from side to side and Lorcan held her, a willing prisoner of mouth and lips, fingers, teeth and tongue.

When she thought she might explode, when every sense and synapse cried out for release, Lorcan suddenly raised up on his knees, moved close, rubbed the thick head of his cock in the moisture between her legs and thrust, hard and fast and deep.

Amanda screamed. His fingers tightened on her buttocks and he held her close, lifting her hips and burying himself even deeper, thrusting harder. She wrapped her legs around his trim waist, felt the thick pressure of his cock against the mouth of her womb, the heavy weight of his balls pressing into the crease of her butt, the fiery shock of climax taking control, lifting her higher, harder, faster, brighter than she'd ever gone before.

Gasping, sobbing, she threw her arms around Lorcan's neck and held him close, clinging to him. Her pussy clenched, the muscles unwilling to let him go. Her fingers and toes went numb as every bit of feeling centered between her legs, inside her pulsing, shuddering, weeping body.

Lorcan thrust once more, then again. Suddenly he stiffened in her embrace, his fingers tightening around her buttocks with bruising intensity. He threw his head back, cried her name. "Amanda! Mandy, Mandy my love, Amanda." The last he whispered against her ear as he lowered her to the bed and collapsed across her shivering body.

She felt each pulsing release flooding against the mouth of her womb, bathing her with his seed, each hot breath that tickled her throat below her ear. Her fingers stroked his sweaty back, fluttering over ribs and muscle, tracing the hollows of his muscular buttocks.

The stray thought flitted across her mind that they'd not used any protection, not once when they'd made love, something she'd never done in her life. Rather than feel fearful or foolish, Amanda smiled, wondering if Elves and humans were compatible, if this amazing lover of hers could give her a child.

If only they could actually consider a future together.

Impossible.

Lorcan belonged in some mystical land he called the Northern Realm, a land where Elves ruled and Dragons flew.

Amanda's future lay in a kingdom just as mystical but not nearly so wonderful… the corporate fantasy that was Hollywood.

She'd always loved her life, her career, her chosen path, no matter how frivolous it often seemed. Why now, when this man offered her something just as insubstantial but twice as magical, did Amanda find herself afraid to follow a dream?

They made love once more, a sweet and tender coming together of two souls afraid of the truth. Lorcan had sworn his love for her. Had promised her a life in his kingdom unlike anything Hollywood might ever imagine.

Amanda had done her best to show him her love with her touch, with her mouth, her body, her heartfelt response. Unable to say the words, she'd let him take her back to her bungalow for a few hours' sleep before the day began.

A soft knock on the door awakened Amanda. Disoriented, she sat up quickly and shoved the tangled hair out of her eyes. She vaguely remembered showering with Lorcan after they'd reached her room, but he'd gone as promised and left her alone.

Except for that incessant knocking. "Just a minute." She wrapped a robe around herself and opened the door. Lester stood just outside.

He looked worried, almost distraught.

"Les?" Amanda opened the door wider and stepped back to let him in. "What's wrong? You look upset."

Lester nodded and entered the room. Without any preamble, he turned with his hands on his hips and an accusatory tone in his voice. "The prince says you won't marry him. Why not?"

"What?" Amanda's hand went to her throat. "I didn't actually say no..."

"You didn't say yes, either. The man loves you. He said he'd apologized for acting like such an ass the first night, that he thought you cared for him, but..."

Amanda sighed and reached for the coffee pot. She had a feeling this discussion might require a lot of caffeine. "Les, I've known him just a couple of days. Not nearly long enough to fall in love."

"Are you implying I don't love Tady?"

Amanda shook her head. "Of course not. It's obvious you two have a special connection, that you're meant to be together... I'm not sure that's what I share with Lorcan. I need more time, Les. It's a huge decision to make."

Les sighed and took both her hands in his. "Remember, sweetie, it's a decision that affects all of us."

"What do you mean?" Amanda looked down at their linked hands, his twice the size of hers, dark as the coffee trickling into the pot yet more gentle than any hands she'd ever known.

Except Lorcan's.

"It would break my heart to leave you, sweetie." Lester squeezed her fingers tightly. "You're the sister I wished I'd had, the daughter I'll never have, the mother I never knew. You're more important to me than I ever imagined and I love you so much! You are all the special women in my life, rolled into one perfect package. You. I need you."

He took a deep breath and his shoulders slumped. "Thing is, I've found a love with Tady so far beyond anything I've experienced in my life, a love so complete that I can't make myself give him up. He loves his prince the same way I love you. It puts us in a terrible conundrum -- does he leave his world to come with me, or do I leave mine to be with Tady? I can't ask Tady to give up his life -- he's a Dragon, sweetie! A gorgeous, full-sized flying Dragon and he lives in a world we've only imagined. They're not immortal, but almost. If we go to the Northern Realm, our life spans will be just like theirs. We'll eventually grow old, but not for a long, long time."

He smiled, but there was no humor in it. "Think about it. I really don't have a choice. Tady can take me to his world and make me a part of it... what can I offer Tady in mine?"

Amanda bowed her head. "I need time, Les. We've still got a few days. I would never ask you to stay with me no matter how much I love and need you, not at the risk of your love with Tady. I have to figure out where my life is going, where I want it to go. Most of all, I need to sort out my feelings for Lorcan."

She raised her chin and looked deep into Lester's amber eyes. "Les, you are my one true friend. I depend on you more than I've a right to. I love you and I admire everything about you. I will miss you terribly if you go with Tady and Lorcan, but I would never ask you to stay. All I ask is a little time. Can you give me that?"

Lester leaned over and kissed her full on the mouth. "You know I'll give you whatever you want or need, including time. The question is, what about the prince?"

Sighing, Amanda pulled her hands free of Les's gentle grasp and turned to pour each of them a cup of coffee. "What about the prince?" She smiled and handed Les a cup. "Time, Lester. A little bit of time alone, without his amazing presence affecting my decision." She laughed, but there was very little humor in the sound. "I find it very hard to think rationally when he's near."

It was no easier to think rationally when he wasn't near. Amanda sat under the shade of a palm tree and gazed at the waters surrounding Chimera. Dazzling turquoise blue sea, snow-white sands -- it was too perfect to be real.

How much of what she'd experienced these past few days had been illusion, how much reality? This was, after all, Chimera. She'd discovered the island not only welcomed Elves, there were other creatures beyond belief, vacationing, meeting, falling in love. She might have been vacationing on a Hollywood set, for all the fantastic things going on around her.

If she went back to LA, would this all be but a dream, an insistent memory of something that might have been?

The thought of returning had begun to fade. Was that the island's doing as well? Was she somehow being coerced into making a choice that wasn't her choice at all?

What would she be giving up if she took the chance this was real, gave into her heart's desire and went with Lorcan as his bride?

She had no family waiting for her. Very few friends. Friendships and Hollywood didn't really go together at all.

Her only true friend would be gone, living with the one he loved in a magical kingdom where men became Dragons -- and a prince could fall in love with an aging Hollywood actress.

She was thirty-eight years old. Ancient by Hollywood's standards. William, her agent, had grown distant, the parts coming her way fewer and farther between. The audience was still there, but were they looking for the young ingénue they recalled or actually enjoying the traces of age beginning to show on her face?

William had mentioned plastic surgery.

Actually, he'd more than mentioned it. He'd given Amanda the business card of a well-known surgeon and suggested she set up an appointment as soon as possible.

Lorcan hadn't noticed the lines around her eyes. Lorcan had feasted on her beauty, the beauty of a woman well into her prime. He hadn't missed the bloom of youth long past.

He thought she was beautiful. More than that, he loved talking to her, teasing her, experiencing new things with her.

Am I so superficial I worry more about appearance than substance?

The idea left her cold. Was she really willing to give up a mystical, magical love with Lorcan for a few more years of shallow adulation from her fans?

A shadow fell across her. Amanda looked up and smiled. A large and particularly beautiful Dragon blocked the sun as it landed lightly on the sands in front of her. His huge, iridescent wings beat once, twice, then folded neatly along his back and sides. There was a brilliant green strip of silk wrapped around his neck. It matched the color of his eyes.

"Will you come fly with me?"

Fly? Of course! Why not? Laughing, Amanda rose to her feet and kicked off her sandals. Lorcan crouched low and dipped his neck. Without thinking beyond the moment, Amanda tucked her sarong between her legs and straddled his smooth, scaled back.

Lorcan raised his head and unfurled his wings. They glistened in the sunlight. "Hold on tight. Wrap your arms around my neck and grab onto the fabric. It'll give you a better grip."

Amanda did as she was told, hooking her heels beneath the large muscles where Lorcan's wings attached to his body and tightening her grip around his long neck, the silk bunched tightly in her fists.

The Dragon lifted off with a huge jump and a powerful thrust of his wings. Rising quickly, following warm air currents over the island of Chimera, Lorcan flew in an ever widening arc, spinning higher, farther out over the sea, then back toward the broken caldera of the volcano. Amanda found herself caught between watching the gorgeous landscape unfolding below and studying the smooth undulations of muscle and sinew as Lorcan carried them aloft.

This was magic. Unexplainable, unbelievable, inexplicable... magic.

It came to her, a flash of lightning so obvious, so real, Amanda laughed aloud. What kind of idiot wouldn't trade Hollywood for this? There she only pretended at fantasy, merely acted emotion, passion and love.

The only magic she created was scripted, directed and paid for.

With Lorcan, she would live it. Real, heartfelt, sometimes painful, always honest, true passion and emotion, the raw unedited fantasy of life... the magic she'd always wanted.

He landed high on the western flank of the volcano, way above the tiny bungalows barely visible along the edge of the jungle at the point where it met the perfect sands.

Setting down gently, Lorcan dipped his neck low so Amanda could slide off. Her hands were numb from holding on so tight and her bottom felt bruised from her seat on his muscular neck.

She'd never felt better in her life.

Lorcan shifted, his image wavered, and he stood before her, naked but for the fabric sliding down over his shoulders. Amanda realized immediately it was a sarong, just like Lester's. Lorcan tugged it free then wrapped it around his hips and tucked the ends beneath the waistband.

Then he looked at her, his eyes filled with love, the question in them obvious. "I know Lester said you needed time..."

Amanda smiled and shook her head. "I've taken all the time I need." She stepped closer, so close her breasts beneath the light silk sarong she wore pressed against Lorcan's warm chest.

So close their hips met and his arms seemed to come up of their own accord and wrap her even closer, hold her even tighter.

Amanda reached up with her left hand and touched the side of his face, gently shoved the black hair back to reveal his perfectly pointed ear. "I love you, my prince. I love everything about you. I don't know why or what I doubted. I'm not sure how to make the break from my world to yours, but if you'll still have me, I'm yours."

She raised up on her toes to kiss him, met his lips as he bent down to hers.

Magic.

The thought crossed her mind. Somehow it all seemed so right. She'd gone in search of the magic. Here on Chimera, the magic not only found her, it stole her heart away.

Epilogue

"Uncle Lester, Uncle Tady, look at me!"

Les and Tady glanced up from their game of chess as Micah, Amanda and Lorcan's eldest son, raced into the room. His hair was as black as his father's, his eyes the deep, penetrating gray of his mother's, but he was all seven-year-old boy and always a handful.

"Watch me."

Lester grinned at Tady and they both turned their attention on Micah. You never knew what the little monster was going to come up with next, but with two doting uncles, a grandmother who spoiled him rotten and a little sister who thought he hung the moon and lit the stars, a bit of attitude was to be expected.

Suddenly Micah stood very still. His forehead wrinkled, his eyes shut in concentration, his pointed little ears practically quivered. His wiry form wavered, misted and shifted.

Tady looked at Lester and shook his head. "We're in for it now, ya realize?"

Lester nodded and stared at the perfectly formed Dragon sitting in front of the chess table with a big toothy grin on its face.

Micah's voice squeaked out of his Dragon chest. "Cool, isn't it? Mom freaked."

Lester laughed. "I bet she did. She has enough trouble with you when you're a regular little boy. What'd your dad say?"

"His father said he's never to shift without permission and is absolutely forbidden to fly unless Tady or I are with him." Lorcan sounded stern, but Lester could see the pride in the prince's eyes clear across the room.

"I told him he'll have to answer to Uncle Les if he doesn't mind his father." Amanda followed behind Lorcan with four-year-old Meggie clinging to her hand. Only a month away from her delivery date, Amanda still looked youthful and absolutely gorgeous. "We all know what a meanie Lester can be."

Even Micah laughed at that one. Then he shifted, reformed, and was once more the little boy everyone loved.

Lester glanced up and caught Amanda's gaze. There were bright tears in her eyes and a huge smile on her face.

Les felt his own eyes well up, figured he was grinning like an idiot -- but he also knew that Amanda, more than anyone else in the room, understood exactly what he was feeling. Mainly, because he knew Amanda felt it too. They'd left the world behind in search of magic. Both of them had found love.

Without a doubt, the greatest magic of all.

Kate Douglas

For over thirty years Kate Douglas has been lucky enough to call writing her profession. She's produced ad copy for radio, flown over forest fires in a spotting helicopter as a photojournalist, drawn a weekly comic strip for a worldwide health agency, co-authored a cookbook and written numerous freelance articles. She's won three EPPIES, from the international authors' organization, EPIC -- two for Best Contemporary Romance in 2001 and 2002, and a third for Best Romantic Suspense in 2001. Kate's also won EPIC's Quasar Award for Cover Artists.

She and her husband of over thirty years live in the northern California wine country where they find more than enough subject material for their shared passion for photography, though their grandchildren are most often in front of the lens.

Visit Kate at www.katedouglas.com. For regular updates and a chance to win copies of Kate's books and other cool stuff, sign up for her newsletter by sending a blank email to KateDouglas-subscribe@yahoogroups.com.

A.O.E.M.: 4 Play
Eve Vaughn

Chapter One

This day couldn't possibly get any worse.

Trina brushed an angry tear away as she made her way down the block toward her small ranch style house. No, she wouldn't cry.

I knew I shouldn't have gotten out of bed.

The day started out lousy when she woke up at eight-thirty, the time she was supposed to be at work. Her live-in boyfriend Tim snored loudly beside her, oblivious to the predicament he'd placed her in. He'd unplugged her alarm clock again. She wasn't going to let him get away with it without saying something this time. Trina shook him. "You jerk!"

Tim's response was to turn around and open one light brown eye. He pushed a thick dreadlock from his eyes, giving her that lazy smile of his, which usually made her knees weak. "What's the matter, baby?" he asked in his deep Barry White-like voice.

"Don't you 'baby' me. You pulled the plug on my alarm clock after I've asked you time and time again not to. Now I'm late. Thanks a lot, jackass," she admonished before scrambling out of bed.

Tim sat up looking unapologetic and unconcerned, further pissing her off. "You know how I hate the sound of that screeching alarm. Why don't you set it to music?"

"Because I'd sleep right through it, that's why."

"Well, the sound of your alarm disturbs my aura," he said, not sounding a bit repentant. He grinned at her as he sat up, the cover dipping lower to reveal his muscular, golden chest. She was a sucker for a nice body. His sexy bedroom eyes lowered, surveying her scantily clad body.

She felt her pussy getting wet with the seductive look he sent her way. Damn him for doing this to her. She placed her hands on her hips, determined not to let him manipulate her as he normally did. "You know what I find disturbing? You've been without a job for nearly two months now and it doesn't seem as though you're putting much of an effort into getting another one."

"What am I supposed to do? I can't work just anywhere. I'm an artist."

"No, you're a bum, and you had better get your lazy ass in gear, because I'm tired of paying all the damn bills."

He pouted, looking offended. "I'm trying as hard as I can, but it's hard for a brother to find work out there in this depressed economy, especially when the *man* is constantly trying to hold him down."

Trina rolled her eyes in exasperation. She didn't have time to get into it with Tim and listen to another one of his conspiracy theories. It was always someone else's fault, never his own. The *man* wasn't Tim's problem -- his laziness was.

"We'll discuss this when I get home from work, but I hope you drag your butt out of bed long enough to straighten the place up a little bit. The last thing I need is to come home to find your clothes thrown all over the place."

"I'm not the damned maid." A petulant expression fell across his face, detracting from his handsome looks. He poked his lip out, looking all of five years old instead of thirty-five.

"I'm not saying you are, Tim, but after working full-time, I shouldn't have to come home to find your stuff thrown all over the place."

"I thought you liked doing stuff for me. You said nothing pleased you more than to take care of your man," he pointed out.

She was sure she'd never said any such thing, but she supposed she had done everything for Tim, so it really wasn't a wonder why he took advantage of her now. In the beginning, she'd been smitten with him and made pleasing Tim her priority. Now it was getting old.

"Look, all I'm asking you to do is to clean up after yourself. At least put your clothes in the washer."

"But I like the way you clean my clothes." He smiled at her as though he knew he'd get out of it as he usually did.

"Tim, this is not up for discussion. Don't you think I get tired sometimes? Besides, I'm tired of cleaning your funky-ass underwear. I don't know what you've been doing lately, but there've been a lot of skid marks in your briefs. I don't buy toilet paper for nothing, you know."

"Stop talking like you're my mother. I'm a man, damn it."

"Well, start acting like one and I won't act like a mother. Clean this place up!"

"I live here too, you know. I'm not a cleaning service."

She could have pointed out that her name was the only one on the deed, but she was late as it was. By the time she finished preparing herself for work, she was forty-five minutes late.

Luckily, her job was only ten minutes away. Unluckily, her fifteen-year-old Jeep didn't feel like cooperating. She wasted another twenty minutes waiting for the bus. By the time she made it to work, Trina was nearly two hours late. The minute she set foot into the bank, she could feel a malevolent set of eyes follow her progress to her desk.

Stephanie.

God, she hated that bitch. Trina was sure Stephanie had already pointed out her tardiness to their boss. As she sat down, her boss walked over to her desk. "Miss Davis, do you know what time it is?" Mr. Peterson asked in his usual condescending tone.

"Yes, I do. I left a message on your voice mail."

"That doesn't change the fact you're two hours late."

"You're right. I'm sorry. It won't happen again," she said through gritted teeth. She knew from experience that it wasn't a good idea to contradict her boss. No one liked to be wrong, but he made being right all the time a science. Heaven forbid if someone pointed out one of his numerous errors. It wasn't above him to make his employees miserable. She was still paying for correcting a mistake he'd made a year ago. If she had not been with this bank for seven years and enjoyed what she did, Trina would have quit a long time ago.

"I know I'm right. Of course you know I'm going to have to write you up."

"But I've never been late before," she protested.

"So you say, but it's been brought to my attention that you leave earlier than you should." He folded his arms across his chest, hovering over her in an intimidating stance.

He was her boss, but she wasn't about to be reprimanded for something she wasn't guilty of. "I'm here until five o'clock on some days and past that on most others. I take pride in my job, and I've never left early."

"Are you calling me a liar?" He raised a brow, a frown marring his corpulent face. He stood so close to her she could smell stale coffee and eggs on his breath. Her stomach turned.

"I'm not calling you a liar, but I'm saying whoever informed you I leave early is." She briefly glanced over her shoulder to see Stephanie Nash looking at them with a satisfied smirk on her face. Stephanie couldn't get over the fact that Trina continuously beat her every quarter for bringing in loan revenue.

Trina would have been happy to share her secrets, but Stephanie thought she knew everything and brushed aside any of her friendly overtures. The redhead eyed Trina with a look of triumph in her frosty blue eyes.

"Miss Davis, if you've finished daydreaming, I would appreciate your attention." Trina could feel her face grow hot as she turned her head to look up at her boss. His loud voice seemed to fill the entire bank. His beady brown eyes drifted to her breasts. It took every ounce of her self-control not to slap the nasty out of him.

"As I was saying, I'm going to have to write you up so there's no point in arguing. The next time you're late, you'll be on probation. I'm sure you know what will happen after that."

"But --"

"That will be all." He turned away then. She watched his bulky frame disappear behind the closed door of his office. He didn't even have the decency to take her aside in order to speak to her privately.

She thanked God she was dark-skinned, otherwise she was sure she'd be beet red. Trina felt humiliated, which she believed was what he'd intended. Bank employees and customers alike watched her as she started up her computer.

"Are you open, miss? I've been waiting for an hour for someone to help me." An impatient looking woman tapped her toes -- arms akimbo. Trina was sure the woman hadn't been waiting that long, but knew better than to argue with a customer.

Trina rubbed her temple, feeling a headache coming on. She knew this customer would be difficult and she was right. After running Mrs. Sherman's credit report, Trina found she didn't qualify for the requested loan. Instead of crying or begging as some clients did upon being declined, Mrs. Sherman spat at her, with the spit barely missing her face. She called Trina every possible name under the sun.

Trina sat back in her chair in stunned silence, mortified that this was happening to her. The security guard rushed over to drag the screaming woman away. If she were inclined to violence, Trina would have run after that old bitch.

The regional bank manager, who happened to be visiting that day, rushed over to see if she was okay. She must have looked pretty shaken up, because she was sent home. As Trina left the bank, she could see Stephanie looking on with an amused gleam in her eyes.

Bitch.

Now here she was, fresh off the bus. She was tired, her heel had broken stepping off the bus, she was sure she looked a mess, and it wasn't quite noon. Trina hoped to God Tim had at least dragged his sorry ass out of bed. Why the hell did she put up with him anyway?

Because he has a big dick, you're thirty-four, and scared to be alone.

Perhaps there were worse things than being alone, like being in another dead-end relationship. As Trina rounded the corner of her house, she spotted her best friend Twan's Volkswagen Golf. What was Twan doing here in the afternoon? Her flamboyant friend and Tim couldn't stand each other.

The sound of loud groans greeted her the second she stepped foot across the threshold. What in the world? This could not be what she thought it was. She had to be imagining things.

"Oh lover, give me every inch of that caramel voodoo stick. Fuck my ass, cowboy!" Twan's familiar high-pitched voice cried out in obvious delight.

No. She shook her head in denial, despite what she heard. She just knew her boyfriend wasn't in their bed screwing her male best friend -- she just knew it.

Careful not to make a sound, she slowly headed toward the bedroom. She peeked inside the slightly ajar door. Although this was exactly what she expected, she couldn't help being surprised at the sight that greeted her.

Twan was on his knees holding on to the bedposts. His dark chocolate body glistened with sweat as a look of pure ecstasy clouded his face. Tim's cock was planted so deep inside Twan's ass it seemed as though they were one. Her boyfriend's long dreads flowed down his back as he arched his head back with gritted teeth. They almost looked like a beautiful work of moving art -- gold on black.

"Don't think this means anything to me. I'm not gay."

"Yeah, you say that now, cowboy, but that hasn't stopped you from fucking this tight ass to your heart's content for the past couple months," Twan taunted. "It also didn't stop you from letting me play with yours either."

"A little ass-play doesn't make a person gay."

Trina's jaw dropped. They had been having an affair that long? How dare they? How dare Twan betray a ten-year friendship by screwing her man in her bed? And how dare Tim do this to her, in her bed no less. Still, she stood frozen to the spot, unable to tear her eyes away from their act of betrayal.

"So you say, cowboy."

"Shut up, bitch, and take this cock," Tim groaned.

"Give it to me. Give it to me hard. Don't hold back, baby," Twan begged.

"God, I'm almost there!"

"Shoot it in my ass, every single drop, cowboy!"

"Aargh!" Tim yelled, obviously reaching his climax. The two burly men collapsed on the bed as Tim finally withdrew his now semi-erect penis from Twan's wet anus. They wrapped their arms around each other, pressing their bodies close. Their heads came together for a long, hot kiss, their tongues dancing in an almost choreographed movement.

Twan pulled back with a smug smile on his dark face. "I bet you Trina doesn't give good ass like I do."

"She doesn't give me ass at all or I wouldn't need you and if you say anything to her, I'll fuck you up," Tim threatened.

Twan pursed his lips. "Hmm, I don't think you're in a position to make threats. Anyway, I don't know why you're with her if she doesn't know how to treat a man like you in bed. I would give you everything you need."

"Except a pussy."

"Who needs fish, when you can have beef. Besides, if her pussy was that damn good, you wouldn't be with me."

"She pays the bills. Besides, I've grown used to having her around so you had better not ruin my good thing."

"I could take good care of you, cowboy. Forget about her."

"She's your friend. What's your deal?"

"When I see a good thing I go after it. Anyway, you know what they say -- all's fair in love and war. Trina's a nice girl. She'll get over it and she's cute enough to find someone else. My poor clueless friend, she thinks we can't stand each other. What would she say if she could see us like this?" Twan's throaty effeminate laughter filled the room and that was the last straw.

Those bastards!

Trina couldn't remember being this angry in her life. She turned around and stalked toward the kitchen. She opened the cutlery drawer, and pulled out a butcher knife. One or both of them were going to lose their nuts today. She walked back toward the bedroom and kicked the door open.

The two men looked up with stunned expressions on their faces. "Trina! What are you doing home?" Tim asked, hopping out of bed, his limp dick swinging between his legs.

Twan on the other hand, once he regained his composure, looked totally unrepentant. "Well, girlfriend, I told you he was cheating, but don't worry, I was taking good care of him while you were at work."

"Son of a bitch!" Trina screamed, lunging at her former best friend with the butcher knife. Twan screamed like a teenage girl in a horror movie as he scrambled out of the bed with catlike reflexes.

"Save me!" he squawked as Trina brought the knife down in a slashing arc.

Tim grabbed her from behind as Twan dashed out of the room so fast he would have made Carl Lewis proud. "Baby, I can explain."

She was too enraged to listen. Trina brought her heel down on Tim's bare foot, causing him to loosen his grip on her. She pulled herself out of his arms and turned around, raising the knife with the intent of cutting off Mr. Happy.

Tim pulled back just in time. "You're crazy!"

"You're damn right I am. Crazy for putting up with you for so long."

"It wasn't me, baby."

Tim's lame excuse was enough to make her pause. "Wasn't you?" she asked incredulously. Did he think she was an idiot?

"No, baby. It wasn't me."

"Oh? So who did I see fucking my so-called best friend in the ass?"

"You were seeing things, baby, but if you put the knife down, I'll forgive you and we can get past this little incident."

"You're kidding, right? You forgive me? Ha! You've got some damn nerve, do you know that, Tim? Get out of my house!"

"Please, baby --"

"Don't you 'please baby' me. Get out now!" she screamed, raising the knife again.

Tim must have read something in her eyes because he turned and started to run. She chased him down the hallway with the knife hovering in the air. His dreads flew behind him. Trina reached out to grab one, yanking him back. He had her by a good sixty pounds, but her rage gave her superhuman strength. He stumbled backwards, falling on his ass.

She raised the knife higher.

"Don't do it!" His arms came up to shield his face. A puddle of urine formed underneath him and he burst into loud embarrassing sobs.

What the hell was wrong with her? She wasn't a murderer and Tim definitely wasn't worth going to jail for. Trina lowered the knife before dropping it to the ground.

"Get out of my house now, and don't come back," she sighed, leaning against the wall.

"My stuff --"

"Will be forwarded to you if and when you send me your new address. Get out now."

"My clothes!"

"No, you mean my clothes. I paid for those clothes. Now get out before I kick your sorry ass," she said, leaning down to grab the knife. She had no intention of using it, but he must have thought so because he got up in a hurry and dashed out of the house.

Trina had no idea where he was going or how far he would get without clothing and she didn't care.

"Why me?" she groaned.

Tim wasn't the first loser she'd dated. There was Larry, who didn't inform her he was married with three kids before they dated for nearly a year. Then there was Kwan, who was tied so tightly in his mother's apron strings he asked for her permission before taking Trina anywhere. Julio was a serial cheater who thought he was God's gift to women, and Chuck... well, Chuck had a very interesting fetish involving feet and a bear suit. She'd dated men of all races, age ranges, and sizes and had come to one conclusion -- they were all dogs no matter the package.

Was there no end to the losers in her life? Was she a loser magnet? Maybe there were worse things in life than being alone. That's it. No more men. They were trouble and caused too much heartache. The only person she could depend on was herself.

"Damn, I need a vacation."

Chapter Two

Roar watched as Bayoh and Talh positioned the naked maiden on her knees. Nika's golden tail swished back and forth in her delight. Her white bottom was turned up in his direction in an enticing pose. She was beautiful with silvery tresses that looked as though they were kissed by the moonlight, creamy white skin that begged for a lover's caress, and feline green eyes that seemed to promise many hours of pleasure.

Yes, she was magnificent, but Roar felt absolutely nothing for her. Nika shot him a coy look, as though inviting him to join the ménage, but he remained still, choosing to observe his friends from the wall. She pouted when he shook his head, but her frown soon changed to a smile as Bayoh slid his cock inside her pretty pink pussy.

Talh stroked Nika's head before inserting his dick between her parted lips. She moaned as her head began to move back and forth over Talh's cock. Talh pushed his dark red, waist-length hair out of his face, before clasping her head between his large hands.

Bayoh pumped gently in and out of Nika's sheath, gritting his teeth with concentration. "Your pussy feels wonderful."

"So does your mouth," Talh added.

Roar watched dispassionately, wishing he could feel something for the scene he witnessed before him. Even as his hands reached inside his soft elkskin pants to stroke his cock, he couldn't muster up enough excitement to even enjoy watching.

This was becoming a growing problem. It wasn't that he could not become aroused. Actually, he was quite virile and often told what a good lover he was, but unfortunately Nika was not the woman for him.

As a member of the Alpha Triad, one part of the ruling faction of the Manani people, he knew it was their duty to mate and produce heirs. However, Bayoh and Talh, the other two parts of the faction, had different ideas of who their mate should be.

The male to female ratio was six to one and women were scarce among their people. Because of this, each female had three mates to take care of her every need. Of course there were males who chose to mate with each other, but there were still enough males who sought female mates for it to be an issue.

Females were allowed to be pickier in choosing their mates than the males, even though it was a male-dominated culture. Among their people, when a male child was born, an elder would read his soul sign to match him with two other males. These three males would live under one household and be forever bonded through brotherhood and friendship.

It was ordained before he was born that he, Bayoh, and Talh would lead the Manani: Roar the healer, Bayoh the chief hunter, and Talh the war chief. They were all respected and revered among their people living in the mystical land of the Laiocean, a land not visible to human eyes.

They were generally a peaceful people, but territorial of their land. There was no one Roar felt closer to than his two friends -- his brothers. He would gladly give his life for either one, but the dissension between them was growing. The three couldn't agree on a mate.

For instance, Roar found Nika extremely attractive, but he saw her as a bratty little sister as they had all grown up together. She didn't make his heart beat faster with just a glance. Bayoh and Talh seemed taken with her. On the other hand, there were women he found attractive that his friends didn't.

Even though there was a short supply of women, the Alpha Triad had more of a choice because of their higher status. Still it didn't help their situation.

Nika purred in the back of her throat as the two cocks slid in and out of her quivering body. She tore her mouth from Talh's cock. "Oh, fuck me harder!" she demanded, slamming her hips back.

Bayoh began to thrust harder before Talh reinserted his dick in her mouth. Feeling bored, Roar shed his clothes before shifting to his natural form. He needed to get out of there to think. He sauntered out of their dwelling to take a stroll through the forest, reveling in the feel of the soft earth beneath his paws.

He stared down at the lake he came upon, looking at the reflection beneath him. His usually aquamarine eyes were now amber-circled with a ring of hazel. His long, shaggy golden mane rested around his broad face. He looked like he could use a little grooming.

Roar sat back on his hind legs and began to lick his paws. He took pride in his beautiful caramel pelt and cleaned himself at every chance. His ears pricked up as he heard approaching feet. Two pair. He looked up to see Bayoh and Talh coming toward him. They were both dressed in a pair of soft leather pants and thigh-high boots. Their chests were bare.

He was secure enough in his own masculinity to recognize and appreciate their male beauty. Bayoh with the short dark brown hair stood six feet six inches, the same height as Roar in humanoid form, while Talh with his waist-length auburn hair stood an inch taller.

They both had lean but well-muscled bodies with broad shoulders, finely chiseled faces, full lips, and penetrating aquamarine eyes like his. They almost looked like true brothers. When Roar was in humanoid form he knew he looked a lot like them, except with short spiky blond hair.

"Nika was very randy today. She is eager to mate with the three of us." Talh sat down next to him.

Maybe there's something wrong with me, but I just can't get excited about her. Roar projected his thoughts to them.

"But she is the most sought-after female among our people, and her pussy is so damn tight and juicy, it makes me hard just thinking about it. She's made it known she's interested in being claimed by us," Bayoh said with his hands on his hips. He was the most excitable of the triad, and it was obvious to Roar that Bayoh was the most impressed by Nika's charms.

She may be interested in being with us, but I'm not really too thrilled to claim her. The thought doesn't excite me. She's very beautiful -- I won't dispute that, but... I don't feel she's the one.

"This is ridiculous, guys. We'll need to mate soon. We can't retain our positions as leaders among our people if we don't," Talh interjected.

"But we can't agree on a mate. What do you suggest we do?" Bayoh raised a dark brow.

"There's always Chimera," Talh suggested.

"Chimera? If we can't agree on our own women, what makes you think a human female would hold our interest," Bayoh snorted, kicking a pile of dirt under his heel.

"There are men who've journeyed to Chimera and found their mates. Human females are one of the few species who can bear our cubs," Talh shot back.

The human women generally take lots of time to adjust to our ways. Would it be worth doing? Roar looked up at his redheaded friend.

"It's worth a try and, to be honest, Nika stirs my loins, but not my heart."

"I don't like the idea of mating with a human. Remember the human Tegor, Rain, and Geho brought back from Chimera? She screamed every time we shifted to our natural form. I have no time for weak human females. Nika will give us strong cubs to carry on our line, and not to mention, she's insatiable in bed," Bayoh argued.

Have you forgotten we all have to agree on a mate?

Bayoh's lips flattened into a thin, disapproving line.

"Let's compromise. If after a week we don't find a female who interests all of us, we'll come back and take Nika as our mate." Talh spoke, being the voice of reason.

It was fair.

Bayoh grunted his agreement, although it was apparent he wasn't as into the suggestion as Roar and Talh.

Roar eagerly nodded his head in agreement at the chance to find a mate and vacation on a beautiful tropical island in the middle of the Bermuda Triangle. Surely the three of them could find a mate among the women on Chimera.

Roar certainly hoped so.

* * *

Trina clutched her invitation close to her chest as she stepped off the plane. She could hardly believe her luck. Trina read the letter one more time to assure herself it was real.

> *Congratulations, Trina Davis. You've won an all expense paid week on beautiful Chimera Island. Located in the geographical center of the Bermuda Triangle, Chimera Island offers both mystery and natural beauty beyond compare. Only the most adventurous traveler is welcome on Chimera, and we've determined that's you, Trina Davis. Absolutely no obligation, but you must book now. Call 1-800-555-4AEM or visit www.margaretriley.com/aoem.html today to book your fantasy trip of a lifetime.*
>
> *Margaret Riley,* CEO

Shortly after kicking Tim out of her house and out of her life, she'd called her travel agent to book a quiet vacation away from civilization, but when it came time to pay, she found her credit card maxed out.

Tim.

If she hadn't already kicked him out, Trina would have killed him. It'd been a hassle to cancel all the cards and get the banks to credit her accounts some of the funds she lost. Going through that mess had only strengthened her resolve to live a man-free life.

One day after coming home from another tough day at work, she'd found a letter in the mail stating she'd won an all-expense-paid vacation to the island of Chimera, a place where dreams came true -- whatever that meant. At first Trina thought it was some kind of timeshare scam, and planned on tossing it in the garbage, but something held her back. She figured it wouldn't hurt to call the number. When she did, a representative assured her she was chosen randomly from the residents of her area.

The only thing she had to do in return was give them feedback on how much or how little she enjoyed the island. Kind of like a focus group member testing out a new product, but instead she got to enjoy the pleasures of a tropical island.

Things like this didn't happen to her. She had the worst luck imaginable. She was basically alone in the world with deceased parents and no siblings, so Trina had been taking care of herself since the age of seventeen.

She'd worked very hard from the time she was a teenager until now, so she was looking forward to this vacation where she would be pampered and her every need would be seen to for an entire week.

From now on she would be single and love it. Her theme song would be Destiny Child's "Independent Woman." Besides, men caused too much heartache.

* * *

The island was absolutely gorgeous. Trina gasped in awe as she took in the beauty of her surroundings. This was truly Paradise. She felt as though she had just landed on Fantasy Island and the only thing missing was Mr. Roarke and Tattoo.

Trina giggled to herself as she thought about the look on Mr. Peterson's face after she quit on the spot when he wouldn't grant her the time off. Good riddance to that job. She was good at what she did, and there was enough in her savings to get by for a couple more months until she found another job.

A large valet took her bags. "Welcome to Chimera, Miss Davis."

There was something odd about this man, who stood close to seven feet tall. Was she imagining things, or did this guy have a bluish tinge to his skin, and what was up with his Spock ears?

Too weird.

Oh well, she didn't care about the appearance of the island staff as long as her vacation brought her the peace and quiet she sought. The tall, hulking valet led her to a limo. "This car will take you directly to your bungalow. There's a restaurant, a nightclub, beach activities, horseback riding, and much more. You'll find a pamphlet in your room that lists all of our amenities."

"Thank you very much -- uh -- what's your name?" She searched his floral shirt for a nametag, but found nothing.

"Triel. I'm number 67 on speed dial should you need anything. Have a great vacation and may all your dreams come true." He smiled at her with tiny jagged teeth. Eww. What had he done with his mouth? Poor fellow. He probably wouldn't be kissing many women with those choppers.

As the limo drove her to her private bungalow, she pondered over Triel's last statement. *May all your dreams come true.* He said it as though there was some hidden message behind those words. No matter, it was probably something all the staff members said to the guests.

Trina's jaw dropped when she arrived at her bungalow. She'd been expecting something nice, but didn't think she'd be housed in such luxury. Trina pinched herself to make sure this was real. "Oh my God," she muttered in amazement and awe.

Soft orchestra music played from a Bose stereo system. Exotic flowers filled the grandly decorated house. There were four rooms: the kitchen, the bathroom with a whirlpool tub, the huge living room, and the bedroom with a large California king-sized bed, but the only person who'd occupy it this week was her.

She flung herself on the bed, rolling around, laughing with joy at her good fortune. "This is the life."

Trina got back to her feet, racing from room to room to check out every intricate detail. It was immaculate. "I've hit the jackpot."

She hurriedly unpacked her suitcase and changed into her pink paisley string bikini, unable to wait to hit the beach. She wanted to feel the sand beneath her toes and the sunshine on her skin. Just thinking about it was heavenly.

Yes, this was going to be the best vacation ever. Trina was looking forward to enjoying her man-free week in paradise.

Chapter Three

"This island is crawling with beautiful women, yet no one has caught my interest," Bayoh sighed, raking his fingers through his dark hair. His aqua eyes scanned the beach as a tall brunette sauntered by, turning his frown to a smile.

"What about her? Look at the way she swishes those hips back and forth. I bet she knows how to ride a cock." Talh jerked his thumb in the bikini-clad brunette's direction.

Roar studied her intently. She was pretty enough. But he supposed there was something about her he didn't quite like. "She's okay, but if she walks with her head any higher, she's going to trip. The last thing we need is a haughty mate. Why do you think I didn't have any interest in Nika? Our mate must help us lead, not cause us problems."

"You never mentioned this before," Bayoh said with a puzzled expression on his face.

"I never had a reason to until now. How about we go to the bar. I need a drink. I'm sure there are some ladies there. It's getting dark and we've been standing out here all day."

"No, I think I want to check out more of the night scenery," Talh said with a grin on his face as a petite redhead with tight leather pants walked by them, flashing a huge bright smile. She winked at the three of them, obviously assured in her feminine charm. Roar sensed she was confident without being conceited and he admired such a trait. His eyes took in her full lush body.

"Yes, I think I'll stick around too," Bayoh murmured.

Bayoh and Talh seemed to like what they saw, their tails swishing behind them eagerly.

She was beautiful, but then again, nearly every woman on this island was beautiful and Roar wasn't interested. "I'm going to the bar to get a drink. I'll catch up with you two later."

His friends merely nodded, giving their attention to the redhead. Roar walked toward the seaside grill, stopping short when he heard a female screech, "You rotten, lying, two-timing, pointy-eared lizard. How dare you!"

Uh-oh. Someone was in trouble. Whoever the woman was yelling at, Roar didn't want to be in his shoes. He paused, not wanting to walk into this lover's quarrel.

"You don't un --" he heard a male voice pleading.

"You're damned right I don't. After what we... how we... oh hell! Why did I believe anything you said, you bastard!"

Roar heard the clicking of angry heels pounding against the floor and knew the mystery woman was coming his way. A magnificent picture of blonde fury stormed out of the bar. He'd only caught a glimpse of her face, but what he saw, he liked. As though his legs had a mind of their own, they began to walk toward her.

She halted as though she sensed his presence. His first impression was correct. She was magnificent. Standing a few inches over five feet, her body was firm, supple, and gently curved. Her breasts jutted forward, full and high, encased in her silk dress as though they waited for a lover's hands to caress them.

He bet her body looked even better without clothes than with them. His eyes drifted to her face -- also noteworthy. Her gorgeous heart-shaped face with its flashing gray eyes and soft-looking sensual lips made her one of the prettiest women he'd seen since arriving on Chimera.

A glorious mane of honey blonde hair rested on her delicately curved shoulders. She raised a blonde brow as though she were waiting for him to speak. Roar sensed a deep sadness within her. It was obvious whomever she'd been yelling at in the restaurant really upset her. What a fool that man was to cause this beauty pain. He wondered what Bayoh and Talh would think of her.

"Do you need any help?"

She shook her head. "No, I..." She broke off, giving him the once over. He smiled at her thorough perusal of him. Good. Maybe he could take her mind off the mystery man in the restaurant. "Actually, I'd love a drink. Would you care to join me?"

She tilted her head back to meet his eyes and she flashed him a big white smile. There was something behind that smile, but he couldn't put his finger on it. To be honest, he didn't care. For now, he wanted to get to know her better.

He held his arm out to her, which she eagerly latched on to before they walked back into the restaurant. Once they found a table and ordered their drinks, she turned that bright smile on him again. "My name's Amanda. And you are?"

"Roar. My name is Roar." He handed her a glass of sparkling white wine. "You look distressed."

She hesitated before answering; her eyes darted away from his. "I'm okay. I was just a little upset over, well, nothing." Her smile widened. "I'm fine, thank you."

As the hour passed, he asked Amanda questions about herself. He learned she was a Hollywood actress taking a much-needed vacation with her personal assistant. Throughout the conversation her eyes kept straying to the bar to a dark-haired elf.

Roar suspected this was the mystery man she'd argued with. It was apparent Amanda's heart lay with the dejected-looking man. The poor bastard, he looked miserable. Great. The first woman who'd actually captured his interest on this island and she was taken. He supposed it was just his luck. Roar hoped Amanda and her mate could work out their differences before the end of the week.

He was about to ask her about the elf when he felt a hand on either side of him. Bayoh bent over to whisper in his ear. "We've found her."

How could you have found her if I have yet to see her? Roar shot back.

"Trust us. She's the one."

Roar let out a mental sigh. *Okay. Let me say goodbye to my friend first.*

Bayoh straightened up, shooting Amanda an apologetic look, giving her his best 'I'm sorry' smile.

"I have to leave. Maybe we can walk you home?" Roar offered.

She shook her head. "I'm fine. Thank you though for the company. For helping me out."

"My pleasure," he said, reaching across the table to cover the sexy blonde's hand. "Thank *you*. May all your dreams come true," he said, straightening up before turning around to follow his companions outside. "This had better be good, damn it," he growled, not happy at being interrupted from his drink. Although he figured nothing would happen romantically between him and Amanda, he had enjoyed talking to her. It was the first intelligent conversation he'd had with a female on Chimera.

"Okay, where is she?" Roar asked when they stepped out of the restaurant.

"On the beach. Let's hurry. She might not be there anymore," Talh said, dashing off toward the beach with Bayoh on his tail.

"Hey, wait for me!" He took off. When he finally caught up with his friends, they'd already stopped. Roar followed the direction of their stares.

His jaw dropped.

Standing on the beach was the most enticing vision he'd ever seen. Her arms were stretched out, neck arched against the gentle island breeze. The vision's eyes were closed while a smile rested on full, glossy lips. She had to be around five six, give or take an inch. Roar's fingers itched to caress her creamy dark skin - - skin as dark and rich looking as a coconut husk.

Her nearly black hair was tucked adorably behind her ears, resting on her jaw line. Her round and softly curved face was nothing short of exquisite with high cheekbones and a pert nose. Roar's mouth watered as he studied her body.

A tiny waist spanned out to wide hips and one of the roundest asses he'd ever seen. With a backside like that, he wanted more than anything to push her onto her knees and take her from behind with his balls pounding against that juicy ass.

He was sure he could span her waist with his two hands. The beauty's head and body straightened then as she put her arms back down to her sides to reveal a large pair of dark brown eyes and the biggest endowments he'd seen on a woman her size.

The white strapless dress she wore emphasized her delectable body. Roar had visions of spreading those dark creamy thighs apart and fucking her until she screamed his name. Damn, it was dangerous for her to walk around with a body like that.

She stared at them like a frightened doe. Her eyes widened as she looked at the three of them. Before he could go to her, she scrambled off as though she were being chased. What was this madness?

"She's magnificent, isn't she?" Bayoh asked with a smug look on his face.

"More than magnificent," Talh added.

"She's the one," Roar said in agreement, his head nodding as he watched her fleeing figure. The way her big ass jiggled when she ran made his cock stir.

In his culture, true mates were hard to come by because of the female shortage, but when a Manani triad found their true mate, it was instant. His heart beat erratically, his breathing quickened, his mouth went dry and his balls tightened. The soft leather of his pants rubbed against his sac, making his balls even more sensitive.

Whoever this woman was, Roar knew without a doubt she was their true mate.

"Doesn't she realize the harder she runs the harder we'll chase her? Shall we?" Talh asked, raising a dark red brow. A gleam of anticipation flashed in his bright eyes, and his tail swished back and forth in his eagerness.

Roar knew his friend was ready for the hunt and so was he. "Let's go."

They started after her. No human could outrace a Manani, and though they would have moved faster had they shifted, he realized she probably wasn't ready to see them in their natural forms.

He could hear her panting for breath as they closed in on her. When he was mere inches away, Roar reached out and grabbed her, pulling her against him. She began to scream, squirming and writhing as though she were fighting for her life. "Let me go, you jerks! Let me go right now!"

Roar clasped his hand over her mouth to stop her tirade. This only seemed to make her angrier. She brought the heel of her shoe down on his foot. Hard. "Oof!"

He released her; however Bayoh and Talh grabbed her arms when she tried to bolt again. She fought like a wildcat. Her hair whipped from side to side and her breasts threatened to pop out of her dress. Already he could see the top of dark aureoles. Damn, he wanted to see those large mounds fully exposed to his gaze.

"Let me go, you perverts. I'm not going to make it easy for you to rape me, you big gorillas," she hissed, kicking out at them.

Roar managed to sidestep her foot, but only just. Perverts? Rape? Is that what she thought?

"We don't take unwilling women," Talh said, sounding offended. Where they came from, the charge of rape was taken very seriously and it was an automatic death sentence to anyone found guilty.

She stopped struggling and turned her head to look up at Talh. "Then why did you start chasing me and why are you holding my arms so tight? This isn't exactly the way to get a lady's attention, you know."

"Then why did you start running? We only wished to speak with you... get to know you better," Bayoh pointed out.

Her dark eyes narrowed as she snatched her arms out of his friends' grips, before pulling up her dress. Roar was sorry to see that. Had her dress dipped any further, he would have been able to see her breasts. "Well, chasing after me isn't going to get you what you want," she huffed, smoothing her hair back into place.

He noticed she didn't fully answer the question.

"We wouldn't have chased you if you hadn't run." As Roar stepped forward, she took a step back, looking as though she were ready to flee again.

"What did you expect? You guys were looking at me like a juicy slab of steak and I have no intention of being your main course, thank you very much. Look, you fellas seem nice and all, but I'm not into any kind of kinky stuff, okay? As a matter of fact, sex is the last thing I came to this island for, so if you three don't mind, let me enjoy the rest of my man-free vacation in peace."

She turned around as though to dismiss them, but Roar wouldn't let her walk away from them until she knew she was theirs. He grabbed her arm to turn her back around. "Didn't I tell you --" she began.

"What did you mean by kinky stuff?"

A confused look crossed her face before comprehension dawned. "I'm not letting you guys run a train on me. What kind of girl do you think I am?"

Now it was his turn to be confused. Run a train? What did that mean? He looked at his friends who looked equally baffled, before turning back to her. "Run a train? Explain, please."

"You know. When a girl is with more than one partner. I'm not a hoochie, so you and your friends can take your tired asses out of my face."

He watched in amazement as her head worked in a circular motion. She spoke intelligently enough, but some of the phrases she used went over his head. He had no idea what a hoochie was and his ass didn't feel tired in the least.

Hmm, perhaps there were common phrases among humans. Yes, it would take some effort. "This running a train you speak of doesn't sound like it's a favorable thing to you, but in our culture, our females mate with three mates at once, for life."

"Huh? What country are you from? I've never heard of a place where this happens."

"You wouldn't have heard of our homeland. Not many humans have," Roar answered with a smile. She was so lovely, it nearly hurt to look at her.

She shot them all a skeptical look. "Uh, yeah. Pull the other one. If this is your cute little attempt to get a piece of ass, it's not working. It's obvious the three of you have been smoking the wacky weed, so how about letting me go on my way and we'll pretend we didn't have this conversation." She placed her hands on her hips, looking as fierce as any shifted Manani female.

Roar had no doubt she would make a fine leader among his people.

Talh spoke for the first time in minutes. "But you see, we don't want to forget this conversation and we don't want you to forget either."

"Why the hell not?"

Roar exchanged a secret glance with his companions before turning back to the bewildered-looking woman. "Because you're our mate, and when this week is over, we'll take you back to Laiocean to live with us."

She gasped.

Chapter Four

Trina wasn't on Fantasy Island -- she was in the Twilight Zone. What normal person approached a woman with a line like that? Admittedly, when she'd spotted the three men staring at her so intently, she'd paused, stunned by how damn good-looking they were. They were by far the most beautiful masculine specimens she'd ever seen.

They stood around the same height. If she were to guess, she'd say six feet five or six. Though they weren't overly muscular, each one of them was cut like the Soloflex model. One had short, spiky blond hair, the second, dark brown, nearly black hair, and the last one had long dark red hair that hung to his waist.

They wore leather pants of different shades and long sleeved Renaissance-style shirts opened to the navel showing off their well-toned pecs. Each possessed a face that looked as if it were molded by the hands of God himself. The redhead had a scar, slashing from the corner of his eye to his jaw line, but instead of detracting from his looks, it only enhanced them.

Their aquamarine colored eyes had seemed to look right through her as though they could see her soul. Trina had felt her panties go wet as three sets of eyes traveled over her body. She knew she wouldn't mind having a *ménage a quatre* with these hunks.

What? Was she crazy? This was supposed to be a man-free vacation, yet the island was crawling with gorgeous men. She'd stood there ogling three hunks who looked as though they wanted a slice of Trina pie, so she did the first thing any rational person would have done in a situation like this. She ran.

The thing she hadn't figured on was them catching her and giving her this line of crap. "Umm, I'm your mate?" she asked at a loss for anything else to say.

"Yes. That's why we've come to Chimera, to find a mate -- to find you," the blond spoke, looking at her with his ocean-colored eyes. He spoke the most. Perhaps he was the leader. Maybe if she could reason with him, they would let her go.

"Well, I came here to relax and the last thing I need is to be harassed by the likes of you three. Now, if you don't mind, please excuse me or I'll call the authorities," she threatened.

"What kind of authority would stop us from claiming our mate? Haven't you realized what kind of island this is?" the redhead asked.

What did he mean by that? What kind of island was this? Were things too good to be true after all? "I don't know what you mean and frankly, I don't care. Just leave me alone, okay?" She turned to leave, but the blond grabbed her arm.

That was it! Trina turned around to smack him across the face. Who the hell did these guys think they were?

He caught her wrist in his large hand before bringing it to his mouth to plant a gentle kiss against it. Trina gasped as her body shivered. The touch of his lips on her skin was electric.

"You feel it too, don't you?" the blond asked smugly. She looked away from his face, but a movement from behind him caught her eye. Holy shit. Did he have a tail? No. She had to be imagining things.

Trina looked up at him. "Look, this isn't funny. I'm not interested. Perhaps where you come from you can walk up to a woman and say she's your mate and then proceed to go caveman on her, but it doesn't work that way where I come from. Now be good little boys and let me go on my way." She yanked her arm away from him.

"Why are we standing here talking? Let's take her," the dark-haired one spoke.

Trina turned to him. "Excuse me? Who do you think you are? *Take her*? I'm not an object for you to take as you please. You can all go to hell for all I care."

She looked around, desperately combing the beach for someone to help her out of this mess. It was obvious these

Neanderthals had no intention of leaving her alone. No one walked by. Where the hell was everyone? The place had been swarming with people earlier. Now when she needed someone, no one seemed to be around.

Perhaps the best way to deal with the situation was to outwit these three goons. She looked up, giving each of them the biggest smile she could muster. "Okay, you win. I don't know what I was fighting so hard for. How about coming to my bungalow for a private party?"

"Yes. I'm glad you see there's no point in arguing with us. Besides, there's a lot we need to discuss and prepare you for," the redhead said.

"Of course, but you have to allow me to freshen up and slip into something a little more comfortable. How about you guys come to my place in an hour."

"Is an hour necessary? Why can't we follow you there?" the brunet asked with a thunderous expression on his face.

"I want this to be special." Trina ran her tongue suggestively over her lips. She let her eyes drift down to their crotches and knew she was having the desired effect. They were hard as rocks. My God, exactly how hung were they? Judging from the bulges in their pants, she guessed the answer was very hung.

An image of three sets of hands caressing her body filled her mind, a cock in each hole. She could feel her body grow hot, her nipples stiffening. They noticed too, because their eyes fell on her chest, glancing at it appreciatively.

Snap out of it, girl. You don't want anything to do with these three lunatics.

These three very gorgeous lunatics.

"Umm, so how about it, fellas?" she asked, taking a step away from them.

"What's your name?" the blond asked.

She said the first thing that popped in her mind. "Louise...uh Louise Jefferson, but my friends call me Weezy."

Blondie's eyes narrowed. "That's your name? It doesn't suit you."

"Well, it's not like I could help what I was named. Is there anything wrong with that?" She cocked an eyebrow in challenge.

"Uh... nothing I guess... Weezy. I hope you don't mind, but I'd prefer Louise. I'm Roar, this is Bayoh and Talh," he said, pointing to the two other men who eyed her with an equally intense look.

"Nice to meet you guys. Okay, I'm going to get going now so I can freshen up. I'll see you boys in an hour."

Trina was hoping she could finally make her escape, but Roar halted her again.

"What's your bungalow number?"

Damn, she thought she'd be able to get away without giving them that information so she made it up. "Bungalow 227. Okay, gotta run."

This time they didn't stop her.

She couldn't believe those guys. What was wrong with them? Perhaps the question should have been, what was wrong with her? She'd only been on the island for a day and had seen some strange things. Was she the only normal person on the island? Maybe coming here without checking this place out was a mistake. Sure it seemed like paradise, but she had a strange feeling it wasn't what it seemed.

Trina headed toward her bungalow, but decided to take a walk to clear her head. There obviously had to be something wrong, if she even briefly entertained the idea of sleeping with three strange men at once. It didn't matter they were so gorgeous that looking at them made her heart flutter. She was supposed to be off men and there were three of them and one of her. Trina wasn't that kind of girl -- or was she?

She must have walked for nearly an hour before finding herself in front of the island's nightclub. Did she want to go inside? No. Being around a rowdy crowd right now wasn't her idea of fun at the moment. When she turned around to go, she noticed a tall dark man swaggering over to her. Trina could tell he was drunk, but it didn't excuse the fact that his eyes were firmly glued on her breasts.

As he got closer, she gasped. What the hell? He was definitely one of the oddest-looking men she'd seen so far, yet he was beautiful in his own way. He had to be at least six five, with onyx skin, cornrows that fell past his butt, and a thin neatly trimmed goatee with a soul patch. His eyes were beautiful -- black with a ring of amber surrounding them. She did a double take when her eyes traveled to his ears, which looked like elf ears. Was this Halloween Island or something?

Granted there was a whole bunch of weird stuff on Chimera, but this took the cake. Opals and onyx adorned his ears and a long thin gold chain hung from one of them. He obviously liked jewelry because he was covered in it.

His outfit was rather unusual as well. He wore a belly blouse and drawstring pants, which showed off his muscular tattooed body. As strange as his appearance was, Trina wasn't about to let him ogle her as though she was some dime store hooker.

She placed her hands on her hips. "Can I help you?"

He lifted his head up, giving her a confused look. "How did you do that?" His voice was very deep and gravelly.

"How did I do what?"

"This." He began to move his head in an erratic circular motion. She looked at him in stunned silence. He looked like a demented clucking chicken.

Suddenly she realized he'd been mimicking her. Did she really look like that when she became agitated? She'd been told by her friends that she was queen of the sister girlfriend neck roll. Trina burst out laughing at the comedic sight.

How could she possibly take this guy seriously? "Thank you. I needed that. I came to this island for a relaxing vacation, but it's been everything but so far. The men around here run around like a bunch of horny school boys."

"Really?" A look of interest crossed his face as though the thought pleased him. What was up with this guy?

"Yeah, really."

"Which way did they go?"

"Why?" Was he for real? He acted as though he was eager to find other men, yet his eyes kept straying to her breasts.

He bounced up and down with seeming impatience. Oddly, she didn't feel threatened by him. Actually, she felt quite comfortable talking to this man. Trina took a step back as she noticed wings slowly sprouting from his back. They were the same mother-of-pearl shade as the tattoos on his body. "What the..."

She didn't hear a word he said as he began to answer her question, because she couldn't tear her eyes away from his wings. It felt as though she were the one who'd been drinking. Trina was just waiting for the little pink elephants to start walking by.

The wind gently brushed against the black tips of his feathers, making them ripple. Her eyes drifted lower as the already impressive bulge in his pants steadily grew larger with each passing second, threatening to push free of his already low-rise pants. The tip of his cock peeked out.

Trina didn't know whether to run or stare some more.

"Not that I don't find you attractive, but I have to be gay by the end of the week. I mean, I am gay, but I have to prove it or I'll dishonor my family and lose them," the winged man explained.

He thought he was gay? With a boner like that? No way. "You're no more gay than I am," she said, pointing to his erection. "How can you be gay when you haven't been able to take your eyes off my breasts throughout our entire conversation?"

"Well, they are nice breasts. It's just that I'm not supposed to notice." He blushed, turning a deep purple. "How can I be gay when getting winged and hard over some woman's breasts," he muttered more to himself than to her.

It took every ounce of Trina's willpower not to laugh out loud at this situation. Why was he fighting so hard to be something he obviously was not? "Have you ever thought that maybe you're not gay?"

"No. I have to be gay. It's tradition."

"Why are you letting tradition dictate who you screw?"

He paused as though to think. His tongue ring clicked against his teeth. "Honestly, I don't know."

Trina felt sorry for this very confused man. In her experience, people who struggled with their sexuality tried to be straight, not the other way around. Regardless of what his sexual orientation was, he had to be true to himself. He couldn't please everyone so he might as well please himself.

She stepped closer to him to pat him on his dark shoulder with sympathy. "Who you choose to be with is your affair."

"Only in a perfect world."

"I know how you feel. In a perfect world, I wouldn't be so stupid where men are concerned," she said with more bitterness than she'd intended.

"What man would harm such perfection, would mar the inner beauty which marks the outer beauty you downplay."

Her breath caught in her throat at his eloquent words, which touched a part of her soul she thought was dead. "Didn't you know? I'm an asshole magnet. I came home to find my lover of two years in bed with my so-called best friend who happens to be male. *He's* gay -- you're not."

"He's unworthy of you and clearly at fault. Honesty is all in a relationship and this male -- not a man -- deserves nothing but your contempt. How can your decision-making skills be at fault when you are the one who decided to end the relationship -- hopefully after you ran your foot up his well-used ass."

She giggled at the thought. "Well, I did nearly pull a Lorena Bobbitt."

"Who?"

"Uh, long story, but let's just say her now ex-husband is not quite the man he used to be. We've made some advances in reattaching severed body parts, but I'm sure it doesn't work half as well as it used to."

She couldn't believe how much she was enjoying talking to this large, strange man. Trina casually glanced past him and groaned. The three men from the beach were fast approaching.

She had to get away to save herself from them, but more so to save herself from her.

"Oh Lord, not them again. Well, it was nice meeting you --"

"Tal."

It sounded a lot like the redhead's name. "Tal, I have to run. Do me a favor and say you never met me."

As she turned to go, he reached out to catch her hand. "What's your name?"

She felt she could be honest with him. "Trina. Trina Davis," she said, yanking her hand away. "Sorry, I have to go."

Trina took off like a track star, and didn't stop running until she reached her bungalow.

Chapter Five

Roar, Bayoh, and Talh saw Trina talking to a tall dark Fairy in front of the nightclub. Who the hell did he think he was to make moves on what was rightfully theirs? As they neared, she saw them coming and ran off. Because the Fairy's wings were blocking the way, he didn't see which direction she went.

"Let's get her," Bayoh said.

"There will be time for that. I want to let this Fairy know not to mess with what's ours," Talh argued.

Roar was in agreement with Bayoh, but when Talh made up his mind to do something it was hard to deter him.

Talh confronted the dark Fairy, his tail swishing in an angry motion behind him. "Stay away from our woman!" The Fairy reached up and plucked out a large cream-colored feather from his wings. The feather transformed into a glowing blade.

Roar's eyes narrowed. This Fairy thought he could intimidate them with this little toy? He had no idea who he was dealing with. "What woman is it you seek?" the Fairy asked with a knowing smirk on his ebony face.

Roar knew very well the Fairy knew who Talh was referring to. "Don't play games with us, Fairy."

"Why, thank you for recognizing both my heritage and my sexuality by human standards," the Fairy answered.

Roar was taken aback by the Fairy's odd comment. He glanced at Bayoh and Talh who seemed equally stunned. He turned back to the Fairy. "You prefer men?"

"Well, I feel comforted that a somewhat-male like you would draw my attention. Now be a good boy and let me speak to the real man, okay? If you're good and quiet while the adults speak, I may give you a piece of candy, but not my lollipop. I doubt you could handle it." The Fairy grinned indulgently as though he were talking to a child.

"Somewhat male?" Roar's usually even temper was at its breaking point. "I don't have time to trifle with you, Fairy --"

"You forget your place, cub, and the fact that I have no desire at all to trifle with an almost male." The Fairy turned to Talh, obviously thinking he was the leader of the three of them. "Can't you control your cubs? In my homeland, until a child is allowed to participate in adult conversations he is taught to keep his mouth shut."

That was it. The Fairy was dust. Uncaring that he was fully clothed, Roar shifted to his natural form. He wasn't going to let this confused Fairy tell him he wasn't a man, especially when the Fairy was experiencing some kind of sexual identity crisis.

As he was about to pounce, he found himself bound to the ground. He couldn't move a muscle. Damn. Fairy magic. The Fairy laughed before addressing Talh again. "And I thought redheads were supposed to have the tempers. Can't you control your pets?"

I can't break free, Roar communicated to his companions.

"You --" Bayoh was about to charge forward, but Talh held him back. "Stand down, Bayoh. It seems there is more than meets the eye to this effeminate male. Release my friend, Fairy, and tell us where the woman went," Talh growled.

Roar continued to struggle against the invisible force holding him down. When he got free, he intended to rip that damn Fairy to shreds.

"You should have more mature playmates, but I will give you what you need if it's not necessarily what you want. She went that way," the Fairy said, pointing to his left.

"If you've lied to us, we'll be back. By the way, you may call my friends nearly men, but they're men enough to know who they really want to fuck. You're no more gay than our Trina is a man." Talh looked the Fairy up and down with contempt.

"Well… shit," the Fairy muttered as though he'd been knocked for six.

Roar felt the Fairy release him and would have jumped on him, but Talh stopped him. "There is not time for that. Let's go get her."

Roar gave the Fairy, who now had his back turned toward them, one last glare before following Bayoh and Talh in the direction the Fairy had pointed.

Before we leave this island, I'm going to have it out with that bastard.

"Do you think he gave us the right direction?" Talh frowned.

Bayoh cursed. "I have a sneaking suspicion he didn't. Damn. Already we've been all over this island looking for her. If only we could have marked her, we'd have no problem locking on to her scent."

Roar pointed out, *I know what you mean, but my cock was too hard to think straight. Besides, marking her would have required us taking her back to her bungalow for a little privacy.*

Talh had a pensive look on his face. "Perhaps she's back at her bungalow."

It's possible, but she's already given us a false name and bungalow number. She's slippery. Where in the world did she come up with an awful name like Weezy? Since we now have her true name, it shouldn't be too hard to find her bungalow number. We can ask around, Roar said, scanning the area, knowing Trina was long gone.

There must be someone around here who's seen her. Let's split up and meet back here in an hour. In the meantime I'll go back to our bungalow and put some new clothes on. These are ruined. I shouldn't have shifted without undressing first.

"Okay, that sounds like a plan. When we find her, this time, we won't let her go," Bayoh swore.

* * *

Trina rested her head against the side of the whirlpool tub, letting the bubbles massage her tense body. It was so soothing she found herself drifting off to sleep. What an odd day this had been. It started out as a nice laid-back day as she'd intended, but then she began to see things that shouldn't exist. On the way back to her bungalow, she could have sworn she saw a Merman, not to mention Tal, who'd sprouted wings before her very eyes.

As disturbing as that was, the scene which kept playing in her mind was of Roar, Bayoh, and Talh. Why the hell did those three nuts have to be so damn good-looking? And why did the thought of them make her heart beat faster and her pussy grow wet? Was she greedy for lusting after three men or wondering what it would be like to be with them all at once?

Tim had once suggested they try a threesome, but the thought repulsed her at the time. Why now did she think about three partners simultaneously? Did it make her a slut? Whether it did or not, she shouldn't have been thinking about it at all. This definitely wasn't what she'd visualized when she came to Chimera. It seemed as though her vacation was doomed, especially if she spent all her time avoiding Roar, Bayoh, and Talh.

Had it been simple lust perhaps she could have dealt with it, but Trina sensed there was something more to this thing she felt for them. It was absolutely nuts, because she'd just met them.

As she lay in the tub, thinking, someone knocked on her door. "Damn," she muttered, as she reluctantly stood up in the water. She grabbed an oversized terry cloth towel, wrapping it around her before stepping out of the tub. The knock became louder and more forceful as she made her way to the door.

"Okay, I'm coming. Hold your horses."

When she unlocked and opened the door she immediately tried to close it again because standing behind it was none other than the last three men she hoped to see.

Bayoh stuck his foot in the door, shoving it forward, pushing Trina back.

The three men strode into her bungalow as though they owned it. "Get out!" Trina yelled, clutching the towel around her as though her life depended on it.

"We aren't going anywhere, Weezy, or should I say Trina Davis?" Roar stepped forward menacingly.

She gasped, taking a step back. "How did you... how did you find out my name? How did you find me?"

"It's not a very large island, you know. It wasn't very hard once we realized you lied to us about your name. As for how we found you, someone on the island saw you come to this bungalow, and was quite helpful to us." Talh stepped closer, his light eyes flashing fire.

She knew there was no escaping them this time, but she had to try. "If you guys don't get out of my place right now, I'm going to call the island authorities. You can't just come into someone's bungalow uninvited," she said, trying the reasonable approach.

"Why should we need an invitation to our mate's bungalow? As I said earlier, who on this island would stop us from claiming our mate?" Roar gave her an easy smile as he stepped forward.

Trina stepped back until she found her back against the wall. "Leave me alone!" she screamed, grabbing the first thing she could get her hands on which just happened to be the television remote. "Stay away or I'll brain you!"

"You won't be able to keep us away with that puny thing," Roar chuckled, pissing her off.

Before he could duck his head in time, the remote caught him just above his left ear. The smile left his face. She refused to plead with them, however, because she was only trying to protect herself. "Just leave me alone, okay?" She held out her palm to ward them off.

"You will pay for that, but later. Now, we will get to know you better." He smiled at her again. Before she could respond, Roar grabbed her against him. Trina struggled, caught in his strong muscular arms.

"Let me go, you big blond ape." She raised her hand before smacking him in the face. When she lifted her hand to him again, the cold look in his blue-green eyes made her stop in her tracks. This time she realized she'd gone too far.

"That is the last time you will strike me, woman!"

She would not cry. She would not cry. "Please. What do you want from me?"

"I thought we'd already said, we want you," Bayoh answered.

"Why me? There are other women on the island -- willing women."

"But we don't want other women. If we did, we wouldn't have gone through so much to find you. If I let you go, will you sit down and listen to what we have to say?"

Should she trust these guys? She had no reason to, but it was three against one. What if they hurt her?

"We wouldn't hurt you," Roar said as though he'd read her mind. His cheek was still red from where her palm had connected. She winced. It wasn't in her nature to strike people, but her fear had made her act out. The only time she could ever recall getting violent with anyone else was Tim, when she'd caught him in bed with Twan.

"I'm sorry about hitting you."

Roar's eyes lit up. "If you give me a smile, I will forgive you."

She did, and his own smile widened. Damn, he was fine. They all were.

"Give us your word you won't try anything like running off, and I'll release you."

"Give me your word none of you will touch me and I won't," she countered.

Talh shook his head. "We will touch you, because you belong to us."

"Do you guys hear yourselves? I'm a person, not a thing. I'm no one's possession. Now please let me go. This isn't funny."

"I agree. It isn't funny. I wish you would listen to us with an open mind." Roar leaned over, whispering in her ear. The sensual undertone of his voice made her tremble. Trina could feel her nipples hardening.

He must have noticed too because he started to smile again. "See? You're not as averse to us as you say you are. I think you want us, just as much as we want you." Roar brushed his lips against hers. She was too stunned to react as his tongue slipped between her parted lips.

He tasted so damned good -- so hot, so male. She found herself surrendering to his hungry kiss. She was so caught up in Roar's mouth moving diligently over hers she didn't notice the other two men remove her towel until she felt cool air against her skin, causing her to shiver. Trina pulled her head away from Roar's. She moaned, "No, this isn't right."

"That's where you're wrong. This is very right. Perhaps we've been going about this the wrong way. They do say actions speak louder than words." Roar lifted her into his arms before carrying her to the bedroom with Bayoh and Talh trailing behind. She knew she should struggle, but it was as though her brain had shut down.

He placed her on the bed. Trina's breath caught in her throat as the three prime hunks of man flesh began to undress. They were just as perfect without clothes as they were with them. She longed to run her fingers over their nicely cut bodies. As they removed their pants, her eyes widened as the men revealed three of the longest, thickest cocks she'd ever laid eyes on. They would have made John Holmes proud. Dear Lord, she'd have to be a yoga master to take on all three of those donkey dongs.

As Trina marveled over their length and girth, she noticed something else -- what she'd originally thought were belts were actually tails.

Dear Lord, they had tails. So, she hadn't been imagining things on the beach. Each possessed a long thin tail, the color of the hair on their heads. Trina scrambled off the bed to the other side of the room, putting as much distance between them as possible. "Why the hell do you have tails?"

They all held a puzzled look on their faces as though she were the weird one. "The same reason you weren't born with one. We were made this way. Now come to us. Let us show you why we belong together," Bayoh beckoned.

Trina shook her head, crossing her arms over her breasts. She must have been crazy to let them in here without raising a bigger fuss, then allowing things to get this far. "I wish the three of you would stop speaking in riddles."

"After talking to some of the islanders, haven't you figured out why you're here?" Talh asked.

What was he talking about? "To enjoy a free vacation?" she asked hesitantly.

Bayoh chuckled. "Even where we come from, we know nothing in life is free."

"What do you mean? What kind of place is this?"

"This island is the cover for a dating agency. Before we came, we sent out preferences and a list compiled with our likes and dislikes. A number of women fitting the profile were invited to the island for a *free* vacation. We chose you," Roar explained.

Holy hell. She was right. This was the Twilight Zone. Trina suddenly felt faint. The next thing she remembered was everything going black.

Chapter Six

Roar rushed to Trina's side with Bayoh and Talh on his tail. They reached the fainting woman just in time to catch Trina before her body hit the ground. Roar lifted Trina up into his arms and carried her limp body to the bed.

Roar placed the beauty in the center, as gently as he could before brushing his knuckles across Trina's soft cheek. By all that was sacred, Trina was by far the most beautiful creature Roar had ever laid eyes on. Had they not come to Chimera, they'd never have met such perfection. A feeling of gladness rushed through him.

"I almost feel guilty looking at her like this when she's unconscious," Talh mused.

"She's ours to look at as we please," Bayoh huffed.

Roar silently agreed, but it would take Trina some time to get used to the way things were going to be. "Yes, she's ours, but how do you think she will feel when she wakes up. She may not like it."

"I'll get her something cool to drink," Talh said, leaving the room.

"Good idea. I think she may be a little dehydrated, judging from the pallor of her skin."

Roar caressed Trina's smooth brown flesh again. Unable to resist, he bent over, brushing her lips with his.

Bayoh crawled over the bed, sliding next to her. "Hey, you've been hogging her, my friend. She's just as much mine and Talh's as she is yours."

"It's not my intention to monopolize her attention, but I'm sure you know how I feel when I look at her."

"Yes, she's everything I ever hoped to find in a mate." Bayoh ran his index finger along the side of one plump breast. A deep moan came from within Trina's throat. "She's very passionate. I admit when I'm wrong and I was wrong in thinking we wouldn't find our mate on Chimera. My only concern is her complete acceptance of us. Will she accept us in our true forms?"

"I think she will," Roar said more to himself than to Bayoh. She just had to.

Talh returned holding a glass of water. "Ah, I see you two couldn't wait for her to wake up."

"We didn't try anything with her. I want her to be awake and recognize us when we take her. I want her to feel every touch, every caress --" Bayoh broke off when Trina stirred.

She slowly opened her eyes, surveying their faces hovering over hers. "Oh, God. It wasn't a dream," she muttered with apparent dismay.

"If this is a dream, it's a dream come true." Talh came forward to hand her the glass of water, which she eyed suspiciously. "Take it. I'm sure you're thirsty."

Trina took the glass and gulped down the water.

"Slowly, or else you'll make yourself sick." Roar placed his hand over the glass, forcing her to slow down.

"I must be out of my mind." Trina sighed and leaned her head back against the plush pillows.

"Why do you say that?" Talh picked up a delicately formed foot before rubbing it.

"I'm lying naked in bed with three equally naked strangers."

"We won't be strangers for long," Roar assured her.

"Please try to make me understand. You say this place is some sort of dating service?"

"Yes." Roar began to tell her how they'd come to be here before explaining the Manani people and culture. For the most part she was quiet, only making the occasional gasp of disbelief every now and then. By the time he was finished, her mouth was wide open.

"Say something." Roar gently shook her shoulder.

"What exactly am I supposed to say? What you said shouldn't make any sense, but oddly enough, it does. I mean, I knew this vacation was too good to be true. I... I'm flattered that you guys think I'm your mate, but you see, I can't be. I've sworn off men."

Bayoh grasped her chin, forcing her to meet his eyes. "It's a good thing you have because we won't share you with other men."

"No. You don't understand. I've sworn off all men, and that includes you. I don't want to be in a relationship with anyone."

Roar's eyes narrowed. "Surely you jest. You didn't think a beautiful woman like yourself would remain unmated."

"So what? My looks have nothing to do with anything. You're asking me to be with all three of you at the same time. This isn't right. There are laws against this kind of thing."

"According to human standards it's wrong, but we're not human and in our culture it's perfectly acceptable," Talh explained.

"And you guys don't have a problem with sharing one woman?"

"Our souls are connected. It's almost as though we are one, but with three bodies. It's our way," Roar said, sensing her softening toward them.

"But I can't be with you guys," she protested weakly.

Bayoh cocked one dark brow. "Why not?"

"Because everyone I've been with has hurt me. If I give you three a chance, you'll only end up hurting me too." Her big brown eyes were filled with a deep sadness.

Roar's heart went out to this gorgeous woman who obviously had not dealt with any real men. A real man would've appreciated what he had. Roar could see the uncertainty in her eyes and wanted to erase it.

He leaned over and gave her a kiss on the cheek.

"I -- please don't do this to me." Even as she said it her lips parted slightly as though anticipating his kiss.

"Let us take care of you. We'll make you feel good." Bayoh captured her hand, kissing the back of it.

Trina shivered. No. She was not averse to their touch. Roar could sense her passion. Though the look of uncertainty remained on her face, he could tell she wanted them, too. Roar had to taste those sweet lips again.

He turned her head around to face him. Trina was just as sweet as he remembered. "Open your mouth for me, sweetheart. I want to taste you," he whispered against her lips. The smell of her floral-scented skin wafted to his nostrils, turning him on even more. Everything about Trina excited him -- her soft dark skin, the shy way she returned his kiss, her taste and her scent.

He needed to bury himself between her thick thighs or go crazy. When her lips parted under the gentle persistence of his, Roar's tongue darted forward. He couldn't get enough of her.

She pulled back, gasping for breath. "You're so sweet. I get so damn hard just looking at you. When I touch you, I can't stop. You liked my kisses, didn't you?" he asked knowingly.

Trina looked at all three of them before answering, though she seemed reluctant to do so. "Yes."

"Good. Let us make love to you. We're going to take you in ways you never imagined possible. Would you like that? Do you think you can handle the three of us?" Roar brushed his lips to the pulse of her neck.

* * *

Trina knew she should fight this, but her body seemed to have a mind of its own. She couldn't remember ever being so thoroughly attracted to anyone before, let alone three men. The kicker was, they all wanted her.

She wasn't so sure she was thrilled about this mate thing, or the fact they had tails, but damn she was horny. Perhaps a "no strings attached" affair was what she really needed. They were just as horny as she was so why not give in to their mutual lusts.

"Yes, make love to me. No. Fuck me." She moved until she rested on her knees and had them all smiling. Trina didn't know who to turn to first. She wanted them all.

Bayoh reached for her, pulling her against his chest, kissing her with a ferocity that took her breath away. Unlike the gentle persuasion of Roar's kiss, Bayoh's was rough and hungry. He devoured her lips as though he couldn't get enough.

She liked it.

His tongue stabbed forward, demanding entrance into her mouth. Trina moaned as he wrapped his arms tighter around her, crushing her sensitive breasts against the hard wall of his chest. His unique flavor was intoxicating. Trina felt scorched from the inside out with his forceful kiss. She whimpered as he withdrew. Bayoh looked down at her with hungry eyes, his breathing ragged. "I knew you would be delicious, but I never imagined how much so. Damn, woman, you must have bewitched me."

Trina could feel the heat generating from his body. It threatened to scorch her from the inside out. Her body felt as though it would explode at any minute, and her pussy throbbed with the need to be filled with a thick cock. Trina wanted to try every single one of them. She shuddered in anticipation when she thought of their thick rods.

"I want to taste you too." Talh pulled her out of Bayoh's arms, turning her toward him. His strong white teeth nipped and nibbled on her bottom lip sending little bolts of fire up and down her spine.

Talh pulled back, looking down at her. Just like Roar and Bayoh, he looked at her as though she were the most precious thing in the world. It made her heart flutter at the mixture of tenderness, awe, and passion in his aquamarine eyes. "You are so beautiful, Trina. When I first saw you, I thought I was imagining things, because I didn't think it was possible for a woman like you to exist, but you're here."

Trina's breath caught in her throat at his beautiful declaration. No one had ever said anything so poetic, with such obvious sincerity to her before. She reached up to caress his cheek. Her fingertips danced across Talh's face, reveling in the texture of his skin. He smiled down at her, revealing strong white teeth. "You're beautiful too." Trina returned the compliment.

An amused look crossed his face. "A man cannot be beautiful."

"Yes, they can. Beauty is something that pleases the eye, and I find you very pleasing to my eyes. Each one of you," she said, encompassing them all in her statement. Trina was tired of talking. She wanted to fuck.

Damn, she was horny.

Talh bent down and outlined the seam of her lips with his tongue. His kiss was slow and playful, so when he finally slipped his questing tongue inside her mouth, Trina was hungry for the taste of him.

Each man had his own technique when they kissed, but each drove her past the point of all reasoning. Roar pulled her back, positioning her in the middle of the circle they'd formed around her with Bayoh directly in front of her, Talh and Roar at her sides.

Her heart sped up in anticipation of what was about to happen. She pressed her knees tightly together, squirming with desire. Her pussy was burning with need. If they could make her feel this way after just a few kisses, she didn't know how she would hold up when they finally slid those big cocks inside her. Trina fanned herself at the thought.

Bayoh placed his hands on her knees. "You need not be shy with us. I can smell your pussy. The scent is driving me wild. It's wet and ready for us already, isn't it?" He smiled at her. Trina's heart skipped a beat.

She nodded in agreement. Trina knew she couldn't speak had her life depended on it.

"Good, because I've wanted to touch you there since I laid eyes on you. Before we found you, I daydreamed about touching, tasting, and fucking your pussy." Bayoh pried her thighs apart. His fingers caressed the dark thatch of hair between her legs before parting the swollen, dew-dampened lips of her cunt.

Bayoh's thumb pressed against her clit. "Oh, yes. That feels so good," she groaned. He seemed pleased with her response when he gave her a big smile. He rolled the hot little button between his fingers. It felt so good. So damn good.

Caught up in what Bayoh was doing with his hand, Trina didn't realize Roar and Talh leaned over her until she felt a hot mouth latch onto each of her nipples. Trina looked down. One blond head, one red head, each suckling at her breasts in earnest. The triple stimulation shook her body to its core. "Yes! Yes! Yes!" Trina's head rocked back and forth.

Nothing else existed for her except this moment and the mindless pleasure these men were giving her. Bayoh's thumb continued to caress her clit while he slid two thick fingers inside her wet channel. Never in a million years would she have imagined herself in this position, but it was one Trina found she liked very well.

"Oh God, Bayoh, just like that," she whispered. She'd never wanted anything as badly as this. When he removed his fingers, she felt empty without them inside her. The steady thrusting of his fingers inside her had made her so wet, a puddle had formed beneath her.

Trina watched in amazement as he slipped his drenched fingers into his mouth.

"Delicious, just like I knew it would be."

Roar lifted his head from her breast, letting his cock hit the hard little peak. "I want to taste some of that wonderfully scented pussy as well."

He moved to kneel in front of her, beside Bayoh.

Talh lifted his head and the three men pushed her backwards before spreading Trina's legs as far apart as possible. The redhead returned his attention to her breasts, suckling on one while squeezing and kneading the other with his callused palm. She loved the rough eager way he touched her.

Trina moaned as Talh's long red tail curved around to caress her. Its tip brushed over the taut mounds and slid between the valley of her breasts. It sent goose bumps all over her body as it brushed against the side of her arm.

Roar and Bayoh dipped their heads between her legs. They each held a leg, licking her inner thigh. Her body shook with the erotic picture they created. She could not keep still as she felt one of their tongues brush against her outer labia.

Trina couldn't take her eyes off the three men feasting on her body, as though they couldn't get enough of her -- one at her breasts, two at her throbbing pussy. She watched Roar pull back. With room to move, Bayoh lifted her hips and fastened his mouth fully over her.

She gasped in pleasure-pain at the forceful pressure of Bayoh's mouth on her. His tongue stroked every inch of her pussy, licking her from her clit to the crack of her ass. He licked and nibbled her like a starving man, and all she could do was writhe and shake as he devoured her cunt.

Roar smiled at her. "I know you like this, Trina, but I want to hear you say the words."

"Yes. I like it. I love it. I want more," Trina whispered.

"We want to hear you say it louder. Tell us how much you like it," he demanded, crawling up next to where her head rested. His cock was mere inches from her face. She wanted to know what it tasted like. It was so big she wondered just how much she could fit in her mouth.

"I want you. I want all of you," she groaned.

"Louder. Say it louder," Roar commanded.

"I want you!" she screamed as she felt Bayoh's tongue dart into her channel and Talh gently bite her nipples.

"I see the way you're eyeing my cock. Do you want to taste it?" Roar asked.

She didn't bother to deny it. If she was a slut for doing this, then so be it. "Yes. Please. Give me some of that big beautiful cock. I want to feel every single inch of it."

Roar gently turned Trina until she faced him. He stroked her face with his callused fingers, ran his thumb across the seam of her lips, parting them. Slowly he slid the head of his cock between her lips. Trina shifted, uncaring of the awkwardness of her position, intent on taking Roar's huge pole into her mouth.

She would give him as much pleasure as the three men gave her. Inhaling his scent, tasting the musky flavor of his flesh, she opened her mouth wide, but his cock was so long and thick, she managed only a few inches without gagging.

He moaned, stroking her hair, crooning to her. "Yes, baby, just like that. I knew you were the one when I saw you."

Trina worked her head back and forth, savoring his taste in her mouth. The musky male flavor of him was intoxicating. Roar shuddered with each brush of her tongue, moaning softly when Trina compressed his hard cock with the strong muscles in her cheek. His obvious arousal turned her on even more, filled her with a sense of power, to think she could have an effect on this man. Even more arousing was the thought of tasting Bayoh and Talh as well.

She ripped her mouth away from Roar's cock, as Bayoh increased the intensity of his mouth over her pussy. He fucked her with his tongue until she bucked her hips against his face.

"Yes!" she screamed. "Eat my pussy! Don't stop! Don't ever stop!"

Talh squeezed and plucked at her breasts with fingers, and lips, harder and faster. Trina's body shuddered, so close to her peak.

Roar bent down to fasten his mouth over hers. Trina returned his kiss as though it were her last. Just then her body seized up. She nearly blacked out as one of the most explosive orgasms she'd ever experienced shot through her.

Trina twisted her head away from Roar as she screamed. Her body convulsed uncontrollably, rocking her to the very core of her being. Bayoh and Talh lifted their heads with pleased expressions on their faces.

Roar looked equally smug. "I knew you had a passionate nature."

"I don't know if I can take any more," she whispered, her body still recovering from her earth-shattering climax. She felt her juices drip down between her crack.

"But we're not finished with you." Talh smiled. She thought he was going to touch her pussy, but instead, his fingers went straight for her ass. Trina tensed up. The few times she'd had anal, it had hurt like hell, so it wasn't her favorite thing.

"Relax. It will be easier for you that way." The redhead smiled in reassurance as he ran his thumb over the tight bud of her ass.

She forced her body to relax. Trina realized by taking on three partners at once, one of them was bound to want her ass, but she hadn't really given it a lot of thought until now. "I... I'm not sure I like that."

"We won't do anything you don't want to do. If you want me to stop touching you here then say so and I will," Talh promised.

The stimulation of his fingers rubbing her anus didn't feel bad. Actually it was beginning to feel quite nice. "Do you want me to stop, Trina?"

She shook her head. She didn't want him to stop touching her. He slid a finger inside her ass, making her body quiver. She gasped. They watched her as though trying to gauge her reaction. Oddly it turned her on to have three pairs of eyes watching her so intently. Trina raised her hips slightly allowing the finger to go deeper inside of her. So far so good.

By the time Talh added another finger, her body began to respond to the anal stimulation. Perhaps she had never enjoyed anal sex before because no one had prepared her, going at her pace instead of just thrusting into her as though she had no feelings.

When he added a third finger, Trina was so hot, she wanted to feel his cock inside her. "I don't want your fingers. I want you," she pleaded.

"And you shall have me, my beauty."

Talh removed his fingers before pulling her close, with her back against him. She felt his cock pressing against the crack of her ass. His fingers were one thing, but his dick was quite another. She tensed up again. "Relax. Remember how good I made you feel? I'll make you feel that way again. If it becomes unbearable, you only need to say the words," he whispered against her ear.

She relaxed as he'd instructed, crying out as she felt him slide the head of his cock inside her ass. Trina felt a slight discomfort, but it wasn't nearly as bad as she'd imagined it would be.

"See? It isn't so bad, is it? The worst part is over. You were made for us. You will have no problem taking our cocks inside you." Talh grazed the side of her neck with his teeth.

He reared forward, sliding his full length inside her ass. It felt so good. She wanted to move up and down on the thick pole deep within her ass, but he held her firm with one hand while he fingered her clit. Trina thought she would die from the mind-numbing pleasure. "Your pussy is so wet. I think you need a cock inside it, don't you think?"

She nodded, surrendering to the seductive tone of his voice. Talh lay back on the bed, taking her with him. His cock never left her ass. Bayoh came forward then, covering her body with his. When he slid his cock into her dripping cunt, all she could do was moan at the sensation of her pussy and anal wall being deliciously stretched by such big cocks. She hadn't thought it was possible for them to fit inside her because of their size, but somehow they did, and it felt good. Real good.

Trina looked to Roar, who watched them. His fist wrapped around his cock. "Don't you --" she began.

"I will have my turn with you. I take as much pleasure in knowing how much you are enjoying this. I like watching the expression on your face as you shudder with pleasure." Roar smiled at her, stroking his cock with his hands.

His words brought out the exhibitionist in her. Knowing that one of them watched as the other two fucked her turned Trina on nearly as much as the act itself.

Bayoh and Talh began to slowly pump into her pussy and ass, filling Trina with a desire so strong she felt she would die with pleasure. The scorching heat building inside her threatened to set them all on fire.

Trina's gaze locked with Roar's. The intensity of his stare was just as arousing as being fucked. She wanted to taste him again, but in this position she knew it would be difficult. The next time they tried this, she wanted to take them all at once.

"Yes! Fuck me harder," she moaned, not able to get enough.

The two men sandwiching her moved in an almost choreographed motion matching rhythm for rhythm as they slammed into her.

"Trina, I could fuck your pussy all night," Bayoh groaned.

Talh nipped her shoulder. "This ass is so tight and snug around my cock I don't think I'll be able to hold back any longer."

"Don't hold back," she cried. "Give me everything you have. I need you all so much."

She moved with their cocks, until she didn't think her body could take any more. Suddenly she stiffened. A wave of passion swept through her that was so strong she began to scream and couldn't stop.

"That's it, baby, show us how much you like this." Roar smiled, obviously pleased at her reaction.

This had to be the most powerful climax she'd ever experienced. Her body shuddered and shook until she went limp from exhaustion. Instead of finishing inside her, like she thought he would, Bayoh pulled out and shot a greenish fluid on her belly.

If she weren't so weak after such a thorough fucking, Trina would have questioned what the hell was spewing from his cock. Instead she just stared as he sprayed the strange fluid over her. Bayoh collapsed onto his side when he finished.

When Talh eased his way out her ass, she felt empty. He moved to position himself over her, and he too shot a greenish fluid from his cock. This time it covered her breasts.

He moved aside, letting Roar take his place. The blond held his stiff rod in his fist, jerking it back and forth. Trina watched, unable to take her eyes off this action. She instinctively knew he was about to do what Bayoh and Talh had just done. She was right.

Roar moaned as the greenish liquid fell over her chest. When he finished, he began to rub the fluid they'd spilled into her skin as though it were lotion. It almost felt as though they'd just performed some ritual with her.

When Roar finished his task, he smiled at her. "Now you are truly ours. For life."

Chapter Seven

"What would you like for dinner tonight, Trina?" Roar gazed over the menu with disinterest. He wasn't particularly hungry for anything except for Trina's pussy.

"Hmm, I think I'd like the house salad. It's much too hot for anything else." She pushed the menu away from her, giving him a small smile.

Roar knew he'd never get tired of watching this beauty. It made his heart race whenever she looked at him like that. He was sure Bayoh and Talh felt the same way. He glanced over at his two friends to see they were as enchanted as he was.

Roar wondered what Trina felt when she looked at them. Did her heart beat faster when they looked at her? Did she melt on the inside with just one glance from any of them?

Trina turned to look out the window, her expression pensive. Bayoh grabbed her hand in his. "What are you thinking?"

She turned back around with a small smile on her lips. "I was just thinking I must be the luckiest woman in the restaurant. I'm sitting with the three most handsome men on the island. It's hard to believe the three of you would want to spend your time with me."

"Why would you wonder about that? Surely you know what you look like." Bayoh smiled at her. He brought her hand to his lips before letting go.

"I know I'm not ugly, but looks aren't what makes a person. This island is full of beautiful women. What I don't understand is... I mean... why me?" The confusion in her beautiful brown eyes made Roar want to take her into his arms to assure her of her worth.

He gathered from the little Trina had told them about her past that someone or a handful of someones had hurt her. What was wrong with the men in her homeland to not recognize just how special Trina was? Roar agreed with her that the island was indeed crawling with beautiful women, but had they merely been looking for a beautiful woman, they would have settled for Nika. No. Trina was special. He sensed an inner strength and beauty within her that shone through. Roar was sure Bayoh and Talh felt the same way too.

Roar liked the way she moaned their names in the heat of passion, the way her ass jiggled when she walked, and her lovely face and body. Those were superficial things however. What he loved about her was her laugh, the way she smiled at them, the way her eyes sparkled when she told a joke, the wistful look that would enter her eyes when she spoke of her life dreams. Roar loved the whole package.

He knew she was reluctant to give her heart to them because of her past, but the more time they spent together, the more determined he became to change her mind. "Trina, there's more to a woman than just physical beauty. Yes, there are beautiful women on this island, but there were beautiful women on Laiocean. Where you come from, isn't there such a thing as instant love?"

She lifted a delicately arched brow. "You mean love at first sight?"

Roar nodded. "Yes. If that's what human call it. Love at first sight isn't something common among our people, but it happens. It happened to us when we saw you."

The incredulous look on her face told Roar she wasn't convinced. "But I don't --"

"You don't feel the same way? This is just an island fling to you?" Talh asked with a knowing expression.

Trina looked away momentarily before turning back to look at them. "Look, I was upfront with you in the beginning. I can hardly believe I've even done half the things I've done with you guys. I'm sure there are plenty of women out there who would return your love, no questions asked. I may not be that woman, but I already know how special you are. The obvious love the three of you feel for each other is a bond any woman would be pleased to share."

"But not you?" Bayoh asked.

She hesitated for a moment, as though searching for the right words to say. "I don't think I'm capable of loving anyone anymore."

The forlorn way she said it made Roar's heart ache. He silently cursed the men who'd hurt her. Damn them all. If he or his friends had three seconds with any of the men who'd trampled on her heart, they'd be shreds. "Trina, just because a few men didn't appreciate what they had doesn't mean we would hurt you. Where we come from, women are given the utmost respect."

"I still don't understand how it is you guys don't mind sharing me with each other. I mean, when other men look at me, the three of you go berserk, but you don't mind sharing with each other. I don't understand this concept." Trina picked up her club soda and took a sip before putting it back down on the table.

Roar took her hand in his. "It's hard to explain to someone who hasn't grown up in our culture, but the best place to start is understanding our history. Our people have existed on another world long before humans. At one time women were plentiful among us. The Manani were more warlike then, and went by another name. Those who were in charge back then wanted to pillage our neighboring land. Our ancestors wiped our neighbors out. It turned out to be a big mistake, because the inhabitants of the land were the chosen people of the Ancient Ones. The Manani were cursed before being banished from that world."

Roar paused to take a sip of his gin and tonic. Trina's eyes were glued to his. "What did the curse do to your people?"

"Our females died, little by little until there were few left. Very few females were born. Our ancestors went back to the world they were banished from to plead with the Ancient Ones. They took pity on us, making it possible for three males, sharing the same soul sign, to be with one woman. Among humans and most other species, it only takes one male and one female to procreate, however, it takes three Manani males to impregnate one woman. Bayoh and Talh and I were bonded from our birth. It's impossible to feel envy for one who is connected to your soul."

"It seems like the males of your tribe get the short end of the stick. Don't any of you feel the need to have one woman apiece?" Trina asked with an incredulous expression on her face.

"No. I suppose you can say it's just the way we were created," Talh joined in.

"What made you come to Chimera?"

Bayoh chuckled. "You're very inquisitive tonight, Trina."

"Well, shouldn't I be? I mean, shouldn't I get to know the men I'm having an affair with?" She shrugged with a nonchalance that bothered Roar. He knew from the beginning Trina wouldn't be easy to sway, but it cut him on the inside when she seemed so casual about their coming together.

Roar sighed. "It's more than an affair, Trina, but we will argue on the point later. The reason we came to Chimera is partly because of the women shortage but mainly because we could not agree on a mate. The three of us are the Alpha Triad. It's not as hard for us to find willing females because of our status, but we're not so different from humans in that we wanted to find a mate who would love us for what's inside our hearts, and not for who we are. Sometimes it's easy to be blinded by surface beauty, as the three of us have been, but one thing we did agree on was we wanted the total package. We saw that in you, Trina."

Trina's tongue poked out to run along her lips. "When you speak like that to me, I almost believe you."

"Why shouldn't you believe us? We only speak the truth." Bayoh scooted his chair closer to her.

"Well... just because."

"Why would we have any reason to lie to you?" Talh asked.

"I don't know. I've long since given up on trying to figure men out."

"Well, tell us something about these men, Trina. What exactly have they done to make you this way?" Roar wanted to know what he was up against, feeling the unfairness of the situation. Why did they have to pay for others' past mistakes?

"To sum it up, I've been cheated on, lied to, hit, made a fool of, stolen from, used and that's only to name a few. Let's face it, guys. I'm a loser as far as relationships go."

"It doesn't have to be like that, Trina. Love can be a beautiful thing if you allow it to happen. We came to Chimera to find a mate and not only did we find you, we found love. It's too precious an emotion to let slip away. Those other men didn't love you. If they did, they could never have treated you in such a shabby manner," Bayoh said with obvious anger.

It upset Roar to know what she'd been through. He looked over to see Talh with a similar thunderous expression. Roar grasped Trina's chin between his fingers, forcing her to look at him. The sadness in her big brown eyes made him ache. He wished he could erase her pain. "Bayoh is right. Love is a gift. Where we come from, it's not something one takes for granted."

"You make it sound so simple," she whispered.

Roar let go of her chin and caressed her soft cheek. "It is that simple."

The waiter appeared at that moment and took their food orders. When he left, Roar thought it was best to steer the conversation in another direction. Pushing her too hard would only make her retreat further in her shell. At least Trina seemed comfortable enough to confide in them. For now, that was enough, but eventually he and his friends would want more.

Much more.

Chapter Eight

Trina laid on the beach, letting the sun caress her bare skin. She'd untied her bikini top when she positioned herself on her stomach. It wasn't as though she needed a tan, but she liked the way the sun felt. This was the first time in four days when Roar, Bayoh, and Talh were not by her side.

The three of them decided to get something to eat, but she wasn't hungry. Besides, she needed a little breathing space. It was still hard to believe she was having an affair with three men at once. Their first night together after Roar made his little declaration, they'd taken her to the large shower and cleaned her body.

When they finished the task they took her back to bed where Roar positioned her on her knees before sliding into her pussy, which by that time was wet again. Bayoh stuck his cock in her mouth and she sucked him with wild abandon. Talh watched with a satisfied gleam in his eyes.

This time when they finished, there was no green fluid. Roar shot his seed inside her pussy and Bayoh into her mouth. She'd never been one to swallow semen, but oddly, she wanted to ingest every single drop of Bayoh's essence.

Trina didn't think she could take any more, but the three of them made love to her well into the daylight, fucking her in every conceivable position. She was surprised her body could contort in so many different ways. By the time they finished with her, she was so exhausted she couldn't move.

She woke up the next morning slightly sore but sated. From then on they never left her side. If she went to the beach, they were with her. They ate, showered, and did activities with her. Trina had to admit she enjoyed their company. She couldn't remember a time when she'd had so much fun.

On their third night together, they revealed their true forms to her. It scared her in the beginning, but they'd prepared her for what she would see before they showed her. Besides, there were so many mysterious things on Chimera, she wasn't that surprised when her three lovers shifted into huge cats before her very eyes.

They all looked like giant lions, but they weren't quite lions. They had big shaggy manes and broad lion faces, but that was where the similarities ended. Their pelts were the shade of their hair, and they all bore markings in various shapes.

Another odd thing happened -- when they shifted, they could only communicate telepathically, but she understood them. It was very weird.

They wanted to screw her in their natural form. This took some convincing, but by the end of the night, she let them, and loved it. If anyone would have told her she'd be making love to three giant cats, she would have laughed and called them sick, but that was exactly what she did. They assured her that they would be in humanoid form most of time, but there would be times when they needed to shift.

She could handle the fact that they were very demanding lovers who kept her up through all hours of the night, making her body sing with pleasure. She could handle them not being human. She could even handle them wanting to be by her side constantly. What she could not handle were the feelings she was developing for each of them.

When she'd agreed to sleep with them, unbeknownst to them, this was supposed to be a "no strings attached" arrangement. When the week was over, she'd get on a plane and go back to the real world, despite what they thought. Now she wasn't so sure. It still baffled her how she could feel this way about three men at once, but she did.

Each one of them attracted her in their own way. She loved Roar's intelligence and conversation. He was very insightful, always having something deep and meaningful to say. Although each claimed there was no established leader, it was Roar who usually led, and the other two followed, but she noticed how Roar always deferred to them first.

Trina liked Bayoh's forceful manner. He was a man of action who took what he wanted, but there was a sensitive side hidden behind his gruff demeanor. He had the soul of a poet. One night, the four of them sat watching the sunset, and Bayoh compared Trina to the beauty of that sunset in such a beautiful way it'd touched her soul.

Then there was Talh. He spoke the least of the three, but when he did he would not be ignored. He was sometimes stubborn in his manner, but not overly so. He was very affectionate, always finding reasons to touch, kiss, or cuddle with her. They all did these things, but Talh more so than the other two. He was a sweetheart.

There were qualities in every one of them that made her heart race, and to be honest, there wasn't one she liked above the other. That was the problem. These feelings would get in the way of leaving them behind. They were feelings she didn't want to have for men she hadn't known that long. It was irrational, but Trina had deeper feelings for them than she cared to examine. How was this possible after she'd sworn off men in her life?

Love hurt and Trina didn't want to be in love, not this quickly after another broken relationship, and not with these three men who had the power to break her heart in a way that none of her exes had.

She knew she had to go back home, because staying would only open her up to more heartache. Knowing her luck with men, she knew it was a matter of time before something went totally wrong. What if she did give in and go to Laiocean with them? Then what? Once she bore them children, would she be cast aside? How did she know they wouldn't cheat or abuse her?

She didn't think they would abuse her physically, but they had the power to hurt her emotionally, and that wasn't a chance she could take. No, when the week ended, so would their affair.

Trina must have dozed off, because the next thing she remembered was a pair of hands rubbing something cool on her back. These hands didn't belong to any of her lovers. She would have known their touch anywhere. Trina stiffened, lifting her head to see who had put their hands on her.

She looked up to see a tall blond man. She supposed he would have been cute if he weren't blue. "Umm, who are you and why are you rubbing my skin like you have the right to do so?" she asked.

The man removed his hands. He looked stricken and Trina felt a little guilty for speaking so sharply to him. "Many pardons, miss, but skin such as yours should be protected from the sun's rays. I only thought to rub some sunscreen on your back. As you can tell, I'm thoroughly sunburned myself, and I'd hate for the same fate to happen to you."

Trina tied her bikini top together before sitting up. "I'm sorry for snapping at you, but you can't just go up to people and start touching them without their permission."

"I'm so sorry. I didn't mean to offend you. I only wanted to help, really. I will leave you alone."

The blue man looked a little distressed as he began to get up. She felt so guilty, although she had no reason to be, she grabbed his hand. "Wait, you don't have to go. What's your name?"

He sat back down with a big smile on his face, showing off little white teeth. "My name's Morel Hyyor, of the Hyyor wood nymphs... and you are?"

"Trina Davis. Nice to meet you, Morel." She smiled back at him. He briefly shook the hand she held. His grip was strong at first. Morel was actually kind of cute.

"And it's very nice meeting you, Miss Davis. You're the first woman who's even talked to me on this island."

"Well, you were nice enough to rub sunscreen on my back, but I can't imagine a handsome guy like you not getting any female attention."

He blushed, looking pleased. "Well, not really. Actually, I've been slapped in the face a few times, told to get lost, and called a loser. One woman told me to go fuck myself, whatever that means. If I could do that I wouldn't need a woman."

She felt sorry for him. The poor fellow didn't seem to be having much luck. "Well, give me an example of how you approach women."

"Well, I do what all wood nymphs do when they're greeting their women. I grab them between their legs and squeeze. It's the way our males tell a female we're interested. Had you not been lying on your stomach, I would have greeted you in the same manner."

"And I would have knocked you back into next week. I can appreciate that greeting a woman in this way is what your people do, but for people not of your culture, it's insulting because it's not what they're used to."

"But I know no other way. I knew coming to this island was a big mistake, but it was either this or marry Swinla."

"What's wrong with Swinla?"

"She's been my betrothed since we were children, but I don't see her as anything more than a little sister. Yes, she is beautiful, but she doesn't make my heart beat faster. I want the real thing. My people mate for life, and I can't imagine being stuck with someone I only feel a mild love for, for the rest of my life."

"How does Swinla feel about you?"

"She loves me, at least she says so, but I need to find someone who isn't her. My brothers were able to choose their mates. Just because I am my father's heir why can I not choose my own?"

Trina had the sneaking suspicion that Morel was here more out of rebellion than anything else. "Have you given the relationship a chance?"

"Well... no, but I know it's not what I want."

"How do you know if you don't give it a chance?"

"I never thought about it to be honest, but it's just not fair," he pouted with a petulant expression on his blue face.

"Life isn't fair. Look, from what you're telling me, it doesn't seem like you're doing so well here on Chimera. Why not go back home and find if there can be anything between you and Swinla, and then if things don't work out, you can come back to Chimera."

He paused for a moment as though thinking over the possibility. "Well, I guess that doesn't sound like a bad idea. My mother said the exact same thing, but..."

"Sometimes it's easier to take coming from an objective third party, right?"

"I suppose. Thank you, Trina. I appreciate the advice. I've been miserable since I've been here on this island anyway."

"I'm sorry to hear that."

"How is your time on the island? Are you enjoying yourself?"

"Yes, I am actually."

"I'm surprised to see you alone on the beach. A beautiful woman like yourself should have swarms of men around you."

"Thank you. Actually I've met three men. They're all very nice."

"Three men? And they're okay with sharing you?" he asked with evident disbelief.

"That's what they say. They're Manani."

"Oh, yes. I've heard of them. In that case, I had better go." He had a worried expression on his face.

"Leaving so soon? You don't have to go." She reached out for him, catching his wrist.

"I may not know everything about the Manani race, but I know how possessive males are. I'm sure you've been marked by them, and though I won't back down from a confrontation, I'm not in the mood to fight because I was seen talking to you."

Marked? What was he talking about? Trina frowned. "Umm, they can't tell me who I can talk to. They don't own me."

"But you've been marked, haven't you?"

"I don't even know what you mean."

Morel looked over her shoulder before abruptly standing up. "If I guess right, I see your three angry suitors coming this way. Pardon me if don't stick around. Thanks for talking to me, Trina."

Before her very eyes, he disappeared. What an odd man he was, but she supposed he was no worse than anyone else on Chimera. She turned around to see Roar, Bayoh, and Talh approach. Morel was right -- they didn't look happy.

The three of them hovered over her, with not too pleased expressions on their handsome faces. What were they so mad about? It was Roar who spoke first. "Who was that you were speaking to, Trina?"

She didn't like his tone one bit, but decided it was best not to get into an argument about it. "Morel. He's just a nice guy I met on the beach. We were only talking."

"I didn't particularly care for the way he was looking at you. Didn't you tell him you were already mated?" Bayoh asked.

"No. Why should I? We were just talking. What's the harm in that?"

Bayoh shook his head. "No harm to you of course, but much harm to him if he thinks he can make moves on our woman."

"I don't like to be discussed as though I'm a piece of meat. We've gone over this already and I'm not your possession, and if you guys are going to act like this every time I talk to someone, I would rather end this thing right now." She stood up to face them, her hands planted firmly on her hips.

"If you think you can end things just like that, you're sadly mistaken. You've been marked, which means you're ours, and this is something not up for discussion." Roar grabbed her arm, pulling her against him.

"Marked? What the hell are you talking about?"

"Don't you remember the first time we made love? We sprayed you with our love nectar," Talh explained.

Trina suddenly realized what they were talking about. The green fluid they'd sprayed on her was not semen. She should have suspected something was up when they rubbed it into her skin, but she'd been too damn horny at the time to think straight.

"So what? So you shot some green stuff on me. That means less than nothing to me. I am a woman with my own free will who has the right to pick and choose who she wants to be with."

Roar brought his face down to hers until their noses were almost touching. "But you see, that green stuff, as you so delicately put it, means everything to us. It means you're ours, and when you let us, you gave us your permission. We're bound for life now, and you can protest all you want, but it doesn't make you any less ours. When this week is over, you will come home with us."

"The hell I will. That's it. I'm not going to be treated as though I don't know my own mind. I don't want anything else to do with you three, do you hear me? Absolutely nothing."

"Do you think we're just going to let you walk away from us after what we've shared? Don't deny that you feel anything for us, because I see it whenever you look at us, touch us -- respond to us. You're so scared to admit you care for us, because of something a bunch of immature assholes have done to you. You've been waiting for an excuse to end this all week, haven't you?" Roar demanded.

She gasped. How did they know how she felt?

"Ah, I see the surprise on your face, but you still don't seem to get it. You belong to us and you always will. We know your feelings and your moods. We probably know what's in your heart better than you do. Don't think we didn't know you were treating this as a casual affair. We indulged you because you've had a bad time with love. This week we've done the things you've wanted to do to ease you into this relationship with us. You hold nothing back when we make love to you, but you want to put a wall between us. Well, we will not let you do so anymore."

When Roar finished with his speech, Trina could only look at them with wonder. "If you know how I feel, then how can you think I would want anything long term? This is not a game, this is my life we're talking about here. I thought by coming to this island I would be taking charge of my life again, but you guys just want to control me."

"We don't want to control you, and wouldn't dream of it. We just want to take care of you, and treat you in the way you deserve to be treated. You deserve the best of everything and we want to give it to you," Talh said, approaching her. He cupped the side of her face in his palm. As always, when any of them touched her, her body responded. Damn them for being able to do this to her traitorous body.

"If you knew what was best for me, then you'd know the best thing for me is to leave me alone. I can't deal with anything long term."

"Life is about taking risks. If you get hurt once, it doesn't mean the next person is out to hurt you," Bayoh reasoned.

What he said made sense, but her scarred heart made it difficult for her to believe them. It was a risk she didn't know if she had the courage to take.

"You guys talk a good game now. You tell me that you love me and want to take care of me, but then again, that's something all men say to get into a woman's pants. If I went back to you with Laiocean, how would I know that you wouldn't hurt me like the others?"

"You don't know, Trina, but that's what loving is all about. Loving is about trust. You will just have to trust that we will cherish and take care of you for the rest of your days. You're not the only one who's scared. We were worried about coming to Chimera and not finding our mate. We were worried we'd be stuck with a mate the three of us couldn't agree on. We were scared a human woman wouldn't be able to accept us for what we were, but we found you. We took a big risk to come here. Now we're asking you to take a risk in us. Let us love you." Roar kissed her gently on the lips.

Her eyes welled with tears. Dare she love them?

The image of Tim and Twan flashed in her mind. Love led to pain. "I can't. I'm sorry, but I just can't."

"I see. It distresses us to hear it though. I guess there's only one thing left to do," Roar said with a note of resignation in his voice.

Were they letting her go? Why did the thought bother her so much when she'd just pleaded they do exactly that? "What are you going do?" she asked, swallowing the lump that had formed in her throat.

"We're just going to have to take the choice out of your hands," Talh answered.

Before she realized what they were talking about, Roar hauled her up in the air and threw her over his shoulder as though she were a sack of flour, before heading back to her bungalow.

Chapter Nine

Trina wiggled and squirmed, trying to break free of Roar's vise grip. "You can't do this to me!" she protested.

"It's funny you should say that because it's exactly what I'm doing. Now stop wiggling so much before I drop you." He brought his palm down on her bottom.

It didn't hurt, but it surprised her. She cried out in outrage. "You brute, put me down this instant!" She lifted her head to look at Bayoh and Talh who followed closely behind. By the amused looks on their faces, she could tell they would be no help. They actually seemed to enjoy seeing her like this.

She knew when they went to her bungalow what they would do, and her body began to shiver with the very thought of it, but the feminist inside her protested this display of Cro-Magnon male.

By the time they reached her bungalow, she was exhausted from struggling so hard. The moment her feet hit the ground she glared up at them. "That wasn't necessary, you know. I could have walked."

"But would you have let us walk with you? Besides, as I've already said, the choice is no longer yours. We're going to do what we want to do, and we want to make love to you. This time, you're going to take us all at once," Roar declared as he peeled off his swim trunks. Instead of taking her to the bedroom, they remained in the living room.

This was the moment she'd been anticipating since she'd started this affair with them. She wasn't sure about the mechanics, but knew they would find a way. Why did her body always seem to take over when she knew her mind should be in control? The thought of taking all three of those big cocks inside her at the same time filled her with fear and lust.

Bayoh and Talh followed suit, and as always, she stood amazed at the beauty of their bodies. Unable to help herself she reached out to the one closest to her, which happened to be Roar. She ran her hands over his sinewy chest. His nipples stiffened as her thumb brushed over them.

Trina leaned forward to run her tongue across one tiny disk. He tasted of musk, salt water, and something else she couldn't quite put her finger on, but she liked the taste of him. He groaned, grabbing her head against his chest, and she sucked the hard little peak into her mouth. "Do you like that?" she asked.

"You know I do, woman. I love it when you touch me," he groaned.

"But I bet you especially like it when I touch you here, don't you?" she said, feeling bold as her hand slid lower and grasped his cock in her fist.

He nodded, speechless.

She stroked his cock back and forth, knowing he enjoyed it, feeling high off of her feminine power. Knowing she could make this big strong man react to her this way aroused her as much as when they touched her. As she jerked his cock in her hand, her tongue continued to tease and lick his nipple. Trina transferred her attention to his other nipple.

Roar pulled away from her, his breathing ragged. "Woman, you are going to be the death of me."

Trina smiled at him. "I thought you liked it? Perhaps Talh would appreciate my touch." She turned to the tall redhead whose eyes flashed with untamed desire. She kissed the smooth expanse of his chest, drawing his scent deep within her nostrils, savoring his unique flavor. It was similar to Roar's but different. Touching their hard, lean bodies was becoming an addiction she couldn't quite get enough of.

She felt a strong pair of hands pull her back, making her protest. "I need you too, Trina. I need you badly," Bayoh whispered in her ear.

Bayoh stood behind her and began to undo the ties of her bikini. She could feel her breasts harden. They felt as though they wanted to burst from her top. He kissed the back of her neck, causing her to lean against him. His hand reached around to cup her breasts, making them harder than they already were. She could feel the swell of his hard cock pressing against her bottom and Trina wanted him inside her in the worst way. His hands squeezed and caressed her flesh. "You have such soft, beautiful skin. I like the way my pale skin looks against your dark flesh. I also like the way you moan for me when I touch you like this," he whispered against her neck.

Her breath caught in her throat as Roar knelt down in front of her to slide her bikini bottoms down her thighs. She lifted her legs, one at a time, to step out of them. She looked down at Roar just in time to see him insert his long middle finger inside her slick folds. The finger grazed her clit before moving further down to slip into her channel.

"That feels wonderful," she sighed, rolling her head back and forth against Bayoh's shoulder.

Roar lifted one of her legs and placed it over his shoulder so that he could have better access to her sopping pussy. He slid another thick digit inside her, and the added stimulation created an urgent need within her so strong she didn't think her knees would support her for much longer.

Roar fucked her with his fingers, looking up occasionally as though trying to gauge her reaction. "Your pussy is so wet and fragrant. I don't think I can go a second longer without tasting it," he growled, parting her dewy folds with his free hand before leaning forward and placing his lips against her pussy.

She gasped as his teeth captured her clit. He nipped, nibbled, and teased before sucking it into his mouth. Between Roar suckling on her clit and Bayoh's hands on her breasts, Trina didn't know how much more pleasure she could take. It amazed her still that each time she was with them it always felt like the first time.

Talh didn't seem content to watch this time. "I want to taste those sweet lips of yours," he said, stepping closer, gently guiding her head toward him.

As his mouth came down to close over hers, Trina opened her mouth to welcome the invasion of his questing tongue. The kiss was slow and deep. He explored her mouth, tasting every inch of it. The heat of passion was evident as the kiss became more forceful -- hungrier.

Trina opened her mouth wider, letting her tongue taste his, running it along his bottom lip. It was delicious, heady, and hot at the same time.

The three men seemed to know exactly where to touch, where to push, and where to stroke. They seemed to know how to make her moan, as though they had mastered her body, and she supposed they had.

As good as this felt, she wanted more. She needed to feel their cocks within her or she thought she'd expire with need. Trina was drowning in lust, needing to be filled, as only these three men knew how. She ripped her mouth away from Talh's. "Fuck me. I can't take this anymore."

Roar, who'd been eating her pussy in earnest, took his time lifting his head. He removed his fingers from her pussy. "I think I could stay between your thighs all day. I can't get enough of this sweet cunt juice." He stood up then and rubbed his juice-dampened fingers across her lips. Trina's lips parted at the insistent poking of those fingers. "See how good you taste. It's delicious, isn't it, darling?"

She sucked on his fingers. Trina had never tasted herself before but the taste wasn't unpleasant. The intimacy of the act was more of a turn-on than anything else, and she was turned on. Very turned on.

Before she could say anything else, Bayoh dragged her to the couch, pulling her onto his lap with her back against him. She knew then what was about to happen. Nerves took over and she began to shake.

"Don't be nervous, Trina. Remember we told you we'd never hurt you. We wouldn't begin to now, either. You'll have to trust us."

Trust.

There was that word again. Why couldn't they understand trust wasn't something that came easy to her anymore?

"Relax," Roar said as though he sensed her unease.

Bayoh pried her legs further apart and began to stroke her already soaking wet cunt. "That's it, Trina. Relax, baby. You're already so hot and wet for us. I can feel your heat without even touching you."

"Yes, I'm ready for you. Please don't tease me anymore. I don't think I can take it," she moaned.

He slid his finger lower to glide over the tight bud of her anus. "This isn't teasing, baby. You'd know it if I were teasing you. I enjoy touching your tight pussy and ass. You know what I'm going to do, baby?" he asked as his thumb continued to rub her asshole.

"What?" she said, almost unable to get the word out when she felt him insert his thumb into her butt.

"I'm going to fuck your ass. Will you like that? Will you like the feel of my thick cock slamming in your big round ass? Your ass was made for fucking and I think you're going to enjoy it as much as I will, won't you?"

His words of seduction sent shivers up her spine. She wiggled over his thumb, wishing he would stop talking and fuck her. "Fuck me," she begged.

"Oh, I'm going to. We all are." Another finger joined his thumb and Trina nearly blacked out from the pleasure of it.

Roar and Talh looked on with an expression of anxious anticipation on their faces, waiting to take their positions. She didn't know how, but during this past week, she'd developed a taste for being watched.

Bayoh continued to tease her ass with his fingers, until she begged him. "Please, give me your cock. Please! I can't take it anymore."

He chuckled, twisting and thrusting his fingers inside her ass. Her body shook with the warm sensation of lust coursing from her head to her toes. Bayoh slowly removed his fingers, causing her to gasp with the sudden emptiness she felt. "Anything for you, my love. You're so hot and ready for me I'll have no problem sliding my cock inside you."

"Hurry. Please." She moaned and lifted her bottom, ready for the entrance of his cock. When he slipped his thick rod past the tight ring of her ass, she sighed in relief as he filled her. The sensation was like none other. Trina began to move up and down on his cock, but he grasped her hip.

"Uh-uh, my greedy little vixen. Not yet," Bayoh halted her. He bent over and nipped her on the shoulder.

"Please," she begged.

"Oh, we will please you all right," Roar said, coming from the side of the room to stand before her, his stiff cock bobbed up and down with each slow deliberate step he took. He looked so beautiful standing there. Her mouth went dry. She couldn't wait to feel him deep inside her.

Roar positioned himself in front of her, straddling his knees over hers and Bayoh's. He grabbed his cock, teasing her clit with its head. Trina threw her head back and shouted, "Give it to me! I want every single inch of you."

Roar licked his lips with apparent anticipation. A fierce gleam of passion shimmered in his aqua eyes before he slipped his dick inside her wet pussy. She sighed with pleasure, feeling whole once again to have these two big cocks filling her. The only thing missing was Talh.

As though he sensed her need for him, he stepped forward. "Turn your head this way." Talh cupped her face in his hands before guiding her head to his cock. Her lips closed hungrily over him, hungry for his taste.

Her head bobbed back and forth over the length of him, his cock going deep inside her mouth. "Yes, that's it, Trina. Suck it, baby, just like that. Not too hard." He guided her head on his cock, thrusting his hips forward.

She moaned in delight as his long pole slid in and out of her mouth. The musky, bittersweet taste of it titillated her senses. The heavenly sensation of sucking his cock felt as good as being fucked in her pussy and ass. "Your mouth feels like heaven," Talh moaned, digging his fingers into her hair.

Trina could barely make out what he said to her because she was too caught up in the rapture of their three cocks moving within her, fucking her, claiming her, conquering her.

She felt as though this was meant to be -- being fucked so thoroughly by the three men she loved.

Loved?

Where did that come from? She couldn't love them in such a short amount of time. How was that possible? No, this was lust, and when this vacation was over they would go their separate ways. For now, she would just enjoy the deliciously delectable sensation of the moment and not think of later. She only wanted to think of the here and now, savoring every inch of their cocks as they thrust into each one of her hungry holes.

They screwed her with an almost synchronized rhythm and she knew this wasn't the first time they'd done it. The thought bothered her more than it should have, but it wasn't enough to stop her enjoying what was going on. The pleasure was mind-blowing.

As they fucked her, their hands caressed and fondled every inch of exposed skin they could get their hands on, leaving a fire in their wake. This was heaven, she thought, as sparks danced before her eyes signaling how close she was to reaching her peak.

Heat spread through her in pulsing waves. Trina's body was burning up with the heat the four of them generated, but it was the kind of heat that could only be doused by feeding this incredible lust.

When she came it was more earth shattering than it had ever been with them. Trina tore her mouth from Talh's dick and screamed out. "Oh God, yes!"

"That's it, baby, don't hold back," Roar murmured, thrusting forward with one last powerful thrust, his sweat-glistened body slamming against hers. She felt the powerful explosion of his seed shoot through her.

Bayoh lifted his hips up, thrusting into her tight bottom, until he shuddered beneath her. She could feel essence dripping from her pussy and ass to slide in a puddle beneath her.

Trina turned her head expectantly to Talh, wanting to taste him, to feel the salty, bittersweet essence of his desire slide down her throat. "I want to taste you." She looked up at the redhead pleadingly.

"And you shall have me," he said, placing his cock back in her mouth. She eagerly wrapped her lips around him once more to suck it. Mere seconds passed before she felt the explosion of his seed in her mouth. She tried to swallow as much of it as she could, but some still dripped down the side of her mouth.

She slurped greedily, sucking and licking him as though he were a particularly tasty lollipop, although in her opinion, this was far better than any lollipop she'd ever tasted.

Talh groaned loudly as he stroked her head. "Your mouth is magic, so soft, and wet, and made just for this purpose."

She looked up at him, giving him a wicked grin before turning her attention back to his cock. Trina didn't think she could get enough, but they apparently had other ideas.

She pouted when Talh pulled away from her. "We must clean you up."

"More," she whispered.

"You're greedy tonight," Roar chuckled as he pulled out his now semi-erect cock. "You have no need to worry, there will be more. Lots more." He stood up over her, and she could feel the cool breeze of the air conditioner hitting her exposed empty pussy.

When Bayoh slid out of her ass, she felt like crying. They might have been finished, but she could go another round. "Is that it?"

Roar pulled her up, taking her into his arms. "Is this the same woman who wanted to end things with us only a short while ago? Where did she go?" he asked, lifting a knowing brow at her.

"So I like to fuck. It doesn't make any difference, you know," she said, peeved at how easily they could make her body succumb to the pleasure they gave her.

"It makes all the difference. Do you respond to other men the way you do us? Do you beg for it afterwards? Can any other man satisfy you as thoroughly as we do?" Roar challenged.

She didn't answer because she couldn't. No one had ever made her react this way sexually before and she doubted anyone else could, but in the back of her mind she kept thinking about the pain of falling for someone only to be disappointed.

As they had made love to her she'd actually begun to believe that they cared for her. Yes, they screwed her voraciously, but there was something else too. The way they'd touched her had been so tender at times it made her want to cry.

It's just sex, she told herself, trying to silence her foolish heart. "No. Other men have never made me feel this way, but that means less than nothing. A good relationship is not all about sex. We can't have sex all the time."

"So what you're saying is that you will have sex with us, but that's it?" Roar asked with narrowed eyes.

"I've been saying it since we started this thing."

"Fine, we'll give you all the sex you want." Roar scooped her up in his arms and carried her to the shower. The stall was large enough for the four of them. They pushed her under the spray. Their hands caressed her, and her body went up in flames as it usually did, but something was different this time.

There was no finesse, no tenderness, just a demand for a response, any kind of response. When Roar pinched her nipple a little too roughly, she gasped. "Please, not so hard," she protested.

"This is what you wanted, Trina. This is just sex, and this is what 'just sex' feels like. You can't complain because we're giving you what you want." He smiled at her without humor.

She wanted to cry out and demand they do the things to her that they did before. There wasn't an inch of her body they did not grope. When they finished showering, they took her back to the bed, where they fucked her, without the earlier tenderness.

She soon realized the difference, and wanted to cry, but instead she gritted her teeth and took it.

Besides, her body was as responsive as ever to their touch even though it was different than before. They fucked her as though she were just some random woman they'd picked up on the street, but she refused to admit how much it hurt her inside.

With each stroke of their skillful cocks, they fucked her with a force that took her breath away, but this emotional rape didn't fill the need within her as the other times had.

They twisted and turned her body in different ways as though she were a rag doll, and she let them, because this was exactly what she'd asked for. They used her body until she cried out for mercy, and only then did they relent.

When they were through with her, instead of cuddling her like they usually did after sex, they all got up.

She felt like a whore, and she only had herself to blame.

Trina turned her face in the pillow, not able to meet their eyes. When she heard them leave the room, she started to cry.

* * *

Roar could hear Trina crying in the bedroom and it took every ounce of his self-control not to go back there and comfort her. He hated doing this to her, but she had to realize herself that she belonged to them. No amount of talking would convince her.

"I feel like a jerk," Bayoh echoed his thoughts.

"I do too, but I think this is what she needs. We know she's our true mate, but how good will a relationship between us be if she fights us along the way? It cuts me to hear her cry, but I know that if we go in there, we'll make love to her and comfort her and things will go back as they were. She'll continue to believe this is some fling, while we pour our hearts out to her. No, we deserve someone who will return our love, and if she doesn't realize it for herself, as much as the thought pains me, I would rather walk away," Talh finished on a fierce note.

"I don't know if I can walk away. When I'm not with her, I feel empty inside. Her smile, the way she looks at us, her laughter -- all these things make me glad I'm alive. When I go to sleep, I miss her," Roar sighed, raking his fingers through his hair. He turned to go into the room to comfort her. Each passing second, listening to her cry like her heart was breaking, tore him apart.

Bayoh and Talh grabbed his arms. "No. Don't you think we want to go in there and take her in our arms as well? This was your idea. We can't back down now. Love is a gamble, but hopefully luck will be on our side," Bayoh said, holding his arm in a firm grip.

Roar didn't need them to point out that this was his idea. He cursed himself now for even suggesting such a crazy thing. All he could think about now was going to her and assuring her everything was okay. "But this is a gamble we can't lose. What will we do without her? After having her, can either one of you even look at another woman and not feel cheated? I know I can't. Besides which, there may never be another chance for us to mate."

"This is a big risk for us all. I want to go to her as well, but do you want to go through the rest of your life with a mate who doesn't give us her heart? Someone who's too scared to take a chance on us? It hurts now, but in the long run, I think it would hurt a lot more," Bayoh reasoned.

Roar bowed his head in defeat. They were right. The decision was now in Trina's hands. Would she offer herself to them whole-heartedly or would she run away?

He'd never been more scared in his life.

Chapter Ten

Trina woke up the next morning with an awful headache. She must have cried herself to sleep. She didn't think she'd even cried like this when she caught Tim in bed with Twan.

As she turned her head over she saw a glass of water and two aspirin on the nightstand. So they did care. Her heart fluttered at the thought, but then she noticed something else beside the glass of water -- a note.

She didn't know why, but she was almost too scared to read it. Trina sat up and took the two aspirin and finished the contents of the water glass before turning back to the note. Her hands trembled as she reached for it. Her heart raced as she read the message.

Trina, you may be confused about what happened last night. As much as it pained us to do what we did to you, we could think of no other way to get the point across to you of how much we care. We have always made love to you with not just our bodies, but with our hearts. Last night, I'm sure you realized the difference.

We understand you've been hurt in the past, but not everything will be smooth in life. There will be people who will hurt you, but that's when you have to get back out there and live again, otherwise you let the people who've hurt you win. We love you with every fiber in our beings, but we also deserve someone who will return that love, so we will leave the decision up to you.

We are leaving Chimera tonight. Meet us at sunset on the beach at the spot where we first met. We'll be waiting. Otherwise you'll never see us again. Whatever

*you decide, your happiness is important to us, and we
wish you the best in all your endeavors.*

Love, Roar, Bayoh, and Talh

Trina dropped the letter. They were leaving? Just like that
they would walk out of her life after all that talk about being life
mates? So she'd been right. They'd already gotten bored with her.
She just didn't think it would be so soon.

No. They hadn't abandoned her, but given her a choice,
Trina reasoned with herself. She shuddered as she thought about
the night before. It still hurt her to think of what had occurred.
They'd made her feel cheap and used, but she had a better
understanding of why they did it. Maybe it was the only way to
get through to her thick skull, but did she dare give herself to
them? Could she entrust her heart to these men she'd known for
less than a week?

There was no one she'd felt so strongly for before. Not Tim,
Kwan, Larry or any of the other losers she'd dealt with. What
about the life she'd left behind? Could she walk away from it all?

What exactly do you have to go back to?

She had no job, her so-called best friend had betrayed her,
and she didn't have any family. Trina was alone in the world, so
why not take a chance on love? Why not run to the security they
offered?

The inner struggle tore her apart. The thought of yet another
heartbreak scared her so much she started to shake. Trina dragged
herself out of bed and headed for the shower. She could still smell
their scent on her, and her pussy twitched. She missed them.

After showering she went to the seaside grill to get some
breakfast. Every time she looked up from her meal, she expected
to see them, but didn't. All around her were happy couples
laughing and mooning over each other. Unable to stand it any
longer she left the restaurant.

On her way out, she bumped into Morel. "Trina. I'm glad to
see you again. Where are your mates?"

"They... they're leaving tonight."

A frown marred his blue face. "Without you?"

"I don't know. Maybe." She shrugged.

"I don't understand. Didn't they mark you? If my understanding of the Manani is correct, once they mark a female as their own, they can't claim another woman, unless their mate dies."

They would walk away when they risked going unmated for a very long time, possibly for life? She also knew, from what they'd revealed to her earlier that week, that they could not retain their leadership positions among their people if they went unmated.

They were willing to take that chance on her?

The men she'd dealt with before would have taken what they wanted without a care for her feelings. The fact they risked so much touched her heart in a way she didn't think possible. They must love her an awful lot if they would give everything up for her.

"Umm, Morel, I have to go. Good luck again."

"Wait!" He halted her as she turned to leave.

"Yes?"

"I just wanted to thank you for talking to me yesterday. If we hadn't talked, I would probably still be here on the island feeling miserable. I leave tonight. Perhaps I will see your mates on the plane ride off the island."

"You're welcome. I hope everything works out for you."

"I hope so too. Goodbye, Miss Trina, and may all your dreams come true." He took her hand in his, squeezing it in a reassuring gesture before letting go.

There was that phrase again. If she took the chance maybe this time she could have her happily-ever-after. On the other hand, her dreams coming true could also turn into her worst nightmare.

Trina was torn.

* * *

"The sun has set. I don't think she's going to show up."

Bayoh sounded as dejected as Roar felt. The pain emanating from his friends was so strong he could almost touch it.

"I think you're right. We've been here for over an hour. That should have been plenty of time for her to show up." Talh sighed.

Roar had been so sure Trina would show. How could he have been so wrong? One of the things that had attracted him to her in the first place was the inner strength he'd sensed. He now saw that her heart was too crippled to love again.

"She's been marked, so we can choose no other mate. We will have to step down from our positions of course." Bayoh raked his hand through his dark hair. His tail drooped, switching back and forth in a half-hearted motion.

"I don't give a damn about our positions. It's Trina I want."

"I wasn't implying our positions were more important, Roar. I was just stating a fact. It tears me up inside to find the one woman I know I can't live without, only to find that I have to. I don't know about the two of you, but I don't know how I'll make it through the rest of my life without her. I suppose I can only pray my life won't be too long on this world, because without her, I feel like I have no reason to live."

Roar could see the glistening of tears in Bayoh's eyes, and wished he could offer words of comfort, but he too hurt. This hurt was so deep, he could barely breathe. "Let's go. Our plane will be leaving shortly, and I'm sure the car is waiting to take us to the airport."

The three of them began to walk away, from the beach, away from Chimera, and away from Trina.

They didn't walk more than a few feet when Roar could have sworn he heard someone call out his name. He turned around, with Bayoh and Talh following suit. They must have heard something as well.

Roar's breath caught in his throat as he saw a vision in white running toward them. "Roar, Bayoh, Talh. Please don't leave without me."

Trina dashed toward them laden with baggage. Tears streamed down her face.

Without hesitation, Roar ran toward her, hoping his eyes weren't playing tricks on him. Bayoh and Talh ran by his side, each of them as eager as he to reach the woman of their hearts.

Trina dropped her baggage and ran toward them.

When they were only a few feet away, she leapt into Roar's waiting arms, which he immediately wrapped around her waist, squeezing her tight. His mouth descended upon hers. The sweet taste of her, just as good as he remembered, sent shivers up his spine. Roar's cock stirred. He took his time exploring the warm, delicious cavern of her mouth. Roar loved her so much it literally hurt when she wasn't near.

Trina moaned, wrapping her arms around his neck. Roar could feel her soft breasts pressing against his chest. Her tongue thrust forward to meet his, tasting and savoring him.

The cool, floral scent of her perfume triggered an uncontrollable burst of lust in his loins. Roar wished he had time to lay her on the beach and fuck her senseless, until she never had the desire to be away from them again.

Roar had never been more scared in his life, but seeing her racing down the beach almost soothed the brief ache he'd felt. He didn't want to let her go, but knew his friends were just as anxious to hold her. When he pulled away from her, Roar brushed her cheek with the back of his palm to assure himself she was real. "Don't ever scare us like that again, or we will give you the spanking of your life."

Trina wrinkled her nose, a mischievous gleam in her dark eyes. "Is that a promise?"

"You saucy wench, come here." Bayoh gently pulled her back and turned her around to face him. Trina eagerly went into his arms. Roar watched as their tongues danced to the syncopated rhythm of the ocean waves. Bayoh ran his hands along the sides of her curvaceous body.

Trina pulled back and nuzzled Bayoh's neck. "I missed you so much."

"I missed you too, my lovely Trina. I thought we wouldn't see you again. I wished my life to be short, because without you in it, life wouldn't have been worth living." Bayoh brushed a tear from the corner of her eye.

"I'm sorry to cause you pain." Trina caressed Bayoh's stubble roughened cheek.

Talh stepped closer to Trina. "Do I not get a kiss?"

Trina disengaged herself from Bayoh's arms and turned to Talh. The redhead lifted her in his arms, his palms cupping her round bottom. She dug her fingers in Talh's fiery locks when their lips met.

Just watching Trina kiss his friend with such passion and love made Roar's cock so hard he could barely think. He couldn't wait to get her back to Laiocean.

Talh gave Trina a long, leisurely kiss. She pushed against his chest, laughter in her eyes. "Put me down."

Talh didn't look as though he wanted to, but did. Trina then pulled Roar and Bayoh closer to her so the three of them were within her embrace.

"You came," Roar sighed, feeling as though things were right in the world once again.

"I've been a fool. What you three told me earlier is true. Love is about trust, and life is about taking risks. Although I was scared to trust again or take this risk, I knew I'd be miserable without you guys. Living without your love was more than I could take. Thank you for taking a chance on this broken woman. Can you forgive me for putting us all through this?"

Roar knew he spoke for his friends when he said, "We could forgive you anything. We would never hurt you. When you're sick, we will be there to heal you. When you cry, we'll be there to dry your tears. When you are happy, we are happy with you. We love you, Trina Davis."

A tear slid down her lovely brown face. She was so beautiful it ached to look at her, and she was theirs. Forever.

"I love you, Roar, Bayoh, and Talh. Let's go home." Trina looked up, encompassing them all in her smile.

Roar's heart soared at how easily she'd used the word home. His eyes locked briefly with Bayoh's and then Talh. He could tell they were just as happy. They grabbed Trina's bags and headed toward the waiting limo.

The sun had set, ending their vacation on Chimera, but this wasn't an ending for them. This was only the beginning. Their dreams had come true.

Eve Vaughn

Eve Vaughn has enjoyed creating characters, and making up stories from an early age. As a child she was always getting into mischief, so when she lost her television privileges (which was often), writing was her outlet. Eve likes to read, bake, make crafts, travel, and spend time with her family. She lives in the Philadelphia area with her husband and pet turtle. She loves hearing from her fans, so feel free to contact her at EveVaughn@yahoo.com or join her yahoo group by sending and email to evevaughnsbooks-subscribe@yahoogroups.com.

A.O.E.M.: Sea God's Pleasure
Alice Gaines

Chapter One

The painting had grown a phallus. DeLande's *The Sea God's Pleasure* sported a hard-on that hadn't been there the day before. A really big one. In all her years running the Hollowel Museum of Art, Gloria VanSant had never seen anything like it. Damage from shipping, forgeries, even intentional destruction by delusional art "lovers," yes. Paintings growing body parts, never. After earning a bachelor's degree in art history, an MFA, and almost a decade at the Hollowel, Gloria could spot a fake. If she was any judge -- and she sure as hell was -- DeLande had painted this huge cock with loving strokes of his brush over one hundred years before. So, why hadn't it been there yesterday?

"Gloria?" said a female voice. Tiffany, the latest upstart the agency had sent over with glowing recommendations.

With a huge show coming up and one of the most important pieces still missing, she didn't have time for crap today. "What?"

Tiff gave her the usual *didn't-you-hear-me?* look. "I talked to Overnight Express. They're bogged down at O'Hare and can't get Samuel's *Orpheus* to us today."

"Oh, for Christ's sake. I'm surrounded by morons. Call them back and tell them to get it here, or I'll sue their asses."

"There's a blizzard covering half of the Midwest. No one's flying in or out of Chicago."

"I didn't ask for a weather report. I want my damned painting."

Tiff crossed her arms over her chest. "When did you get to sleep last night?"

Great. Tiff had gone from upstart to nosey upstart. "I don't report to you."

"You didn't get to sleep, did you? When did you last eat?"

"Eating's over-rated."

"Gloria, you're going to kill yourself."

"Is that any of your damned business?"

Tiff held her hands up in surrender. "Sorry for breathing."

"Find a messenger service and have them send a truck for *Orpheus*."

"To Chicago in the middle of a blizzard? That'd take a week."

Add snippy to nosey and upstart. "Get a military plane to go for it."

"Really, Gloria, listen to yourself."

Gloria glowered at her. That glower had been known to send employees scurrying under their desks. Tiff just stared back at her. "All right," Tiff said finally. "Who should I call? The Department of Defense or the Air Force?"

"I don't care. Just call someone."

"Right. I'll come back when you're feeling a bit more rational."

Tiff turned to go, but Gloria yanked her back. "Look at this painting."

Tiff pointed at the *Sea God*. "This one?"

Of all the... "Yes, this one."

Tiff stared at it for a while and then shrugged. "It's a good example of the Pre-Raphaelite Brotherhood, if you like that style."

"Do you see anything odd about it?"

Shrugging, Tiff gave it a closer look for several seconds. "Nope. Do you?"

"You saw it when it got here yesterday. Did it have a phallus?"

"It's a nude. The guy would look pretty deformed without one."

"But was it that... um... big yesterday?"

Tiff gave her an odd look before staring so hard at the god in the painting her nose almost pressed against his erection. "You call that big?"

"You don't?"

Tiff shrugged again. "It's bigger than when most guys come out of the water, I guess."

"You have to be kidding. It's enormous."

Tiff snorted. "If you think *that's* enormous, you need to get laid more often."

"Gee, thanks."

"You're the one who brought up erections."

"You really don't see a huge cock?"

"Gloria, do yourself a favor and reacquaint yourself with a real penis."

"Smart ass."

Tiff turned and walked away. Gloria really ought to fire the little twerp, but she'd been through six administrative assistants in four months, and the hiring process wreaked havoc with everyone's schedule. Instead, she'd file that away in the "needs improvement" section of Tiffany's next performance review.

She turned back to the painting. She'd admired this work in the catalogue for years. Most people in her profession didn't think much of the Pre-Raphaelites, but Gloria had always been a sucker for the lush colors and dynamic use of light. Realism had fallen out of style long ago, but in the hands of a master like DeLande, the almost excessive use of detail transcended mere reality.

The subject of this painting had always held great appeal for her, too. As a lifetime city-dweller, she'd only dreamed of lush, tropical seascapes. The beach where the god emerged was pure white sand, surrounded by jungles full of flowers and birds of paradise. Behind him lay a sun-washed sky and an ocean so clear as to be transparent.

The man captured her attention, though, despite the beauty of the surroundings. The Sea God didn't appear young but rather a male in his prime. This was a man who'd lived long enough to dominate everything and everyone around him with his mere physical presence. His longish hair had some gray in it, but every aspect of his body possessed an easy kind of power. Broad shoulders, massive chest narrowing to slim hips, and muscled legs. Most impressive of all, right in the center stood that amazing rod. Gloria had had a few men in her day, but she'd never experienced a cock like that inside her.

Well, shit, maybe Tiff was right and she'd just gotten horny from a lack of a good fucking. No matter where she looked in Manhattan, she wasn't likely to find a partner like the Sea God, so she might as well forget about it. A painting needed rescuing from O'Hare, and she might as well get to it.

* * *

Back in her office, Gloria sank into the chair behind her desk and rifled through the drawers, looking for the catalogue with the reproduction of the Sea God painting. Memos, faxes, bills of lading, various drafts of the contributors' letter, pens without tops, yellow-lined pads with scrawling all over them, loose paperclips, and bottles of dried up correction fluid. Even the spike-heeled shoes she slipped into during visits from corporate bigwigs. Everything but the catalogue she wanted. In the bottom drawer, she found a box of over-the-counter pep pills. She popped two into her mouth then swallowed them without water.

Her chair squeaked when she swiveled to the credenza behind her. Plenty of art books and catalogues there, but not the one she wanted.

"Richard!" she bellowed.

In a moment, her chief assistant showed up at the open door of the office. "What do you need, love?"

"Where's my goddamn catalogue?"

"Which catalogue?"

"We're doing a Pre-Raphaelite show, and I need the Pre-Raphaelite catalogue. Isn't that obvious?"

He lounged against the doorjamb. "*Someone's* in a bad mood, I see."

"I've told you guys not to lose my things. How'm I supposed to run a museum if you two come into my office and lose my things?"

"No one's been in your office, Gloria. You need to calm down."

Easy for him to say. He hadn't gone to the endless fundraising dinner the night before and choked down two swallows of rubber chicken before giving up and finding an unguarded bottle of champagne -- bad champagne at that. He hadn't come back here at midnight to check the inventory for the show that was supposed to start in two days, only to discover that *Orpheus* was AWOL. He hadn't fallen asleep with his head on his desk, woken up with a wicked kink in his neck, and then gone out onto the floor to find a huge erection on one of the most important paintings in the show.

She put her face into her hands and rubbed her eyes. What would the stuffy contingent among the patrons say when they got a load of the god's boner? Oh gawd, Mrs. Franklin Homersby would have a cow. Gloria had only recently convinced the old bat that penises were acceptable in paintings as long as they were flaccid. The woman would have a coronary when she saw the DeLande painting. There went twenty grand out of next year's budget.

"Get me a cigarette, would you?" she said.

"You gave them up last month, remember?"

"I changed my mind."

"Oh, no. This time I'm holding you to it."

"Damn."

Richard walked to the chair across the desk and sat down. "Rough night, huh?"

She lifted her head and looked at him. "I don't know why I put up with this crap."

"Honey, you create crap. You thrive on it."

"I'm getting too old."

"Tell Auntie Richard what's wrong."

"The DeLande painting. I've wanted to get my hands on it for years."

"The *Sea God*?"

"Have you looked at it yet?"

"Haven't had time."

"Make time. It isn't just the central figure of the god. It's the world he lives in. The ocean, the sand, the jungle. The whole place is magic." Like the stories her parents had told her of Hawaii but hadn't been able to show her for real. "I know it's passé to love realism in this day and age, but I swear, I can feel the breeze on my skin when I look at that painting. I can smell the flowers and hear the surf."

Richard's brows went up in concern. "Is there anything wrong with the painting?"

"It's grown a phallus."

His eyes got wide. "Do tell."

"A great, big, erect cock. The thing's almost pornographic."

"Ooooh. I need to look at that."

"This isn't a joke."

"Believe me, honey, I don't take great, big, erect cocks lightly."

"Damn it. I can't have pornography in my show," she wailed.

He reached across the desk and patted her hand. "Okay, what do you want me to do?"

"Find that catalogue. If the god has a huge boner in that, I'll brazen out the criticism."

"And what if it doesn't?"

"Then we have a case of vandalism and not only can't I use the painting in the show, I have to get the insurance company to pay for some expensive repairs."

"I see the problem."

"Thank you."

Tiffany appeared at the doorway with a bunch of papers in her hand. "Mail."

"I thought nothing was getting through," Gloria said.

"Neither rain nor snow nor dark of night," Tiff recited.

"Great, now she's a poet."

Tiff held out the mail. "You need to look at this."

"Not now. I have other things to worry about."

Tiff walked to the desk and plunked one piece of paper down in the middle. "Read this. Now."

Gloria tried glowering at her again, but again, it had no effect. If anything, Tiff glowered back. So, Gloria picked up the paper, tilted back in her swivel chair, and read.

"Congratulations, Gloria VanSant. You've won an all-expenses-paid week on beautiful Chimera Island."

Gloria looked up at Tiff. "What in hell is this?"

"Just read."

> *Located in the geographical center of the Bermuda Triangle, Chimera Island offers both mystery and natural beauty beyond compare. Only the most adventurous traveler is welcome on Chimera, and we've determined that's you, Gloria VanSant. Absolutely no obligation, but you must book now. Call 1-800-555-4AEM or visit www.margaretriley.com/aoem.html today, to book your fantasy trip of a lifetime!*
>
> *Margaret Riley,* CEO

"Why are you bothering me with this? It's a goddamn time-share."

"No, it isn't. I called. It's totally on the level."

"Come on. How gullible can you be?"

"They told me it was an exclusive resort -- by invitation only. An anonymous sponsor has arranged for you to spend a whole week there."

Gloria set the letter back on her desk. "Thanks. I'll think about it."

"No, you won't. You're leaving tomorrow. I've arranged it all."

"You did what?"

"Your plane leaves in the morning."

"What in hell is wrong with you? Call them back and cancel."

"I've cleared your calendar for the next week. Everyone sends their best wishes for your aunt's complete recovery."

"I don't have an aunt!"

"Easy, love," Richard said. "Maybe Tiff's on to something here."

"She's on drugs if she thinks I'm leaving town before a huge show."

"I can take care of the show," Richard said. "You've done almost everything. I'll check into the problem with the DeLande painting and hang *Orpheus* when he gets here. Everything else will take care of itself."

"I'll pitch in and work the whole show, no overtime," Tiff said. "You need to do this, Gloria."

"No. The two of you are nuts."

Richard crossed his arms over his chest, giving her his best schoolmarm look. "I didn't want to do this, but if I have to, I will. Either take that vacation, or I quit."

Her jaw dropped as she stared at her chief assistant. "You wouldn't."

"Try me."

"You love the Hollowel," she said. "You wouldn't leave."

"I love you more, Gloria. I'm not going to stick around and watch you kill yourself."

"I don't believe this."

"You were just telling me about the magic in that picture. Go and find your own magic, honey. Everything will be here when you get back."

What could she do? She couldn't operate this museum without Richard. Hell, she didn't *want* to operate it without him. He'd been with her since the beginning. Then, too, maybe -- just maybe -- she could find the island she'd always dreamed of on this Chimera.

"Okay," she said finally. "But there'll be hell to pay if everything isn't perfect when I get back."

The two of them grinned at her.

* * *

The minute Gloria got through the door into her cabin, she found the telephone and punched the "0."

"Front desk, how may I help you?" a male voice said.

"This is Gloria VanSant in..." She checked her room key. "Cabin six."

"Ah yes," the man at the other end said. "I hope it's to your liking."

"There must be some mistake. I don't belong here."

"Your reservation starts today."

"I know, but I don't belong here, out in the middle of nowhere." She'd wanted a tropical island, sure, but something like Hawaii where she could wallow in nature for a while before going out for drinks. As far as she could tell from the helicopter, the only building on the whole place was the tiny cabin she stood in right now.

"Cabin six is on the most beautiful islet in the Chimera archipelago."

"Listen, pal. I don't belong on an archipelago. I'm supposed to be on Chimera." The city she'd seen from the plane wasn't much, but it did appear to have a few restaurants and a club. She might get through a week there. Out here with no one but the palm trees to talk to, she'd go stark raving mad in a couple of days.

"Technically, that island is Chimera," the man said. "If you consult a map..."

"I'm not interested in any damned maps. I want a room in a hotel near the closest thing you have to a shopping district, got me?"

"You'd like to change your accommodations," he said as if he'd never heard of anything like that before.

"Yes, mental genius. Yes, I want to change my accommodations."

"I'm afraid that's quite impossible," he answered as if that settled everything.

"The customer's always right, right?"

"Oh, absolutely. But you see, you're not the customer. Your sponsor specifically directed us to put you in an isolated location."

"All right." She took a breath. "Who's my sponsor?"

"I'm afraid I'm not at liberty to say."

"Let me get this right. Someone paid you a lot of money for me to spend a week here."

"Chimera's an exclusive resort, Miss VanSant. We don't offer cut-rate vacations."

"And that person has told you to stick me out here."

"Correct."

"But, you won't tell me who the sponsor is."

"I can't tell you," he corrected.

"All right. Let me talk to the manager."

"I am the manager."

Oh, great. She sank into a chair. "I'm going to contact the Better Business Bureau."

"We don't have such an organization. Everyone's satisfied on Chimera Island."

"I'm not satisfied," she shouted. "I'm very dissatisfied."

"I'm sorry to hear that," he answered.

"Get me another room, stupid, on the main island!"

"There aren't any."

"You didn't look."

"I didn't have to. I'm the manager."

"All right," she said. "I realize that not all islands are run like Manhattan Island, so I'm going to explain it to you in simple words."

"Please."

"I'm not staying on this little fart in the ocean."

"But your sponsor…"

"I don't give a shit about my sponsor." Whoever the hell he was. "I want you to find me a room on the main island. Put me on a waiting list, if you have to."

"But…"

"Twenty-four hours, pal." She looked at her watch. "You have until three pm tomorrow or I'm tail lights."

"Very well, Miss VanSant, I'll consult your sponsor," he said.

"You do that."

"Is there anything else I can do for you this afternoon?"

"Yes, there is. Get stuffed!"

* * *

Gloria woke with the afternoon sun in her eyes and her bladder full. She glanced at her watch -- 2:30. She must have misread it before when she told the manager-bot it was 3:00. That idiot had made her so crazy she'd forget her own name.

She rose from the bed and padded barefoot into the bathroom. After using the toilet, she brushed her teeth. She'd only slept for half an hour, but somehow her mouth felt like fuzzy slippers. Teeth cleaned, she spiked up her hair as best she could. She'd have to find her mousse to get it right.

Her stomach rumbled. When had she last eaten? Not on the plane, that was for damned sure. Not even in first class could you find anything worth feeding to a pet gerbil. Unless the management here expected her to climb palm trees for coconuts, they had to have some kind of room service. Cabin service? Island service? For Christ's sake, how long would it take them to get something out here for her to eat?

She headed toward the phone, going by the cabin door. A smell stopped her there. Fruit. Exotic, ripe fruit. Fruit so delicious the scent went right into her head and to her brain.

She opened the door and found a tray on the stoop. Metal lids covered each dish, but the perfume of fruit escaped into the air.

She bent and picked up the tray. As well as the dishes, it held a carafe of iced tea and a newspaper. She carried the whole thing into the cabin, kicked the door closed behind her, and walked to the table. By the time she sat, her mouth had already started to water. Under the lids lay a dish with cold meats, a selection of cheeses, and a baguette with butter. A bowl held slices of melon, pineapple, and strawberries. She poured herself a glass of iced tea and tore into the food.

The ham and turkey breast were lightly smoked, the cheese tangy, and the bread a crusty dream. She'd never eaten anything so delicious in her life. After just a minute, she'd eaten the whole thing. Fruit next. Juices ran down her arm as she ate all of that too. How did they get so much flavor into the food here? Steroids? Pheromones? All the food gone, she pushed the plates aside, picked up the newspaper, and rested back in the chair to read it.

The *New York Times*, international edition. Perfect. On the culture page, the headline read "Pre-Raphaelite show opens today at the Hollowel." How could that be? The show didn't start until tomorrow.

She checked the dateline -- tomorrow's date. What the hell? The date across the front page said the same thing -- tomorrow. So did the date function on her watch. Today was tomorrow. Time had warped somehow. Either that, or she'd slept for an entire day.

Could she have slept that long? That would explain the full bladder, the cottony mouth, and the fact that she appeared to have woken up half an hour before she'd fallen asleep. After years of too little sleep, she was used to functioning on an hour or two. She never slept for twenty-four hours. For the first time in ages, she felt completely rested.

This was getting too fucking weird.

She got up, walked to the door, and opened it to look outside.

Whoa. There was a whole lot more than just time weirdness going on. She'd somehow missed it the day before -- probably because she'd been so cheesed at being dumped in the middle of nowhere -- but the view from the cabin was the same as the seascape from the DeLande painting. The same white sand and transparent water. The same lush jungle with colorful flowers.

She stepped out of her cabin into the Twilight Zone and walked along the path, down to the beach. Warm sand shifted under her feet as she walked to the water's edge, and a light breeze ruffled the hairs on her arms.

As she watched, a disturbance appeared between the waves. Sort of a lump that rose under the water. It crested after a moment to reveal a person. A man walking straight out of the water as though he'd walked there along the ocean bottom. Broad shoulders, a massive chest. Un-freaking-believable. The Sea God, the man from the painting. She rubbed her eyes, but when she lowered her hands, the image was still there, standing in water that just reached his calves. Sure enough, he sported the same huge hard-on he had in the painting.

Her jaw dropped as she stood there staring at his cock. She ought to scream. She ought to run back into the cabin, throw the lock, and call security to report a lunatic on her island. A lunatic with an enormous boner. But no force on earth could get her feet to move. The sand might have turned into concrete for all the chance she had of walking in it.

"Who..." The word came out as a croak, so she swallowed and tried again. "Who in hell are you?"

The man put his hands on his hips and smiled at her. "I'm your sponsor."

Chapter Two

"You're my sponsor?" Great, now she was squeaking. "But, you're…"

He lifted a shaggy eyebrow. "Yes?"

"You're naked."

"Naked and aroused. I thought we'd mate first and talk later."

Mate. She'd marveled at the size of his member when she'd seen it in the painting. At the time, she'd never imagined she could actually experience taking pleasure with it. In the back of her brain, images exploded. Indistinct and lacking in details, but powerfully erotic. Hands on her breasts. Her body riding on waves while the water massaged her clit. A huge phallus entering her.

She closed her eyes and rubbed her forehead. "I dreamed those. While I was asleep."

"You got my messages."

She opened her eyes again. "You put those dreams into my mind?"

"Promises of what I'd do to you. Images to excite you. Did they work?"

Too well. Gloria's cunt clenched as a surge of energy washed through her. All her breath went out of her, and her knees went weak. She hadn't had a man for months. Hadn't wanted one or missed sex. This man asked to mate with her. He could take that cock and do everything she'd dreamed of the night before. He could give her orgasms strong enough to tear her from reality. Weeks and weeks of doing without, and now she could indulge her senses.

"I'll take that as a yes," he said.

"Yes?"

"The images did excite you."

"Look, I don't know who you are or how you got here, but I don't jump into bed with strangers."

That wasn't exactly true, but it sounded good. She hadn't jumped into bed with anyone for an age, but she could sure do it now with this man and the erection she'd seen in her dreams. Maybe they really did put pheromones in the food, because her cunt was already moist and ready for him.

"I don't plan on taking you to bed," he said.

"You don't?"

"Bed's too far. I'm going to make love to you right on this beach."

"Won't that scare the fish?"

"I hope so."

The man walked toward her slowly, as if she might bolt at any minute. Any sane person would. Most women never encountered a naked man walking up and out of the sea as though his cock was some kind of homing device zeroing in on her. Most women would have run away minutes ago. But, damn it all, she'd dreamed about that cock the night before, and it had driven her wild. Now that she could have it, she sure as hell would.

He stopped a few feet from her and gestured with his hand. Her clothes fell away. The seams split, and the fabric of her dress and half-slip slid along her body to fall at her feet. Her bra and panties dissolved, leaving her completely naked. The sun beat down on her shoulders and breasts. The breeze caressed her skin, and her nipples hardened into peaks.

"How did you do that?" she demanded.

He smiled at her. "It's not important."

"How did you come out of the ocean like that? Where's your scuba gear?"

His eyebrows went up. "Scuba?"

"Self-contained something or other."

He made another gesture with his hands, and a large blanket appeared on the sand. "Will that do for a bed?"

This was all getting too strange. She picked up a corner of the blanket. It seemed real enough.

"A few cushions, perhaps?" he said, and some of those materialized on the blanket. "I don't care, really. I just don't want sand in awkward places."

She skirted around their "bed," holding out her hands to ward him off. "Maybe you ought to rethink this. I mean, I don't know you, and you don't know me. I might have a disease."

"But you don't."

"How do you know?"

He walked around the blanket toward her, but she countered his move.

"I know everything about you, Gloria."

"How?"

"I'm your mate."

She stopped and stared at him. "You're nuts."

"Not at all. I've researched a lot of women, and you're the one."

He moved toward her again, his arms extended, but she danced away.

"I know everything about you," he said. "I know your hair is really red, not black. I know you cry at sad movies. Most important, I know you're so hot right now, you're ready to come."

Damn, he was right. He frightened her, and she wanted him. He might be a lunatic, but she was going to screw him. Right here on this blanket on the beach.

"You've been staring at my cock ever since I walked out of the water. Admit it."

"I could hardly miss it," she answered.

"It's all yours. Every way you want it."

Her mouth went dry, and her breath caught. She had to have a raging case of hormones. She'd wanted his cock since it showed up in the painting, to be totally honest. Now, she could have it, so why was she playing musical chairs with him?

Her hesitation gave him enough time to lunge across the blanket and grab her. He picked her up as though she weighed no more than kindling, let out a whoop, and twirled her around. Images blurred -- sky followed by ocean followed by jungle and then back to sky. Her skin rubbed against him, and her nipples grazed his chest. He was so incredibly strong she ought to be afraid. She ought to scream and kick and bite. Her heart raced and her pulse pounded, but fear didn't cause any of that. She wanted this man. She wanted him to toss her onto the blanket and plow into her until she climaxed.

He did drop her onto their "bed" and came down right on top of her like an avalanche of flesh. Oddly enough, he didn't crush her, but he did cover her, his body swallowing hers up.

He kissed her then. His mouth descended to hers and caught her lips in a searing caress. She slid her arms around his neck and answered with her own mouth. Their tongues met and sparred while his hands roamed over her ribs. She twisted her hips and rolled him onto his back. He'd let her do that, of course, but damn -- what a feeling of power it gave her to command his body that way. She sat up and ran her hands all over his chest. His chest hairs felt like silk under her palms.

He grinned and cupped her breasts with his huge hands, massaging and squeezing them. The sensitive flesh ached and tingled, and she gasped with the pleasure. Tipping her head back, she closed her eyes while she made her hands into fists, clutching his chest hair.

"More, damn it," she said. "More, more."

He raised his head to take one nipple into his mouth. While he sucked, she whimpered and pressed herself against his face. Her cunt throbbed and grew wetter. The sensations were even more powerful than her dreams. Impossible, but true. Nothing in her life had ever felt like this, and soon he'd enter her, making the pleasure even more intense.

She squirmed against him, moving lower on his body until her buttocks encountered the hard length of his erection. While he moved to tease her other breast, she reached behind her and grasped his cock. It felt like sun-heated velvet under her palm. She grasped it and stroked it, rubbing it over her buttocks.

He growled and rolled them over. "You want me."

"Yes."

"How much?"

She pounded on his shoulder with her fist. "I want you. Fuck me."

"How much?"

"Damn you, fuck me."

He parted her legs with his hand and thrust a finger deep inside her. "How much?"

She arched her back and moaned. "Please, please. Fuck me."

He slid a second finger into her and moved them in and out. Moisture spread over her inner thighs as he pumped her. She was aching, burning, ready to burst out of her skin.

"How much do you want my cock?" he said.

"Fuck me. Please, please. I'm begging you."

He removed his hand, placed himself between her legs, and plunged his massive member into her. She cried out and wrapped her legs around him, lifting her hips to embed him as deep inside her as he could go.

"Woman," he said. "You're tight."

"You're huge," she answered. "Don't stop."

"Damn, it feels good." He moved in and out of her in long, hard strokes. She kept pace with him, straining upward, taking him over and over. This was hotter than any dream, more erotic than any fantasy. Urgent, dangerous, irresistible. She floated on a sea of lust while he touched her every nerve. Her spirit soared, just moments away from orgasm.

"Come for me, mate. Give yourself to me."

"Yes!" The climax hit with the force of a hurricane. It stole her breath and stopped her heart as she flew into little pieces. Her sex exploded in one spasm after another. She shrieked, riding the storm until the climax finally ended.

Overhead, birds took flight on flapping wings, some crying with alarm. She lay spent on the blanket and would have laughed if she'd had the energy. They hadn't scared the fish, but they'd done a number on the birds.

The man rested his head next to hers and chuckled. "You sure can come, mate."

"I've never done it quite like that before."

"Enjoying your vacation?"

"Mmmm."

He withdrew a few inches and then surged forward again.

She opened her eyes and looked into his face. "You're still hard?"

He grinned at her. "I'm not through with you yet."

Oh. My. God. He hadn't finished? He wanted to give her more? If she hadn't been lying down, she would have fallen over.

"You do plan to come at some point, don't you?" she asked.

"I'm going to erupt like Vesuvius."

"I'd like to see that." Watching a massive cock like his spew had to be an experience.

"You will, later. Right now, I think you need another orgasm."

Her throat went dry, but her pussy sure didn't. He moved inside her, and she felt the hunger growing again. Amazing.

"A different way this time, I think." He pulled out of her and rolled off. The ocean breeze washed over her sweat-slicked body while the sun bathed her in warmth.

"Kneel here and look out to sea," he said.

"What are you going to do?"

"Nothing exotic. Unless you want me to."

"Regular will do." She smiled. "For now."

He laughed and sat up. She scrambled to her knees and looked out over the ocean as he'd told her. He positioned himself behind her, doggie-style, and slid the tip of his sex into her.

"Mmmm," she crooned. "That feels so good."

"Want more?"

"Please."

He pushed forward, giving her another few inches. She took him easily. Despite his size, she'd grown that slick. She rocked back against him, taking more of his cock inside her. He moaned and surged forward, filling her.

She breathed in sea air and listened to the surf as he thrust into her from behind. He set a rhythm that resonated with the waves on the shore. Powerful and inevitable. Her breasts hung free, swinging as she met his thrusts with backward movements of her own. Though not as frantic as their first coupling, this seemed just as intimate. She could feel every inch of him, sense his trembling as his own passion built. The universe centered where they were joined with his cock deep inside her sensitized cunt. She whimpered as liquid heat pooled in her belly to signal another orgasm. He'd driven her that close again.

He bent and reached around her waist, seeking her pussy with his fingers. When he found it, he parted the lips to tease her clit. She shuddered and moaned with the intensity of the caress. He kept doing that while his cock kept plundering her. The combination went so far beyond anything she'd ever experienced she could scarcely breathe. Tension coiled in her belly, tightening until it was almost unbearable. She was going to come, with him pounding into her. She was going to dissolve into mindless orgasm.

He thrust deeper and rubbed harder. She gasped, crying out as her pussy spasmed around his member. The climax lasted forever, rocking her to her core, and still, he thrust into her.

After a moment, he grasped her hips and pulled her hard against him while he pounded into her a few more times. Massive, violent surges. He let out a roar and buried himself in her to the hilt as he came. Finally, he fell to his side on the blanket and pulled her against him, her back to his chest.

"I was right," he murmured after a moment.

"About what?"

"You're the one."

"The one what?"

"My mate."

She rolled over and looked into his face. "You said that before. What's it supposed to mean?"

"What it sounds like. I'm going to spend the rest of eternity with you."

"I'm here for a week, pal." Six more days, actually, as she'd already slept one day away. "This was good. We can do it again if you want."

"Good?" he said. "It was a lot more than good."

"All right, it was fantastic, but after a week, I'm heading back to New York."

"But, I don't want to live in New York."

"Did anyone invite you to?"

He stroked a finger down her nose. "Mates live together, mate."

She pulled away and sat up. "Stop calling me that."

"What should I call you?"

"My name, maybe?"

He stretched out on his back and put his hands behind his head. "Gloria."

"How do you know that, anyway?"

"I know everything about you."

"So you said."

"You were born in Wharton's Bend, Idaho, and graduated first in your class of thirty-seven students. You can't stand caviar, and your hair is really red and curly."

"Who wants to eat fish eggs?"

"Why do you do that to your hair, anyway? Black doesn't go with your skin, and it sticks out all over the place."

She reached up and touched her hair. "You think?"

He smiled and shrugged.

Wait a minute. She didn't have to listen to his critique of her appearance. He'd walked out of the ocean and given her a good shtupping, but he didn't own her.

"Who are you, anyway?" she said. "And don't tell me you're my mate again."

"I've had a lot of different names over the years. You'd only recognize a few of them."

"Try me."

"The Greeks called me Poseidon, the Maya call me a *chac*. The fellow who did the portrait of me you liked so much called me the Sea God."

"Did you doctor that painting?" she asked.

"I might have." His grin grew outright smug. "I didn't lie about my dimensions, though, did I?"

"You almost gave me a nervous breakdown."

"I had to get your attention, ma... Gloria."

"How did you do that? How did you do all of this?" She gestured all around her. "Who the hell *are* you?"

"Better to ask *what* I am."

"All right, what are you?"

"I'm the sea. I'm the origin of all life. I'm the element water. You've heard of earth, wind, fire, and water. I'm water."

She gaped at him. The man was certifiable. Bonkers. One inkblot short of a Rorschach deck. And she was sitting here talking to him.

"Nice to meet you, Mr. Water," she said. "And thanks for the roll in the hay."

"Sand," he corrected.

"But I have to go. Now that you've destroyed my clothes, I'd better unpack and find something else to put on."

"Good idea. You wouldn't want to burn that redheaded skin. I'll wait here."

"You don't understand. I'm going to go into my cabin and call security to tell them there's a maniac on my island."

"It won't do you any good."

"We'll see." She got up and walked off with as much dignity as she could muster, given that she was naked and had just let the man fuck her out of her mind.

"Yes, we will," he called after her. "We certainly will."

* * *

Quarian could have saved his time reading those self-help books. Women obviously didn't want truth and honesty any more than they used to. He should have tried seduction instead of directly telling Gloria VanSant who he was. Bless Creation, women still loved sex as much as they ever had.

No matter. He had most of a week to convince her she belonged with him for eternity. Unfortunately, she'd gone back into her cabin hours ago and hadn't stuck her nose outside since. Would she really stay in there the whole time while a paradise waited for her out here? A paradise and him.

He'd chosen her specifically for her spirit, of course. A docile female could make for a pleasant dalliance, but eternity with one would be pure torture. He needed a woman who could stand up to him, challenge him, keep him at the top of his game.

An element only mated once. He could have hundreds or thousands of affairs over the centuries, but when time came to create an eternal partner, he got only one chance to choose correctly.

The sex told him he'd chosen very well, indeed. Granted, some time had passed since the little French aristocrat had proved so amusing. But he knew the difference between mere lust and a strong sexual pull toward one particular woman. Gloria had done more than pull him. She'd drawn him in so completely, she'd owned him. Even now, hours later, he could still feel her sweet cunt milking his cock into an orgasm so strong it had held all the power of the ocean's waves. Right now, his prick was growing stiff under his loincloth. He needed her again. So soon.

He would seduce her this time. The sun would set in another few hours. By then, he'd have a campaign planned to win her heart. Wine, flowers, and music. A fantasy straight out of her own memories and dreams.

Chapter Three

Quarian knocked on the cabin door again and got the same response.

"Get lost." It didn't sound nearly as certain as the last time she'd said it, though.

"You wound me to the quick, Miss VanSant."

Silence. He could almost hear the wheels turning in her head. The concept of wounding someone to the quick probably didn't come up too often in her everyday life. She'd be even more perplexed when she opened the door.

He adjusted the lace at his throat.

"I don't know what you're talking about," she said, but she sounded curious this time.

"Does our passion mean nothing to you? I give you my soul, and you cast it aside. I live only to please you."

"Yeah?" She paused. "How?"

"I've brought a modest repast. Quails. Wild mushroom. Crème brulee."

Soft footsteps approached the other side of the door. "Crème brulee?"

"And champagne."

"You didn't murder me this afternoon. I guess you won't do it now."

"I only seek from you the small death that brings us life. In that way, yes, I'd kill you a dozen times over."

The lock turned, and the door opened a crack. "Don't think this means I'm changing..." She took one look at him, and her voice trailed off. "What are you supposed to be?"

"What do you think I am?"

Her eyes widened, and she backed away with her fingers covering her mouth. Clearly, he'd surprised her with his costume.

He entered the room, closed the door, and walked to the table. After setting the dinner tray there, he bowed deeply.

"Don Juan," she whispered.

"At your service, miss."

"How did you know?"

"An astute lover knows how to please his lady." Of course, having access to her most intimate desires helped. The Agency of Extraordinary Mates maintained detailed dossiers on all potential mates. Their exclusive clientele would demand nothing less. He had a whole stock of characters to choose from to win the reluctant Miss VanSant. Don Juan had seemed the most potent, and from her reaction, he might have been right about that. Who cared if her ideal Don Juan held little resemblance to the real person? Her image of the famous lover was what mattered.

"Where did you get that costume?" she asked.

He looked down at the scarlet satin coat and breeches. "I'm resourceful."

"You tied your hair in a queue."

"Do you fancy wigs? I could conjure one if you prefer."

"No. You look…" She stopped and stood for a moment, and then a tiny smile curled her lips. "You look wonderful."

"My spirit soars," he said, placing his palm over his chest. "That you would find my poor person acceptable brings me greater pleasure than I can say."

She giggled. "Hokey, but it works."

"Come, let me give you sustenance." He pulled out a chair and waited until she sat. She looked over her shoulder as he pushed the chair back in. He let his fingers drift to her shoulder. She wore a strapless top, leaving plenty of soft skin for him to explore. When he touched her, she shivered slightly. A good sign. With a flourish, he removed the lid to the tray and set it aside before he sat down.

"This smells delicious," she said.

"I aspire to satisfy all your appetites, dear lady." He snapped his fingers, and lighted candles appeared on the table. In the background, the sound of a mandolin played a love serenade.

"I must be out of my mind letting you in here."

"You allowed me into territory far more intimate than your bedchamber this afternoon," he said. "Priapus is most eager to reacquaint himself with Cunny tonight."

"Why, sir, you make me blush."

Wonderful. She'd entered the fantasy. Even better, she gave him a shy smile, and he could almost imagine that she did blush. Don Juan appeared to be making some headway that Quarian couldn't.

He took her hand in his and raised her fingers to his lips. "A blush becomes you. Over your cheeks and down your throat, all the way to the very seat of your desire."

"I fear I'll need some strength to endure that."

"Let me feed you." He picked up a knife and fork to cut a piece of quail. He lifted it to her mouth, and she took it between her lips.

"You feed all my hungers," he said. "Such tiny, perfect teeth. Like pearls. I'd love to wear a garland of them around the tip of my rod."

She giggled. A thoroughly delightful sound and quite the opposite of what anyone would expect from the hard-edged New Yorker who'd confronted him on the beach. He'd read her history, however, and it described a shy young woman who'd had to scratch and claw her way to the top of the art world. She still had a rich fantasy life, obviously -- one that he could use to good advantage in his quest to win her heart.

After setting the fork aside, he picked up a slice of morel. Creation only knew where the AOEM got a fungus that normally grew in the north woods in the United States. He lifted the morsel to her lips, and she took it into her mouth, giving his fingertips a kiss as she did.

Her eyes closed with pleasure as she chewed and swallowed the mushroom. "Everything tastes so good here. How do they do it?"

"This place is more than an island, fair lady. It's a state of mind."

"I confess it's put me in a state." She gave him a coy smile. "But not by engaging my mind."

He opened the champagne. The cork flew out with a loud pop, which she greeted with more laughter. He smiled at her while he poured two glasses and handed one to her. That done, he moved his chair even closer to hers so that they could link their arms together as they drank.

Her lips came away moist with the wine, so he kissed them. She tasted of fruit and honey. Sweet beyond all reason. He'd kissed human females over the centuries -- some better at it than others. All women were beautiful. All women tempted him. All women could beguile his cock. Only this one could own him with a tender kiss. He had, indeed, found his mate.

She pulled back after a moment, her eyes wide. "How do you do that?"

"Do what?"

"You take me right out of myself. I think I can resist you, but my will dissolves whenever you touch me."

Good. She felt the same pull he did. She could no more fight destiny than he could. He only needed to make her see that.

"We're meant for each other, my love," he said.

"Who are you? Really."

"I've told you. Really."

"Water."

"The most basic element. Life itself."

She rose and walked to the picture window that looked out over the ocean. The candlelight cast a reflection of her in the glass. He made the appropriate gesture with his hand, and a negligee of the finest white lace replaced her top and shorts. The delicate fabric flowed over her shoulders, leaving the tops of her breasts bare, and outlined her form as it fell to the floor.

She gasped.

He walked up behind her and took her in his arms, pulling her back against him. Her buttocks pressed against his crotch and started the chain reaction that would have him fully erect in moments.

"Don't be afraid, love," he whispered into her ear.

"I don't know who you are, or how you can do these things."

"You know everything you need to know about me." He nibbled at her earlobe and then kissed the soft skin below her jaw. Lower and lower he went, all along her neck to the base of her throat. She sighed and grew pliant in his embrace.

"This is the real you, Gloria," he said. "Feminine, romantic. Woman, through and through."

"I can't be. The world won't let me."

"Ah, yes. Your world demands that you have bigger balls than any man, that you deny your loving side. To hell with that world."

"It's the only one I have."

"You love beauty, and yet your world denies it to you. Tell me what your world says about art like the painting of me in your museum."

"It's trite and unimaginative."

"You know better, though, don't you?" He nuzzled his nose against the side of her face. "Your world won't even let you have your own taste in art."

"Modern work is beautiful, too."

"Nonsense. Today, an artist would paint me as a series of little boxes or squiggly lines. Unrecognizable. You want the real thing."

She didn't answer but stood in his arms with her gaze focused on their reflection in the window.

"This is the real you." He raised his hands to cup her breasts, squeezing them gently. "Soft. Giving. Lovely."

She tipped her head back and closed her eyes. "Yes."

"Yes," he repeated. "I need you."

She turned in his arms and tipped her face up to his. "Take me."

He pulled her against him and took her mouth in a kiss. With as much restraint and tenderness as he could muster, he moved his lips over hers slowly. She leaned into him and responded -- at first cautiously and then with more abandon. After a moment, her mouth opened and her tongue grazed the surface of his upper lip. He moaned, answering with his own tongue, taking them deeper while his cock hardened in his breeches.

No woman had ever inflamed him the way this one did. Just a kiss, and she had him throbbing and hungry for coupling.

He bent and picked her up in his arms. She gazed up at him with complete trust in her expression. How far they'd come since the afternoon. Two souls in need of joining recognized each other, no matter how much intellect might try to resist. Tonight, he'd make her his in every sense of the word. His love, his eternal mate. She wouldn't deny him now.

He carried her to the bed and set her on the spread. Lace flowed all around her, and an angelic expression lit her face. He stripped out of his clothes, almost tearing the satin in his haste, and joined her.

He kissed her again, more roughly this time, taking her mouth as a drowning mortal might take air. Her hands moved over his arms and back, creating friction and urging him on. He trailed his tongue along her throat to her collarbone and below. With her chest rising and falling, her breasts seemed to swell as he cupped one and planted kisses over the top of the other. The stiffened nipple poked up into the lace, so he took it between his lips, fabric and all, and sucked.

She drew in a harsh breath and arched her back, pushing her flesh deeper into his mouth. He let his palms wander all over her while he switched to the other breast. He moved his hands over her ribs and along her sides to her hips. As he did, he bunched the lace up in his hands, pulling it upward over her legs and hips. He slid lower, still massaging her. Lower and lower until his face found the mound between her thighs. After pushing the gown upward to her waist, he could gaze on her sex -- his ultimate goal.

"Sweet Cunny," he murmured. "Sweet, sweet Cunny."

"Kiss it, please," she gasped.

He ran his tongue along the folds of her pussy, from the entrance upward to her clit.

She trembled and whimpered. "More, please."

He repeated the caress a few times, each time more firmly. Her hips jerked each time his tongue found her most sensitive spot, so he ran his arms under her thighs to hold her fast against his mouth. Then, he went to work in earnest.

Her clit had hardened into a firm, little nub that he could pull into his mouth. He teased it, sucking and rubbing it with firm strokes of his tongue. Her cries grew louder, her movements more frantic as she strained against his face. Her movements told him she ached to come, but the longer he could draw this out, the stronger her orgasm would be.

He stopped for a moment to let her rest, and she dug her fingers into his hair to urge him on. He teased her some more, driving her closer to the edge this time. Her whole body tensed, so he paused again.

"Don't stop!" she cried. "Please, don't stop."

"You want to come?"

"I need to. Please."

He took her clit back into his mouth and laved it with every bit of skill he had.

Her cries built, one on another until she sobbed. Suddenly, her hips moved right off the bed, and she shouted as she came. He kept up the pressure, pulling every bit of response out of her while she climaxed. The orgasm seemed to go on forever before she finally fell back, limp.

He let her drift on the pleasure for a moment before sliding up beside her and pulling her into his arms.

"Oh, my," she whispered. "I had no idea."

"We're made for each other. Admit it."

"Oh, my. Oh, my, my."

"My lady's pleased, I take it."

"More than I can say, my lord." She reached between them and took his cock in her hand. "I daresay turnabout's fair play."

"Priapus yearns for you. Soon, he'll weep."

She ran her fingers along the length of him and squeezed. "Such an eager fellow."

He groaned at the pleasure of her touch. "Eager to spill my seed into your delicate palm, although he'd quite prefer to do that into your pussy."

She bit her lip and smiled at him. Quite the coquette she'd become. She stroked the length of his rod and then reached further down to cup his balls. "These jewels have hardened, too. Do they pain you?"

"Quite the contrary. The pleasure is exquisite. I fear any more will undo me," he said. "Pray ride me while I jump the final hurdle."

That last was probably too flowery, but his brain had lost touch a few minutes back with anything but the onrushing orgasm. If she didn't let go of his cock soon, he'd cream all over her hand, the bedspread, and everything else.

She did release him, though, and sat up. He rolled onto his back with his member sticking up into the air like a flagpole. It had grown deep crimson, and a drop of pre-cum glistened at the tip. She swung her leg over him, and he gathered up the gown so that it spread over his chest rather than tangling between them.

The lips of her sex found his cock, and she slid slowly onto him. Slick and tight, her cunt grasped him an inch at a time as she lowered herself. Such delicious agony to let her take him this way when he needed to plow into her until he came. Still, if she wanted slow, he'd give it to her somehow even if it killed him.

She closed her eyes as she eased the last inch down to the base of his cock. "You're so large, sir, I fear I may swoon."

"We'll swoon together."

She moved her hips, rocking forward and back with him buried deep inside her. Her muscles gripped him, relaxed, and gripped him again. Damn, she'd done it on purpose -- squeezed him with her hot, wet pussy. Enough. No male could withstand that.

He placed his hands on her hips and pumped into her. She felt like heaven, gliding over the length of him as his climax built.

He couldn't stop now, had to keep thrusting upwards over and over. Blind, savage lust drove him, until...

Yes, now! Starting at his spine and then to his balls. He slammed into her as his cock exploded. Long, hot waves of semen rushed out of him and into her pussy. He growled and roared. Damn, nothing had ever felt like this.

She came, too. Miraculous creature. Her whole body shuddered as her cunt grabbed at his cock in rhythmic contractions. She threw her head back and gasped for breath.

For several moments they hung like that in pure bliss. His, hers, theirs. Shared eternity until she fell against his chest.

He cradled her there and kissed the top of her head. "Unbelievable."

"You're sure something... hey, what's your name, anyway?" she asked.

"Quarian."

"Well, Quarian, you sure know how to fuck."

"Is that any way for a lady to talk?"

She chuckled and rolled off him. "You did that pretty well, too."

"Did what?"

"The Don Juan thing," she answered. "Cute."

"It wasn't a thing, and it wasn't meant to be cute."

"What was it meant to be?"

"I was trying to make you happy."

"You know how to make me happy, all right. You've made me happy four times today, not that I'm counting."

"It wasn't about sex, either."

She looked at him as if he'd lost his mind. "It wasn't?"

"Not completely."

"Don't get your knickers in a twist," she said. "I'll still respect you in the morning."

"Damn." That was the sort of thing human males said to females just before they grabbed their hats and disappeared forever. He'd said that, or something like it, to hundreds of mortal women, so he ought to know what it meant -- absolutely nothing. "How can you make light of what we just shared?"

"Hey, what did I say?" she asked. "What's gotten into you?"

He sat up and swung his legs over the side of the bed. The woman seemed determined to misunderstand what had just taken place between them. Yes, he'd played a game for her, but not to make her think he was cute. He'd planned everything to convince her to spend eternity with him, not to amuse her for a few days.

"This wasn't just an act, you know," he said. Curse the woman, now he sounded petulant.

"Oh, really?" She swung her legs over, too, and sat up next to him. "You dress up in satin knee breeches all the time?"

"I did it to please you."

"And you did. I told you so."

"I want to show you what immortal life with me would be like."

She crossed her arms over her chest. "Not that mate stuff again."

"It's not stuff," he thundered in the voice he used when he wanted humans to cower.

Gloria VanSant just rolled her eyes. "Oh, I'm so scared."

"You're my mate whether you like it or not. At the end of the week, we'll leave here for our life together."

"At the end of the week, I'm going back to Manhattan. You can go to hell."

"Curse you, woman." He stood, towering over where she still sat on the bed. "You will obey me!"

She glowered right back up at him. "And if I don't?"

His hands clenched into fists, and it took some effort to force himself to unclench them again. As much as he'd love to throw her over his shoulder and carry her into the sea, she'd only drown if he didn't prepare her first. Throttling her wouldn't get him anywhere, either. Clearly, he had a lot more work to do with this stubborn mortal, but he had several more days to do it. Angering her wouldn't help.

"I'm going to go outside and calm down now," he said.

"Don't you want to get dressed first?"

He looked at the pile of clothing on the floor. "In satin knee breeches? I don't think so."

She shrugged. "Suit yourself."

Smug little snippet. She had no idea who she was dealing with. She'd learn soon enough, yes she would. Before the week was over, she'd apologize for all her obstinacy and beg him to mate with her. He'd savor every moment of her surrender.

In the meantime, he needed to get out of here before he did something he'd regret. So, he walked, stark naked, out of the cabin and slammed the door behind him. He'd take a nice, long walk along the sea bottom and spend time among some creatures that made sense -- flounders.

Chapter Four

Gloria had to admit that Quarian had knocked himself out every day to give her pleasure. Don Juan, Tarzan, her favorite bad-boy actor -- he'd played them all for her. She'd never had a vacation like this one -- not that she ever took vacations, but still. They'd splashed naked in the ocean and the lagoon he'd found at the center of the island. No one else ever showed up, just trays of the most delicious food and wine discreetly left at the front door of the cabin. She'd stopped moussing her hair or putting on make-up. What was the point if she spent most of her time either swimming or fucking? Life was good, and she'd get to live out the dream of her adult life this afternoon.

Today they sat in the makeshift classroom he'd set up under a palm tree. The set consisted of a podium, a chalkboard, and one student's desk. Bare bones, but it would serve, as would the more... um... unusual props nearby.

He walked to the chalkboard and wrote on it for a moment. *"Story of O."*

He dropped the chalk in the tray and turned, dusting his hands. "I imagine some of the feminists in the class will squirm today, so I want to state right now that I don't want to hear any of your whining."

Quarian didn't resemble Professor Glocket in any physical sense. Quarian stood tall and imposing, making the tweed jacket look like something from the cover of *GQ*. Glocket had been a mangy little weasel who didn't seem to wash often. No doubt, all women found him repulsive. He worked out his anger by humiliating the female students in his class on a daily basis. If the subject matter hadn't sounded so intriguing -- Erotic Literature -- she would never have enrolled in his class. Once in, she hadn't found a way to get out.

"Miss VanSant," he said. "Would you care to discuss the post-Freudian symbolism in the use of implants to expand the woman's anus to accommodate a penis?"

"I'd rather not."

"May I remind you that class participation is a major part of your grade?"

"You always do." That had sounded great in the course description. Who didn't want to get class credit for talking about sex? In practice, though, it meant Glocket could force the women to talk about the most violent, goriest parts of his syllabus in front of a bunch of male students with boners in their pants. She ought to bring harassment charges against the bozo, but that would only mean repeating all of the crap in front of yet more men who might also have boners in their pants.

Glocket smirked at her, his weasel-nose all a-twitch. Quarian had his mannerisms down to a tee. "Freudian symbolism, if you please."

"Well..." She could turn this around if she could think quickly enough. "I can see why you'd need it explained to you. I imagine your penis would fit easily into the tightest of anuses."

In her mind, the other women in the room let out a whoop of victory as Glocket sputtered.

"This is about literature," he huffed. "It doesn't have anything to do with me."

"Oh, really? Then, why do you wear pants tight enough that the outline of your pathetic weenie shows every time you get a hard-on?"

More laughter from her imaginary classmates. Quarian clenched Glocket's jaw and got red in the face. Bless him. She'd have to think of a really great way to thank him for this.

"That's insubordination," Glocket shouted.

"You have to be kidding. For my behavior to be insubordinate, I'd have to be subordinate to you, Glocket. In fact, the other women and I passed you on the evolutionary scale a long time ago."

"May I remind you I'll be grading you at the end of the term?"

"Why not? You remind me all the time, but this time I don't give a shit." Damn, but that felt good. "I'm not twenty-one and trying to get through an MFA program any longer. I'm an adult woman with a responsible job in the art world. You're a dirty-minded pinhead who can't get it up except at some poor woman's expense."

"Miss VanSant, leave the room immediately!"

"Not on your life, asshole." She rose from her seat and approached the podium. Glocket's eyes widened, and his Adam's apple bobbed as he watched her approach. Quarian had nothing to fear from her, of course, but he'd agreed to play the coward for her enjoyment.

"I've had enough of your power trips," she said as she got closer. "Today, I'm going to take your itty-bitty pecker out of your pants and make you cream in front of the entire class."

"You wouldn't dare!"

"Ladies, block the doors," she ordered her imaginary classmates. "I don't want any of the men to miss this."

He backed away. "Don't touch me. I'm warning you."

She followed him, punching her finger into his chest. "Or, you'll do what, little man?"

The two of them continued, Quarian backing up toward the other area where the cast iron rings stuck up out of the sand. Any child could pull them out easily enough, but this was all play-acting and a hell of a lot of fun.

When they got there, she bent and picked up the lash -- a smaller version of a cat-o'-nine-tails -- and flicked it against her leg. "Okay, strip."

"Me?"

"No, the Marquis DeSade. Who else but you?"

"I don't want to."

"Did I ask what you want?" She swished the tongues of leather against her leg again. They created a pleasant smarting sensation.

He held up his hands in surrender. "All right, all right. Don't hurt me."

He shed his clothes in record time, throwing garments in every direction. For almost the first time since he'd walked out of the sea that day, his cock hung only semi-hard. He'd managed that to please her, too. Even in that state, his member was impressively long and thick. She'd have him hard and pounding into her in a minute, which would follow a satisfying fantasy with an even more exciting reality.

She made a circular motion with the whip. "Turn around."

He did so, slowly.

"Stop," she ordered when his ass came into view. "Have you ever seen anything so inadequate as his butt, ladies and gentlemen?"

He whimpered, so she slapped the lash against his buttocks. She'd never hit him hard enough to cause major pain, but his flesh did redden.

His butt was anything but inadequate, of course. Round and firm -- powerful like the rest of his body -- it could win any derrière competition it entered. She swatted it again, for the sheer pleasure of watching his flesh tremble.

"All right, lie down," she said. "And spread your arms and legs."

He stretched out on his stomach, his hands and feet near the iron rings.

"On your back, stupid," she said.

He rolled over, and she knelt next to him. After removing the silk bonds from the pocket of her sundress, she moved quickly around him to tie him to all four rings. That done, she stripped out of her dress -- the only piece of clothing she wore -- picked up the lash, and stood.

"Have you ever seen a naked woman before?" she asked.

"Please, Miss VanSant, let me up."

"Oh, I'll let you up, all right." She bent over and nudged his cock upward with the end of the whip. "You're not very well endowed, are you?"

That last bit was ridiculous. He'd hardened some more, but while still not completely erect, he had several inches on lots of men.

"Have you ever watched a woman touch herself?" she asked. "Most men find that erotic."

He swallowed hard, his Adam's apple bobbing again.

Gloria touched herself, found her clit, and rubbed it. His cock immediately swelled to full attention, and she pictured it inside her as she stroked herself. Damn, it felt good, standing here getting wet while a few feet away, he became more and more obviously aroused.

She plunged two fingers into her pussy and moaned with the pleasure. "Do you want to do this with your prick?"

"Yes."

She teased her clit some more until it throbbed. "Do you want to fuck me until I climax?"

"Yes."

"Do you want to be inside me when you come?"

"Yes, yes, yes."

"Well, you can't." She moved her hand and bent over again. Very carefully, she circled his cock with the tips of the lash. Slowly, slowly, while he whimpered and his eyes went wild with fear. One more circle of his member, and she raised the lash to strike. He closed his eyes, and she brought the tongues of leather down, but across his thighs, not his groin.

"That's a warning to be a good boy and do as I tell you," she said.

"I will. Please don't hit me."

She struck his thighs again to punctuate her order and then tossed aside the lash. "I'm going to make you come now so that the whole class can laugh at your pathetic load."

"No," he moaned. "I don't want to."

"Then do your best to resist, but you will climax for all of us to see."

She dropped to her knees beside him and took his cock into her hand. It hardened even further against her palm -- a sure sign that he was fully aroused now and defenseless against whatever she wanted to do to him.

"See if you can take this," she said as she lowered her face. For a moment, she let him anticipate her next move, and then she closed her lips around his tip and sucked.

"Ah," he cried. "Oh, God."

She moved her lips lower, taking more and more of him into her mouth. He tasted pleasantly salty as she worked his cock, sliding up and down over his length.

"Please, I can't," he shouted.

She pulled her mouth from his rod and squeezed the shaft. A drop of moisture appeared at the tip, and she licked it off. His hips jerked at the contact. He was trying to hold himself in control and losing the effort.

"I'm going to make you cream now, but not in my mouth," she said. "If you get any in my mouth, I really will beat you."

"No," he cried again, but from his tone, his plea might have meant the exact opposite.

She bent to his cock again and rasped her teeth gently against the shaft. His whole body went rigid, nearly rising off the sand. He was only a moment away now, and her pussy throbbed in sympathy. She'd get him to satisfy her afterwards, but she wasn't quite through torturing her sadistic prof yet.

She took him into her mouth again and worked him hard. Up and down, sliding over him at a furious pace. He moaned and thrashed as his climax neared.

"Chimera!" he shouted.

The safe word. She released him and spread out on her back, parting her legs for him. With angry movements, he pulled the iron rings out of the sand. Then, in one fluid movement, he rolled onto her and thrust his cock into her throbbing cunt.

"Yes," she cried. "Oh, yes. Do it!"

His answer was animal grunts as he plowed into her over and over. Massive strength, male power, every muscle in his body driving them both on. The whole world disappeared as he pushed her closer to climax.

"Do it, Quarian," she cried. "I love you. Oh, God, I love you."

He plunged into her, deeper and deeper, past endurance, past anything she'd ever known. He shouted -- a great, booming sound -- as he went rigid in climax. Deep inside her, he spilled his essence, and her own body responded in a massive orgasm. Her cries joined his while her sex squeezed his over and over. Finally, he rested his head against her shoulder.

"Did you mean that?" he whispered. "Do you love me?"

At another time, she might have lied. She might have made up some explanation about the heat of the moment and losing her head. *Besides, hey, everyone says I love you when they're about to come.* At this moment, with him still deep inside her and the reverberations of her own fulfillment still grasping at his sex, all she could do was tell the truth. "Yes, I love you," she whispered back.

* * *

She loved him. Quarian could hardly believe it, but he'd heard her clearly enough. She'd admitted that she loved him in a voice that seemed to come from her soul.

He loved her, too, of course, but then, the moment he'd set eyes on her picture in the catalogue, he'd recognized her as the one woman who could make his life complete. After days with her, she'd taken over every part of him. The sun only shone when she smiled. He had no music but her laughter. His member responded only to her, whether in fantasy or reality. He'd had both with her. Never, in his entire existence, had he made love as he had with Gloria. She kept him constantly hard, and she never failed to satisfy him completely. They'd have that for the rest of time.

All he had to do was give her immortality. Once he'd done that, she'd agree to mate with him. If he'd learned anything about human females over the centuries, he'd learned that once they fell in love, they wanted commitment. No matter how many times they claimed to want only a temporary fling, they wanted happily-ever-after and 'til-death-do-us part. Only, he and Gloria would never die, so they'd stay together forever. Nice job if you could get it, and he'd get it this afternoon.

He didn't have to perform the ceremony right now. He still had two full days before her planned departure. Once he'd realized what he had to do, though, the need hit him with all the power of nature. The ache in his loins told him that the time had come for him to spill his seed for her. Not just any ejaculate, the semen dammed up inside him now held the power of eternal life in it. Mixed with sweet wine and herbs, it would make an elixir to turn his lover into his mate.

The urge was on him now. Primal, like the ocean itself. He couldn't fight it if he tried. Semen, seawater, blood -- the very stuff of life. His gift to her. His very essence spilled into a chalice for her to drink. He could no more put this off than he could stop the earth's rotation.

He stripped out of his loincloth and looked out over the sea from the edge of the cliff at the highest point of the island. All lay calm below him now, but in a moment it would reflect the gathering storm inside him.

He picked up the chalice at his feet and raised it toward the sky. The mother of pearl caught all the blues and greens of sky and sea and cast them into his eyes.

"Creation," he bellowed. "I give You my spirit."

A warm breeze stirred up, ruffling his hair. It shifted directions, now blowing into his face.

"I surrender to Your power. Grant me my deepest need. Give me my mate."

A clap of thunder sounded. The signal, as if he'd had any doubt, that Creation approved. His balls felt heavy suddenly, and his cock throbbed in eagerness. With one hand, he lowered the cup while the other one grasped his erection and began to stroke it.

He'd had more than his share of sex over the years. He'd plunged his member into hot, wet pussies. Women had sucked on it, some shyly and others with an abandon that brought him to orgasm in seconds. Nothing had ever felt like this. While the wind blew and the waves crashed below him, he rubbed his hand over the length of his shaft, from the sac below all along to the head and back down again.

Images filled his vision. Gloria in the lace gown as she rode him, her eyes closed and her head thrown back in rapture. Gloria's sweet ass as he plunged into her cunt from behind. The sight of his cock moist with her juices. Gloria standing over him with a whip in her hand while she fingered her clit with the other.

Damn, too much. He yearned to make this last, but he needed just as urgently to empty his love into the chalice so he could take it to her. He squeezed the base of his shaft, holding off the climax. Fighting against it.

The ocean churned beneath him. Huge waves building higher and higher. They pounded against the cliff as the pressure mounted inside him. He positioned the cup carefully. In another moment, he'd have no control of his motions, and he dared not miss.

All around him the wind whipped into a frenzy. It wailed in his ears with the sound of a hundred lovers screaming in their release, and every one of those cries held Gloria's voice in it.

The ocean rose higher, roiling around the rock and climbing nearly to the promontory. He gave up all resistance and resumed the stroking. His cock came alive in his hand, swelling and throbbing in rhythm with the waves. He pulled harder on it as if he could strangle it into submission.

The climax started in his balls. An unbearable tension almost like pain. He moaned as it hit him and stroked on his cock like a madman. The shock wave ran the length of him and burst from the tip as he sprayed semen into the cup.

He opened his throat and howled as he came in one huge surge after another. His hips bucked with the power of it, but he held firm to his cock, guiding all of his essence into the cup.

This, I give to you, his mind shouted. *And this, and this and this.*

One final ocean wave crested the cliff and sprayed up onto him as the last bit of semen seeped from the head of his cock and fell into the chalice.

It was done.

The ocean subsided, and the wind died down. Birds still cried with alarm, but slowly the island returned to normal. Quarian looked into the cup. All of that had come out of him, and now he'd offer it to his mate along with the gift of immortality. Just as Creation had ordered.

Chapter Five

Gloria watched Quarian approach. Powerful legs carried him quickly over the sand, and his loincloth moved in time with his footsteps. In his hand, he held a goblet of some kind.

He'd grown so beautiful to her over the days. Not just his impressive member, which had entranced her back in New York, but all of him. His smile, his hearty laugh, the way he surrendered totally when they made love. He'd gotten so close to her -- far closer than any other man ever had.

Maybe it was the island. Magic ruled here, enhancing all her senses to overload. She'd pursued beauty her entire life, from her drab hometown through graduate school and on to the dazzle and glitter of New York. How could she have known that she'd discover it on an island so remote she shared it with one other person? But, what a person.

What was she going to do now? She couldn't stay on this island for the rest of her life. She couldn't take someone like Quarian back to her apartment. Imagine what would happen if donors like Mrs. Homersby got a load of him in his loincloth. Maybe they could part for now and agree to meet back here in a year. Maybe she could visit him somewhere in the meantime. Somehow she couldn't let things end when her week ran out.

He smiled as he approached her and held out the goblet to her. "I mixed you a special drink."

She took it from him and studied the chalice. It appeared to be mother-of-pearl, studded here and there with coral of many different colors. "This is beautiful."

"It's quite ancient. Used only for important occasions."

She smiled up at him. "What's the occasion?"

He winked at her. "Drink it and see."

She took a sip. As with everything on Chimera, the liquid exploded with flavor on her tongue. Spices, herbs, and wine that tasted of honey. Underneath all that lay a pleasantly salty tang.

"This is delicious." She held the cup up to him. "Don't you want some?"

"It's all for you, my love. Drink up."

She lifted the goblet to her lips again and swallowed the rest of Quarian's concoction. Finally, she handed the cup back to him. "Okay, are you going to tell me what's the occasion?"

"Come and sit with me for a minute."

Something inside her went way wrong all of a sudden. Her head got light, and her vision dimmed. All the air rushed out of her chest. Her knees turned to water, and she felt herself collapsing. Quarian caught her, helped her down to the sand, and held her in his arms as the world disappeared in a whorl of dizziness. "What's wrong with me?"

"Relax, mate," he said. "It'll pass."

"I'm dying." She'd tried to scream it, but her voice made only a whisper.

"You feel that way, but you'll come out stronger at the end."

"You did this to me!" He was a homicidal maniac, after all. He hadn't knifed her, hadn't beaten her to death as she'd feared when she first saw him. He'd poisoned her. He'd made her love him, and then he'd poisoned her.

"You wouldn't see reason, Gloria. I had to."

"Oh, God."

He rocked her back and forth. "Hush, love. All will be well."

The darkness swallowed her up, pulling her down into a bottomless pit. Her stomach clenched as she fought to stay in the world. Her heartbeat slowed and weakened. She struggled for breath, but no matter how hard she tried, nothing got into her lungs. Quarian's arms were her only reality as he continued to cradle her against his chest. She loved him and he'd killed her, and she'd die with nothing but the memory of his embrace.

She gave up and let death have her. No use trying to hang on. She let herself float as she sank lower and lower into the abyss.

At least there was peace here. She'd never see her parents again. Never see the Hollowel. Never see another sunset. Nothingness awaited her.

Just when she'd started to slip away, everything reversed course. She stopped falling and hung suspended in space and time. Sounds intruded -- distant at first but growing louder. The rhythmic crash of waves on the shore, the calls of sea birds, the rustle of leaves in the wind.

"That's it, love." Quarian's voice. "Come back to me."

Sand appeared under her body. Though her arm felt weighted down, she could stretch out her hand and bury her fingers into the sun-warmed sand. Light burned into her brain, even through her eyelids. She opened her eyes to the glare and immediately shut them again before moaning and rolling onto her side.

Quarian stroked her back. "Feeling better?"

She pulled away from him and forced herself to sit up. Her head swam for a moment and then cleared. When she opened her eyes again, the mists had burned away. The world looked brighter than before, the colors more saturated. Her ears picked up sounds she would normally never have heard. The flapping of birds' wings far above her, the murmuring of sea currents.

"What in hell happened?" she said. "I thought I was dying."

"You were in a way."

"What did you put into that drink?"

"My essence. You're immortal now."

Her jaw dropped, and she stared at him. "You're kidding, right?"

"Not at all. We can be mated now."

"Oh, for Christ's sake." She rose, wobbled slightly, and righted herself. "Not that mate crap again."

He rose, too, and held his hand out to her. "It's not crap. You're my mate, Gloria."

She batted his hand away. "Okay, now I know for sure you're crazy. You slipped some kind of date rape drug into the wine, and you expected I'd agree to be your mate after that?"

"Damn it, woman!" he thundered. "I've been more patient than any god needs to be. You're immortal now. You are my mate, and we will leave here together. We'll go where I say when I say, and you will not argue."

The sound of his voice should have scared her or at least startled her. Instead, it rushed through her like a charge of electricity, increasing her own strength.

"The only place I'm going is back to New York, and I'm not waiting until the week is up. I'm getting off this damned island the minute they can get a boat out here to get me."

"I forbid it," he shouted.

"You can't forbid me anything, pal. You're a maniac, and I'm done playing make-believe with you."

His face turned into the picture of fury and he spread his arms wide. "Do as I say, or I will raise a hurricane and carry you off with me that way."

"Yeah, right. Whatever. I'm going into the cabin now and locking the door behind me. Don't even bother knocking."

She turned and walked off. Let him try to raise a storm. She wouldn't stick around to see it.

* * *

There was a storm that night. Not quite a hurricane, but strong enough to rattle the screen door against the outside of the cabin. Rain pelted the window over Gloria's bed, and the waves slammed against the beach outside. Somehow, in all that madness she could make out each single sound. Damn, but she could swear she heard the birds huddling in the trees. One note came through most clearly, though. A wail. It should have been the wind, but no. A voice. A cry of pure misery.

She sat up in bed and looked out the window. Her vision seemed oddly acute, too. She shouldn't have been able to see anything, but somehow everything came through clearly.

The sea cast its own glow as the froth on the surf shimmered in a ghastly white. A flash of lightning revealed a lone figure on the beach. Quarian stood there with his arms by his sides and his head thrown back. Rain poured over him, and the waves threw water up at his feet. The storm gathered around him, the clouds swarming overhead. One lightning strike and then another hit around him. They should have electrocuted him by now or at the very least thrown him off his feet. None of it moved him. He stood there with that inhuman sound coming out of his throat while the elements went mad around him.

Gloria took a deep breath and lay back down. She should go to him and order him to come inside. But how could she do that without getting herself struck by one of those bolts? Besides, he'd drugged her once in his insane attempts to convince her she should become his mate. She didn't dare trust him again.

No, he'd have to stay out there. When she got to the main island, she could call someone and get him some help. He needed to be in a hospital somewhere where experts could take care of him. She had a lot of her own work to do getting over him and what she'd thought was love.

Sanity would return tomorrow. She only had to endure the storm tonight.

* * *

The door to the cabin opened not long after the sun rose. Quarian rose from the rock he'd been sitting on for the past few hours and watched as Gloria came out. She'd put on tight, black jeans and a clingy black tee shirt that only went to her midriff. She'd painted her face again and spiked up her hair. In each hand, she held a suitcase.

When she saw him, she hesitated briefly. That lasted only a moment, though, before she set her jaw and resumed her determined march to the water's edge.

He walked up beside her. "Are you really going to leave?"

She set down her luggage and stared out over the waves. "Will you let me leave?"

"What do you think?"

"I know now that you can stop me. You really are who you say you are, aren't you?"

"I never tried to hide myself from you."

"What sane person would believe a story like that?"

"I hoped maybe you would. How did you finally figure it out?"

She looked at him for a moment, cold fury in her eyes. "You did make me immortal. I cut myself shaving my legs, and it healed instantly. So, I tried holding my breath to see what would happen. Nothing. I don't seem to need to breathe."

"You don't."

"How could you?" Her voice was low and as cold as ice. "How could you make a decision like that for me?"

He looked down at his feet. He'd never mistreated women before, but he'd never taken them very seriously, either. They were lovely, sweet creatures who could share great pleasure. Eventually, he'd move on, leaving them with wonderful memories. He'd never had to consider their life choices. He did now, and he'd done a piss poor job of it.

"I love you, Gloria," he said. "Do you believe me?"

She ran her fingers through the spikes of her hair. "Yeah, sure. I guess."

"All I can say in my own defense is that the mating urge got the better of me. It's more powerful than even the elements. I must have been crazy with it."

"So, you turned me into... what?" She paused. "What am I, anyway?"

He looked back up at her. "With me, you'd be a part of me. Part of one of life's strongest forces. The ocean, rivers, streams."

"And without you?"

"I don't know." Creation, what had he done? He'd made a being in his own image but given her no choice in the matter. The ultimate betrayal, and she had to see it as such. If only he could undo his actions of the last twenty-four hours... but he couldn't.

"What are you going to do?" he asked.

She sighed, and the sound cut into him like a knife. Damn, how he'd hurt her.

"I haven't decided," she said. "I guess I'll live one life until people realize I'm not aging and then move on to another identity."

"That sounds lonely."

She shrugged. "What else can I do?"

She could come with him, but surely she'd considered that possibility and rejected it. Damn, she'd rejected him.

"What about you?" she said. "Will you get a new mate?"

"I have only one mate -- you."

"You really fucked up, didn't you?"

"I'm sorry, Gloria. I'm so sorry."

"A hundred years from now, I'll be able to speak with authority on today's art because I'll have known the artist personally. I won't be able to tell anyone that for fear they'll have me locked up."

"Damn, I wish there was some way you could kill me."

"I'd like that, too."

"Let me give you one gift before you leave."

She glared at him. "It doesn't involve drinking any potions, I hope."

He raised his hands in surrender. "I'm being completely honest now. I want to show you something that may make up for some of the pain I've caused you."

She sighed again. "What do you want to show me?"

"The sea. I want you to see it the way no one but I have ever seen it before."

"The boat's coming for me."

"It won't be here for some time."

Anger flared in her eyes again.

"I didn't do anything to delay the boat," he said. "I know the schedule."

"Well…"

"Please, Gloria. Just this one thing, and I'll let you go."

* * *

Gloria took Quarian's hand. There had to be some benefits of immortality, although they'd all escaped her when the magnitude of what he'd done had sunk in. Quarian had lived for centuries, and he seemed pretty happy. Maybe he could help her adjust to her new status.

He led her out into the sea. Warm water swirled around her ankles and then her knees as they went. When they got deep enough for the waves to reach her waist, her sodden jeans rubbed between her legs and felt clammy against her skin. Her clothes disappeared -- just vanished -- leaving her naked.

She looked at Quarian. "I'm not having sex with you, if that's what this is about."

He shrugged. "I didn't do anything."

"Then who got rid of my clothes?"

"You did."

"I did?"

"When you have more practice, manipulating objects will come easier."

She glanced down at herself. Her body seemed to belong in the sea, and only nakedness made sense. Anything human-made would get between her and her element. On they went as the water rose higher around her. Over her breasts and to her shoulders. Quarian stopped and held his hand out to her. On his palm lay a clip made out of tortoise shell.

"What's that for?" she asked.

"Put it over your nostrils. Once you're used to doing without breathing, you won't need it."

She clipped it over her nose, cutting off her breath. That strange light-headed feeling returned. Giddy, but pleasantly so. In front of them, a large wave built. A country girl, she'd only encountered the ocean as an adult, and its power had always frightened her. They were already nearly immersed. This swell would take them under. She watched it come, building and building. It couldn't kill her, but it could scare her pretty well.

Quarian took her hand and squeezed. "Trust me."

As if she had any choice. The wave crested right over their heads and pulled them under. A current caught her up and swept her out to sea. It should have terrified her, but Quarian's hand gripped hers to reassure her. Colors rushed past her -- the crystal blue of the water, the greens of seaweed below them, the rich gold of sunlight as it penetrated the water. Like all the paintings she'd ever loved, but not an illusion this time. Everything she saw was real.

The current gentled after a while, and the images took on more solid form. She and Quarian floated slowly to the sea floor until her feet touched sand. She dropped his hand and turned around slowly. On one side, tall blades of seaweed waved in the current, bending and bowing back and forth. Fish colored like jewels ducked in and out of the branches. Red, blue, brilliant black. A mountain of coral in the loudest hue of pink she'd ever seen stood on her other side, with the fish populating the nooks and crannies there, too.

You love beauty above all else. Tell me what you see. It was Quarian's voice, but it came from inside her head.

She turned and looked at him. *Is that you?*

Sound distorts underwater. Best to talk via thought, he answered. *Now, tell me what you see.*

Everything's incredible. The fish, the coral. The way the sunlight penetrates even down here.

Like one of your favorite paintings, no?

Better.

A small shark swam by, no more than inches from her nose. Only a few feet long, the animal stopped to study her briefly, its eyes filled with ancient wisdom. With a flick of its tail, it dashed away again.

What do you have in New York that compares to this?

Good question. She loved her museum, loved her place in New York's intelligentsia. *Art, of course.*

Bah. Reality offers far more than the small vision of modern mortals.

Contemporary painting is beautiful in its own way.

It's clever, not profound. A mere trick of the intellect. He stretched out his hand and a shrimp flew into it. The tiny creature rose up on its tail and waved its legs in movements reflective of the current around it.

This baby has more to teach us than any hundred of the paintings in your museum.

That isn't true, she said, even though every bone in her body told her it was.

You want beauty, Gloria, and they give you fashion. You want enlightenment, and they give you trends. What did they say of the portrait of me you hung there?

That it was trite. That no one did realism anymore.

And what did your heart say? he asked.

She'd had to fight to convince the board to do a Pre-Raphaelite show. Not a single one of the experts wanted the exhibition, and she'd only managed to sneak it past them by claiming it would bring in more money from Philistines like Mrs. Homersby. The truth was that she'd wanted those paintings in one place where she could delight in the colors and play of light, but she hadn't dared to admit that.

Somewhere along the line, she'd grown ashamed of her own tastes and feelings about art. She'd lost touch with everything that had made her happy. No wonder she didn't eat or drink but did snap at her staff. How could you enjoy life when critics had soured your view of everything that made your spirit soar?

Beauty lives in your heart, not your intellect. It grabs your gut, not your cerebrum.

What do you know about beauty?

I've lived for centuries. Millennia. When you have, too, you'll see what I mean.

She looked around her at the majesty of nature. He could be right. Despite her years spent studying art, she'd never seen anything to rival this. She had all of eternity in front of her. Why shouldn't she spend it here? Quarian had tricked her into immortality, but she did love him, and he'd loved her enough to mate with her for all time. If she stayed with him, she'd have company. Besides, she could get back at him for his deception for the next couple of centuries. That would serve him right.

I could show you much more than this. Mountain lakes, for instance. They're too cold for mortals, but that wouldn't bother us.

You mean like in the Alps?

The Alps, the Sierras, New Zealand. I know a lovely place on the South Island no human's ever found.

Oh, my.

We could swim the Amazon. Converse with the manatees in the Everglades.

She stared at him. *You can talk to them?*

They tell me which boats are bothering them, and I put the engines out of operation.

You would.

Come with me, Gloria. What's waiting for you if you don't?

She turned to him. *You really do love me. You wouldn't get tired of me and run off?*

Tired of you? With your appetites and imagination? Eternity wouldn't be long enough.

I'm not joking, Quarian.

He took her face in his hands and gazed into her eyes. The water shimmered between them. Sunlight in his hair. In his eyes. Her own reflection stared back at her -- a water creature, just like him. They did belong together, even if he had tricked her to bring her here.

I love you, Gloria. Don't make me live forever without you.

Yes, Quarian, my love. I will be your mate.

Alice Gaines

Award winning author Alice Gaines has published several sensuous and erotic works. She prefers stories that stretch the imagination, highlighting the power of love and sex. Alice has a Ph.D. in psychology from U. C. Berkeley and lives in Oakland, California, with her collection of orchids and two pet corn snakes, Casper and Sheikh Yerbouti.

Agency of Extraordinary Mates Vol. 2

Aubrey Ross -- Dichotomy

"This story is for ménage fans a must; the story line is great and sex is hot. Ray and Delano being the complementary sides of one other make for an interesting mix of man and definitely spark interest."
    -- Glenda K. Bauerle, The Romance Studio

Willa Okati -- Under Your Spell

"Under Your Spell is a fantastic paranormal romance, filled with magical places, compelling dreams and extraordinary characters. While filled with steamy sex, it also has a compelling plot everyone can learn from. For it to be true, love must be given freely. As always, Ms. Okati gives her readers a great story. One that I wouldn't miss for the world."
    -- Lisa Lambrecht, In The Library Reviews

Stephanie Burke -- Taboo

"Taboo should definitely come with a warning label. This book is so hot it's a miracle the pages don't catch fire. The ending is totally unexpected and a complete surprise, I highly recommend that readers give this book a try."
    -- Angel Brewer, The Romance Studio

Changeling Press E-Books
Quality Erotic Adventures Designed For Today's Media

More Sci-Fi, Fantasy, Paranormal, and BDSM adventures available in E-Book format for immediate download at www.ChangelingPress.com -- Werewolves, Vampires, Dragons, Shapeshifters and more -- Erotic Tales from the edge of your imagination.

What are E-Books?

E-Books, or Electronic Books, are books designed to be read in digital format -- on your computer or PDA device.

What do I need to read an E-Book?

If you've got a computer and Internet access, you've got it already!

Your web browser, such as Internet Explorer or Netscape, will read any HTML E-Book. You can also read E-Books in Adobe Acrobat format and Microsoft Reader, either on your computer or on most PDAs. Visit our Web site to learn about other options.

What reviewers are saying about Changeling Press E-Books

Angela Knight -- The Dark One

"A richly detailed world, filled with strong warriors, enigmatic gods and strong desires. I was caught up in the story, drawn by the obvious love Kaska and Matia had for each other... An intriguing read from start to finish."
-- Sharon McGinty, In the Library Reviews

Elisa Adams -- Night Creatures

"I found Night Creatures to be a very enjoyable, unique and mysterious vampire read. Ms. Adams did a wonderful job of holding my interest throughout this story... their passion was so blazing hot it left me breathless... this thrilling novel will fascinate lovers of erotic romance with a touch of horror added to make things interesting."
-- Contessa Scion, Just Erotic Romance Reviews

Julia Talbot -- The Magic Touch

"...filled with vivid imagination and eroticism... the magic portrayed in this story was described with ease and made very believable... indulge yourself with The Magic Touch."
-- Anita, Fallen Angel Reviews

Nia K. Foxx -- Gargoyle's Quest

"Secrets, sex, love, oh, and did I say steamy sex so hot it gave me blisters? I need more, more, more!!!"
    -- *Dee, Joyfullyreviewed*

Silvia Violet -- Shifter's Station 1: Pilot's Bargain

"4 Tattoos! There are quick plot twists that keep you on edge until the final outcome of the story and it was a great blend of the erotic, sci-fi and shape shifter."
    -- *Louisa Christina, Erotic-Escapades*

Amelia Elias -- Blood Ties

"The passionate sex scenes will leave blisters on the fingertips of the reader. Ms. Elias' attention to detail and explanation of uncontrollable sexual attraction packs a powerful punch. I was so drawn into Blood Ties, I could almost feel the fang marks on my neck."
    -- *Ophelia, Erotic-Escapades*

Cat Marsters -- Sundown, Inc: She Who Dares

"I can't say how much I loved Sundown Inc.: She Who Dares. There are only a handful of short stories that have had characters that I connected to so quickly that I felt immediately teary-eyed with emotion over their pain and successes. Of course, that doesn't dismiss the absolutely fabulous humor this book had. I'll definitely be looking forward to Ms. Marsters' next book."
    -- *Dani Jacquel, Just Erotic Romance Reviews*

B.J. McCall -- Cosmic Cops: Dark Ecstasy

"Hot and steamy love scenes, a real hunk, a galactic adult pleasure playground and a fascinating story. An absolutely satisfying… read. I'm looking forward to the upcoming books of this author."
    -- Stephie, Cupid's Library Review

Belinda Richmond -- Catalyst

"I really enjoyed Ms. Richmond's debut with Changeling and cannot wait until the next book by her. Devin and Talis are hot and hunky and I loved the secondary characters of Devin's sister Keria and her lover Jorran. Hurry your fingers to Changeling and order this awesome book."
    -- Barb Hicks, The Best Reviews

www.ChangelingPress.com

Printed in the United States
98693LV00002B/74/A

9 781595 963628